BURIED FEELINGS

ALSO BY KIT ROSEWATER

All's Fair in Love and Field Hockey

BURIED FEELINGS

KIT ROSEWATER

Delacorte
Romance

Delacorte Romance
An imprint of Random House Children's Books
A division of Penguin Random House LLC
1745 Broadway, New York, NY 10019
penguinrandomhouse.com
getunderlined.com

Smiley face by Vitya_M/stock.adobe.com, hand drawn underline by Mariia Mazaeva/stock.adobe.com, key by oleg7799/stock.adobe.com, and heart shaped lock by dipu/stock.adobe.com.

Editor: Alison Romig
Cover Designer: Carol Ly
Interior Designer: Megan Shortt
Production Editor: Jamie Johnson
Managing Editor: Tamar Schwartz
Production Manager: Shameiza Ally

Library of Congress Cataloging-in-Publication Data is available upon request.
ISBN 979-8-217-03302-7 (trade)—ISBN 979-8-217-03303-4 (ebook)

The text of this book is set in 11.4-point Sabon MT Pro.

Manufactured in the United States of America
1st Printing

The authorized representative in the EU for product safety and compliance is Penguin Random House Ireland, Morrison Chambers, 32 Nassau Street, Dublin D02 YH68, Ireland, https://eu-contact.penguin.ie.

TO AUGUST AND ROWAN—
THE FRIENDS I MADE ALONG THE WAY!

There is still treasure not yet lifted.

      —ROBERT LOUIS STEVENSON, *TREASURE ISLAND*

Time will explain.

      —JANE AUSTEN, *PERSUASION*

Hand-dyed, big mess, cotton, oh my God, you don't even want to know. Stitch, stitch, stitch on the little Singer . . .

Red for life, orange for healing, yellow for sun, green for nature, turquoise for magic, blue for serenity, and purple for the spirit. I like to think of those elements as in every person.

      —GILBERT BAKER

PAST

"Want to go on an adventure?"

I look up as Cam, wearing an oversized denim jacket and a gray beanie, squeezes through my halfway-open window. I'm shoved in the far corner of my room, feet pressed against the wall and back against the side of my bed. I pull a well-creased copy of *The Bell Jar* off my face.

"Another broken vending machine at the laundromat?" I ask dryly.

Cam smiles wide and shimmies the rest of the way through the window. I watch the whole entrance routine: an absolutely terrible somersault across my bedroom floor followed by a quick pop-up to standing, beanie flying off and unruly blond curls bouncing everywhere.

I clap politely. "Very nice. Ten out of ten."

Cam laughs and saunters over to me. "Check this out."

Before I can shift, we're scrunched in together, arm pressed tight against arm. The familiar smells of sandalwood and citrus find their way into my hair. *The Bell Jar* has been kicked under my bed thanks to Cam, and there's now a new book hovering between us. As our hands meet on either edge, I see the rainbow-colored title arching over its cover:

GAY TREASURES

My breath catches so hard that I fumble the book and fall into a horrendous coughing fit.

Oh my God, my brain screams between coughs. *Oh my God, oh my God. It's happening. The talk is happening.*

How does Cam even know I'm gay? I'm frantically backtracking through my memories. Was it the pixie cut I got last fall when we started high school? My ridiculous insistence that we wear pussy hats to all the marches we begged to join as kids?

Cam's breathing has gone soft, and I realize I'm supposed to react in some specific way. As I open my mouth to say something—anything—a thought strikes my head so forcefully that I get a second bout of mental whiplash: What if this talk isn't about me at all? Or what if it's not *only* about me?

Want to go on an adventure?

Did that mean . . . Was that really asking if I wanted to go out with . . .

"My uncle Brian," Cam says quietly.

I turn my head. "What?"

"He died before I was born, and he left this massive trunk behind in our attic. That's where I found *this*."

"Was he gay?" I ask, at the exact moment Cam blurts out, "It's a treasure map!"

We both stare at each other.

"I guess . . ." Cam says uncomfortably. "I mean, yeah. He probably was. That would explain why he had this thing, anyway."

Cam grins and wiggles the book in front of me, as though it's a shiny piece of bait I just can't resist. I take a deep breath, stuffing down every question I was set to ask, every confession I had momentarily considered making. *Of course Cam didn't come here to talk about being gay*, I tell myself. *Cam and I don't talk about things like that.*

It was stupid to let myself imagine it.

"A treasure map," I echo. I sigh and force myself to grab hold of the bait.

The book's spine is so lean that it barely resembles a real book at all. It reminds me of those handmade zines from the 1990s. I thumb through the pages. There are crude drawings of people marching and waving signs, of others standing at podiums and on park benches, speaking to crowds, their mouths open and fists curled. Text fills in the blank spaces behind the people, an angry storm of words in the sky. Various Rubik's Cubes and tic-tac-toe grids with numbers scribbled inside are tucked into page corners. There's a strange urgency in the slant of the writing. Like whoever made these drawings and put this thing together was racing to get it done.

I study one of the Rubik's Cubes. "Well . . . if this really is what you say it is—"

"It is!" Cam interjects. "I'm telling you, this is a real-deal treasure map. Fame and glory are ours!"

"Then you came to the right person," I say, offering a demure smile. "For *research*. We're going to have to Benjamin Gates the hell out of this thing."

Cam frowns. "Benjamin who?"

The book falls into my lap.

"Okay," I say. "You did not just bring an alleged treasure book into my house without knowing who *the* Benjamin Franklin Gates is."

Cam takes a second, then snaps. "Oh, you mean the kite-and-glasses dude!"

"Gah!" I scramble up and grab the laptop off my desk. "That's it! We are watching *National Treasure* right this second."

We've had so many impromptu movie nights and random sharing of online videos that Cam rises as if on autopilot and plops down onto the left side of my bed. I take my usual spot on the right and start searching for the crème de la crème of movies about treasure hunting, or, as the incomparable Nicolas Cage character Benjamin Franklin Gates puts it, "treasure *protecting*." But just as I get the movie queued up, I feel the gentlest touch on my arm.

"Ivy," Cam murmurs.

My whole body freezes, the way it always does when Cam says my name. I peel my eyes off the screen and look at my best friend.

Cam gazes deeply back at me. "You think this is real too. Right?"

I glance down at the soft hand resting against my elbow.

"Yeah," I whisper. "I think it's real."

Then, all too quickly, the opening music swells, lightning strikes over a young Benjamin Gates, and Cam and I snap back to doing what we do best: pretending to be more focused on anything else than we could ever be on each other.

CHAPTER ONE

The view before me is sublime.

A gorgeous girl with thick, auburn hair and cat-eye glasses sits across the café table, her eyes soft, lips parted. Her nails trace the rim of her latte mug, tapping along to cheerful French music as it trips from the speakers. In the background, rows of books with shiny, uncracked spines gleam on the shelves.

Everything in my vision comes together like puzzle pieces. The girl. The coffee. The books. *The girl.* It's all making this perfect picture. But the very best part of it, the biggest piece you can't even see, is the person who isn't here. I get to sit back and enjoy a world of total calm and sophistication without a certain someone—

The gorgeous girl, aka my date, Rachel, suddenly gasps.

"Is that Cam Leonardo behind you?"

I swear, even the violin in the background music shudders.

"No," I say automatically, though I haven't turned my head to look. I scrunch down in my chair and lift my giant mug like a mask.

No, no, no, I think. *Please, God. Not again.*

It can't really be him, I reassure myself. The Cam I know would never show his face here. Rachel and I are parked in a corner table at Lady Business, my favorite bookstore slash coffee shop in San Francisco. We're early to a slam poetry reading Rachel's performing in, and more importantly, we're on our ever-crucial third date.

Rachel adjusts her glasses and smooths her hair, though I notice she's staring somewhere just above my head as she does both things. My heart sinks. While I cannot imagine what the hell Cam would be doing in a bookstore . . . I know from the way Rachel's staring that it's him. No one else makes girls stare the way Cam does.

I clear my throat, hoping this will remind Rachel that, actually, she's on a date with *me* at the moment.

She startles and shakes her head. "Sorry."

"Nervous?" I ask gently.

"What?" Her eyes flick up, then back down to me.

"For your performance." I nod toward the crescent-shaped stage near the doors.

Rachel glances at the stage. She laughs. "Not really. I've been a performer since I was born."

"Hmm." I try to think of some witty response about babies and poetry readings, but every drafted sentence in my head sounds either humorless or just plain stupid. My tongue gets stuck to the roof of my mouth. This is the part where I'm supposed to come off as charming. Cam used to say I could be charming, in my own nerdy little way. But that was forever ago.

I force down a sip of my latte to loosen up a little and . . . Rachel is already back to staring over my head.

"So, when did you know you were gay?" I ask over the coffee shop music.

Rachel looks at me, horrified, and I realize that I might have actually yelled out that last word.

"Queer," she says, correcting me.

"Right," I say. Although, to be honest, I don't get what people have against being called gay. "Gay" can mean whatever you want it to mean, the same as "queer." But whatever. "Queer, of course. So, when did you know?"

Rachel sighs through her nose. "Look, Ivy, I know you're the head of the school's GSA or whatever, but don't you think queer people are allowed to talk about things other than being queer sometimes? Like, can we please be allowed to have some other interesting defining feature?"

"Your neck," a smooth voice says behind me.

I whip around and catch Cam loitering just beyond our table.

"What?" I snap.

My hand itches to fly up to my own neck, where I'm certain Cam meant to give me goose bumps by creeping up behind us like that. But I won't give him the satisfaction. He already has enough of an incessant, self-assured smirk as it is.

"Your neck," Cam repeats, this time nodding specifically to Rachel. "You always look so distinguished in class. A very interesting, very elegant neck. A perfect defining feature."

Rachel beams, her face blooming rosebud pink.

I scowl at Cam.

"Excuse you," I say, mouth pinched. "We're on a date here, if you don't mind."

"Not at all," Cam says, then grabs a chair from the next table and swings it wordlessly to ours. Rachel's eyes glitter as Cam scooches himself in.

He sets both forearms on the table and leans forward, slicing into my view of Rachel. She hardly seems to mind seeing any less of me, with her attention now fully on the beachy-haired, peach-fuzzed, surfer-wannabe idiot tucked between us.

Cam only seems self-assured when no one's challenging him. And almost no one does these days. They're too busy falling over themselves to notice that his carefully manufactured charisma is just a front. But I'm not fooled by all that fake charm for one second.

"For your information," I say, "it's incredibly rude to point out a physical characteristic as someone's so-called perfect defining feature. People also tend to have a sense of humor, or hopes and dreams, or hobbies, or anything more interesting than a giraffe neck."

Rachel's smile drops. She glares directly at me.

Cam only laughs his stupid, easy laugh and leans toward Rachel conspiratorially.

"You can't take this one too seriously," he says, hitching his thumb in my direction as if I were across a football field and not sitting inches away. "She means well. She just doesn't have a filter when she's nervous. Tends to overthink things. A very Benjamin Gates type, if you know the reference."

With every word out of Cam's mouth, Rachel's glare softens. But at this point I don't even care.

"I am not nervous!" I yell. I push my latte away and stand up. "I'm just trying to figure out what the hell my date is doing ogling the shit out of überdude Cam Leonardo twenty minutes before heading onto a stage to recite some crappy *Vagina Monologues* rip-off!"

Rachel stands across from me and snatches her jacket off the chair.

"Screw you," she says. Her delivery is so crisp and biting that instantly my ears go hot. She marches halfway across the length of the coffee shop before she swings around and jabs her finger toward me. "I'm the one performing here. *You* get out!"

"Fine by me!" I say, even though my face feels like it's a million degrees. I plunk my latte mug down onto the clearing tray with as much gusto as I can without spilling the vast remainder of it over the other dishes.

I yank my huge shoulder bag behind me and toss the front door open. As I storm down the sidewalk, I get into a brief boxing match with my coat as I attempt to punch my arms into each sleeve, not bothering to stop for one second to address the fact that I have the whole thing on inside out.

My heart is thumping in my ears. The tiny bit of latte I actually drank starts to churn violently in my stomach. I pinch the bridge of my nose to keep from crying. *It's not fair!* I want to scream. Why does he have to be around all the time? I picture a cat catching a mouse and letting it go, over and over.

I'm so tired of Cam catching me off guard every time I try to do something for myself. I'm so tired of never being able to get away from him.

"Hey!"

As if on cue, footsteps pound down the pavement until a very winded-looking Cam catches up to me.

"What?" I say, upping my pace slightly.

"I have to . . . ask you . . . something," he wheezes.

I stop so abruptly that Cam barges two steps past me and has to turn around. It's nice to see his confidence waver, if only for one second.

"Let me ask *you* something," I say. "What were you doing at Lady Business?"

Cam throws his arms out. "Oh, because I'm—what did you call it—überdude? Is that my new alter ego?"

I huff. "We both know you normally wouldn't be caught dead in a bookstore. It's like someone's paying you to stalk me and ruin my life."

"Damn, wouldn't that be nice." Cam scratches his chin and smiles. He uses every scrap of his four additional inches to tower over me. "Unfortunately, I'm not getting paid."

"Pro bono, then," I say, rolling my eyes. "How noble."

"It's not really life-ruining, though, is it?" he asks.

"Is what?"

"Missing a poetry reading." Cam nudges his toe against the sidewalk. "I mean, if anything, I saved you from a terrible afternoon."

If I didn't know any better, I'd wonder if there was a hint

of sincerity in his voice. Why would Cam care if my afternoon was terrible or not? He wouldn't, of course. He's not sincere when it comes to me. At least, not anymore.

"Thanks for your service," I mutter. I dart around Cam to keep walking, but he catches my arm. His hand feels uncomfortably hot, and I'm relieved when he immediately lets go.

We both stare past each other, not quite making eye contact.

"What do you want?" I ask, adjusting my bag.

"V, come on," Cam says softly. I absolutely hate it when he shortens my name, like we still know each other well enough to shorten names. Like we still know each other at all.

He looks at me and asks point-blank, "Why else would I be in that bookstore?"

His eyes are so warm, his posture so open and exposed, that my glare slips a little. Is it actually possible . . . Is he trying to have a serious conversation?

"Why would you?" I ask, hating myself for how small my voice sounds.

Cam leans closer. He bends his head toward mine. For a moment I'm completely paralyzed, completely silent. I watch him, breath stopped, as his gaze drops from my eyes and down into my bag.

"*Persuasion*!" he shouts triumphantly. "I knew it started with a *P*!"

He takes an enormous step back and claps a hand to his chest. "I totally forgot what book Mr. Kuh assigned for next week. But I knew you'd already have it on you. You always do!"

Cam pivots back to the bookstore, now practically skipping down the pavement. A sliver of air finds its way into my lungs. I pull out *Persuasion* from the top of my bag and hug it tightly to my chest. He just wanted a book. It's always about some stupid book.

I watch my ex–best friend pull the door to Lady Business open. He throws his head back and laughs as he strides inside, already striking up some charming conversation with a stranger. Or maybe with Rachel. It doesn't make a difference, really.

"Asshole," I murmur.

I take a long, rattled breath, then turn for home.

CHAPTER TWO

Even though Life is one of the worst board games I've ever played, it's still better than the game that Cam Leonardo has decided to make of my actual, real life. While we've never spoken directly about it, I assume these are the rules:

1. Cam infiltrates some key aspect of Ivy's life.
2. Cam makes Ivy look like an idiot.
3. Cam flounces away, scoring all the points.
4. Ivy's score always stays at zero.

There was a time when Cam and I used to be on the same team. We were the only two people on our team, really. Us against "the fascist, bootlicking world," as Cam liked to say.

Then, right before sophomore year, I came out as gay.

And *the thing* happened.

That's when everything between us came unglued.

We were hanging out at Duboce Park, one of Cam's favorite

spots for treasure hunting. All we did that summer was look for treasure. Once we realized that some of the clues in *Gay Treasures* pointed to San Francisco, we were hooked. I was in charge of research. Cam was in charge of digging. And even though we kept coming home empty-handed at the end of each day, we knew we were getting closer. We could feel it. Or at least . . . we could definitely feel *something*.

That afternoon we were taking a break and lying together in the grass. I remember the way the leaves fluttered in the trees above us. I kept picturing their shadows as little hands shooing me over and over.

Do it. Do it now, the leaves kept saying. *It's time.*

I turned onto my side and looked at Cam, whose eyes had been closed, soaking up the warmth of the sun. But as soon as I turned, Cam looked back at me, already grinning. Like whatever I had to say would be something good.

"What is it?"

I took a deep breath. It was going to be okay. Everything would be okay.

"I'm gay," I whispered.

Cam blinked. And blinked again. "What?"

"I'm gay," I said again.

I guess I could have added something. Maybe explained how long I'd known or why I hadn't said anything before. When you look back, there are always a million things you could've done differently. To be honest, I didn't realize I would have to explain anything. There was this stupid part of me that thought . . . that was *so* certain that if I could just find the courage to come out, Cam would come out too. And then things would be different between us.

But Cam didn't come out.

Instead, Cam shifted away from me. It was a gesture I should have been used to. The two of us were exclusive, smart-ass nerds, so we didn't mind when classmates at school gave us extra space. But with Cam, the motion physically hurt. It was like our friendship had turned upside down in an instant. I thought that moment was the worst thing that could possibly happen.

Then Cam muttered the four worst words I've ever heard. And walked away.

And we didn't talk a single day the rest of sophomore year.

If you want to know what loneliness feels like, it's not when you're sitting at a table with no friends. Loneliness is sitting at a table and watching your ex–best friend across the room, doing everything possible to avoid eye contact with you. Loneliness is hiding in the metaphorical closet for another six months because the first person you told completely dumped you from their life.

Luckily, the deepest wounds have a way of hardening into the thickest scars. Pain makes for good armor. After a while I stopped second-guessing everything I had done wrong when Cam and I were friends. I stopped thinking about our friendship completely. When I finally came out in the spring, I didn't whisper it tentatively to a few classmates. I took over the intercom at morning announcements and shouted it to everyone. I joined the Genders & Sexualities Alliance club at school and promptly named myself as chair.

I made being gay feel like a kingdom, and I made myself its queen.

Then, after ghosting me for an entire year, Cam had the audacity to show up to Sunset High junior year and pretend like none of it had ever happened. Cam joined GSA the first day of school and came out as transgender, with he/him pronouns. Suddenly, he was the one shouting about how cool it was to be queer. All the members loved him immediately. Because of course they did. Because everyone loves Cam the second he decides they're worth his time.

Less than a month after joining the club, he made a motion to take over as chair. I argued that the role wasn't a popularity contest; it was about organizing meetings and fundraisers, something he had absolutely no idea how to do. Someone in the room suggested we could both be co-chairs, and for the first time in over a year, Cam turned and grinned at me.

Except it wasn't his real grin. It was a Cheshire Cat grin, the kind of grin that told me instantly that this was a battle he had just won.

Cam, one point. Ivy, zero.

The game had officially begun.

Cam's been racking up points on me ever since. He somehow crashes almost every date I go on. He tanks nearly every group project we get roped into together at school. He usurps all my roles, questions every position I take, and generally thrives on being an enormous pain in my ass. But the biggest con of all is the fact that no one else at school even realizes what he's doing. They still think—after everything that's happened—that the two of us are somehow conspiring together, like a fully out Bert and Ernie.

"Gay royalty," I've heard people whisper whenever they find us sitting outside the principal's office because *someone* decided I was serious at the GSA committee meeting when I said we ought to black out every bathroom door label so they'd all be gender-neutral.

But despite what the rest of the student body wants to believe, Cam and I are not some superpowerful queer duo. And we never will be. Which is why, after months of putting up with this new, fake-friend version of Cam . . . I've finally discovered a loophole in his game.

"Hey, Ivy," Julia says from her desk.

I slink into the yearbook office, which also happens to be the basement computer lab at Sunset High. It was the only computer lab until the library installed a brand-new set of computers two years ago. Now the yearbook staff gets to call the old lab home. Although, technically, we call it the Bat Cave.

Sunny and Gabriel look up from their computers and give little waves. I nod and park myself in my usual spot at the head of the room. The majority of our yearbook crew doesn't meet daily. There's around fifteen of us in total, but most members are photographers, tramping in and out, dumping flash drives filled with photos onto our desks. Julia, Sunny, Gabriel, and I are the editors. We're the ones who put everything together. Because I'm editor in chief, I'm the one who has the final say.

Yearbook is an underrated club. For the four of us, it's our version of a digital arts club, which Sunset High apparently doesn't have the "resources" to support. But we're just as much artists as the students who meet to do still-life paintings and figure drawings at the school's official Art Club.

A lot of classmates look at Yearbook Club and think we're just doing this to pad our college applications. Or, worse, they think we're a cohort of nostalgic idiots who want to glorify high school like it's the best four years life has to offer. What no one realizes is that, actually, yearbook editors are the ones writing history. We decide how to tell the story of the school year. Piss us off, and seven months later you'll be handed a permanent, bound book with a photo of you halfway through a sneeze. Or, you know, we can at least threaten as much.

But catching Cam mid-sneeze isn't even my brilliant loophole. The *real* loophole is that, as editor in chief, I get to submit the yearbook as my portfolio for a study-abroad digital arts program at the Paris College of Art. Good yearbooks *are* an art form, and ours is brilliant. The program is strictly for high school seniors, which means—if I do my job right over the next month—this could be my chance to cut out of high school a whole year early.

And get off Cam's game board entirely.

"Ivy, look at this." Gabriel calls me over to his screen.

He's pulled up one of our photos from the Halloween parade last fall, where various clubs dressed up and walked along

Market Street, tossing out candy to little kids. Next to that photo is a much older one from the *San Francisco Chronicle*. It's a Pride parade shot from 1977, and Gabriel has managed to match the angle of the background buildings nearly perfectly to the photo taken just six months ago.

"Damn," I say, clapping his shoulder. "Nice find!"

This is our yearbook's theme. Well, technically it's the theme I introduced to the club this year. We're tying Sunset High's present to the neighborhood's past. But it's not just a simple compare-and-contrast where we're mashing up new and old photos. I'm trying to make a much bigger statement.

Back in the 1970s, San Francisco was a place where one of the most oppressed groups in the country congregated together and showed how much power and influence they could really have. No one got elected in San Francisco without earning the gay vote, which was composed of thousands of young people. And even though the world feels like it's careening into a shithole right now . . . young gay people could totally have that level of influence again. We just have to find the path that history has already laid out for us.

Gabriel digitally cuts the foreground students from our photo and moves them to the archive, keeping several of the background characters from the Pride parade in frame. We'll have to zoom in afterward and check carefully to make sure there are no visible boobs or asses in the final product. I already landed myself in a fair bit of trouble for missing some 1970s butt cheeks that showed up on the midyear teaser reel we submitted to our faculty sponsor.

Julia pulls out a box of slightly crumpled flyers.

"I scanned these last night for our bulletin board page," she says.

She clicks on a file and I see a mash-up of random events and announcements from Sunset High all mixed in with meeting, boycott, and protest flyers we've spotted in old photos around the Castro and Sunset districts.

After months of planning and research, it's incredible to see our ideas finally taking shape in front of us on page after page. We've planted random Sunset High graduates from 1976 into the senior class. We've mixed together club rosters, sports teams, prom queens, and even swapped out some current faculty photos with versions of their younger selves. We've blurred the lines between past and present so thoroughly that on some work nights, when we're already high off sleep deprivation and caffeinated sugar rushes, the four of us feel like real-life time travelers.

I return to my computer and the project I've been working on: the introduction to the yearbook concept. It also happens to be doubling as my mission statement for my portfolio application to Paris.

History isn't forgotten, I type into the document.

We may want to believe that it's all in the past, or that we know so much more now than people did then. But in the end, history will always have a way of catching up with us. Even if we try to put it away in a dusty book on a high shelf. Even if we pretend like it didn't happen at all.

But something powerful can happen if we let history in. We can see a much bigger picture of ourselves, maybe even something that we didn't see before. History doesn't have to be just a snapshot of what people have already done. It can be a reflection of what we're doing now. Or a lesson on what to do differently.

It can even be a map leading to our future.

I pause and look around the computer lab. Julia and Sunny are swapping printed shots and checking over the backgrounds. Gabriel is still clicking away at his computer, his telltale sign of making sure his digital cut is seamless. It feels good to have a group, even a small group, that's just mine—that only I belong to. Cam may think he can invade every part of my life, but he can't stop me from tunneling my way out.

This yearbook project will be the thing that finally gets me away from my own personal history with Cam Leonardo for good.

CHAPTER THREE

San Francisco is, if nothing else, a city of perspective.

Our steep streets might be a pain in the ass to drive on, but they also allow for some of the best city views anywhere around the world. The darkest alley can spill right onto a front-row view of the Golden Gate Bridge. The most unassuming house can reveal the full downtown skyline through a kitchen window. In a lot of ways, real estate prices in the city are based more on what you can see rather than where you can walk to. At least, that's the mantra that keeps renovation architects like my mother constantly in business.

She glides through the front doors to Chez Moi, the French-style bistro she always suggests when I meet her for lunch. If you ask me, the chairs here are way too stiff, and the food portions are never big enough. But Mom never asks me.

"Ivy!" she says loudly as she reaches the table. I stand, and she pulls me into her arms for one of those big, tight hugs usually reserved for a good friend you haven't seen in forever.

I love these hugs. I never get them at home. By the time Mom walks through the door in the evenings, she usually kicks her shoes straight across the room of our narrow apartment and heads directly into the bathtub. At home we're always drained and worn out and all too eager to disappear into our own corners. These lunch dates get to be a kind of fantasy for both of us, where we each pretend we're something different.

When Mom hugs me like this, I pretend I'm an adult already, just fluttering in and out of her life for a quick visit. That way she's happy to see me, every time. And while Mom hasn't exactly spelled it out, I'm guessing she probably likes pretending she's my friend rather than my mother. She always says being a mom has aged her like nothing else. I know she misses when she was young and free to go wherever she wanted, to do exactly as she pleased.

Which is, incidentally, kind of how she got saddled with me.

The thing is, I don't have another parent. I don't know if Mom ever wanted there to be another parent, or if she was dead set on handling things herself. She doesn't really talk about why it's just the two of us, and I don't ask. All I know is, she's really glad I'm almost grown and out of the house.

That makes two of us.

Mom sits across the table and picks up the menu, her eyes skimming back and forth, probably ping-ponging between the only two entrees she ever orders.

"How's school?" she asks.

"Busy," I respond from behind my menu.

This is the answer Mom likes best. If I say "easy," Mom will berate me for being lazy and not pushing myself. If I say "hard," that's even worse, because "public schools aren't supposed to be hard, Ivy." But "busy" is good. It means I'm staying above water but swimming like hell under the surface.

"How's work?"

"Busy," Mom says, sighing heavily.

"Did you finish the hotel this week?"

She shakes her head and pulls a file from her bag, then opens it flat on the table between us. It's a blueprint for the boutique hotel she's rebuilding in Pacific Heights. Mom's finger lands over the central staircase.

"The balustrade rails are spaced one inch too wide," she grumbles. "Three and a half inches. That's city regulation. We'll have to redo all of them."

"Shit." I twist my head, following the staircase on the design as it wraps around to the second and third floors.

Mom leans back in her chair and folds her arms. She's flustered, of course. But she also looks secretly happy whenever she talks about work like this. The page in front of us represents an entire hotel that *she* designed. With construction crews working under her direction. It must feel amazing to create actual jigsaw pieces of the city, crafting doorways and window frames and staircases that could be here for hundreds of years after she's gone.

I push the file gently back toward her. This is exactly the kind of thing I want to bring to a Chez Moi lunch once I get into the Paris College of Art, or even later, when I'm off working on my own stuff. I don't actually know what it is I want to do with art yet. But that's what study-abroad programs are for, right? Someday, one way or another, I'll have an impressive showcase of work I can nitpick and complain about. Something that proves to Mom that the things I'm doing are important too.

"You know . . ." I say. "We're actually getting pretty far on the yearbook layout."

"Mm." Mom stares into her water glass.

"Most of the filler pages are done, which is where we get to be really creative."

Mom snorts.

"What?" I ask.

She shakes her head. "Oh, it's just . . . yearbooks are like grade-school dioramas, aren't they? You can call them creative, but they can't really escape their form. I mean, who's looking in a yearbook for anything other than their own photo?"

"Sometimes yearbook layouts can be artistic," I say carefully. My hands twitch over my bag. Before I can stop myself, I've pulled my laptop onto the table, exactly where Mom's blueprint was. I don't even have to click to find the document—it's always the first thing waiting on my desktop. I rotate the screen to my mom and sit back in my chair.

She flicks her eyes to me. "What is this?"

"It's the yearbook," I say. "This one's not like a diorama, Mom. Go ahead. You can scroll through it."

She sucks her teeth for a moment, then finally leans toward the screen, scrolling and scrolling and scrolling—

"You're going too fast," I blurt out.

Mom sighs. "Ivy, this is how I look at things. Do you know how many seconds a work of classical art gets appreciated for in a museum?"

"You're not even giving it fifteen seconds," I argue. "And this is your kid's work. Don't you think parents should spend a little more time looking at stuff their kids made?"

"As opposed to a piece of actual art?" Mom raises an eyebrow. "God, I hope not."

I lunge across the table and snatch my laptop back.

"Don't cause a scene," Mom says through a clenched jaw. She checks over her shoulder and offers a dazzling smile to no one in particular.

"I'm *not* causing a scene," I hiss. I sniff back any wayward tears and sit up taller. "This is important to me." I chew on my lip a moment, deciding whether or not I want this to be the exact moment I tell her about Paris. Dream scenario, I would wait until I had already received my acceptance letter. Or at least until I sent my application in next month. But there's no point holding off any longer.

I clear my throat. "I'm using this as my portfolio for an art program in Paris."

Mom blinks like a camera flash has just gone off in her face. "Art school? You want to go to . . . art school?"

"It's just one year," I say defensively. I pivot the laptop back to myself and slowly scroll down the document, lingering on all the little details it took hours to get right. "But if I get into the program, then, yeah. I want to go to art school."

I wince and wait for Mom to launch into one of her lectures.

Whatever the topic, I know my mother, and when it comes to anything regarding me or the choices I'm making, she always has plenty of opinions.

But for some strange reason, she doesn't share any of those opinions right now.

She just keeps sitting there, wearing an expression I'm certain I've never seen on her before. Usually I can detect her mood in an instant. I know impatience by the shift of her mouth, pride in the angle of her chin. But the current crease down the top of her nose is all but foreign to me. If I didn't know better, I would say she almost looks . . . pitying?

"What are you thinking?" I ask.

Mom doesn't answer. She presses her fingers to her mouth, clearly working over a response. But here's the thing about Mom: She always says what she thinks. She's not afraid of being blunt or harsh. In her mind, measuring someone with lofty expectations is a compliment in and of itself, leaving her free to share as much detailed criticism as she wants. So something is *up*.

"*Mom*. What are you thinking?" I say it louder this time.

Mom's fingers drop to her chin, and she parts her lips in a sigh. She false starts twice like this until, finally, she splays her hand toward my computer.

"This . . . isn't art."

My mouth fills with tar.

"What," I say. My voice is so dead that I can't even make the word into a question.

Mom sighs again. "It's extreme competence," she explains

gently. Damn it if her gentle voice isn't the cruelest sound I've ever heard. "And, hey, look at me. Architects are masters of extreme competence. But we're not artists either."

I stare at her.

"I tried to do the artist thing, Ivy. I understand where you're coming from. But you can't just show off a little photo collage project and call it art. Art is more than skill, or even mastery, for that matter. Art is . . . bigger. It's narrative."

"I have a mission statement." I murmur this so quietly that I'm not sure if I'm talking to Mom or just to myself. She hears me anyway.

"I'm sure you have some nicely written paragraphs on something like the past and the present intermingling, and that's fine," she says, even though it's so obviously *not* fine that I would laugh if I weren't so close to crying. "But there's no real story in this," she goes on. "*You're* not even in this, Ivy. The problem is—"

Mom's voice becomes a foghorn blaring somewhere over my head.

The problem is, my own mother has just taken a dump on everything I've worked on over the last seven months.

The problem is, she doesn't even think it qualifies as art.

The problem is . . . she might actually be right.

CHAPTER FOUR

I send the SOS text out to Sunny, Julia, and Gabriel early the next morning. Seconds later, my phone pings.

Julia: Where are we meeting? And who's bringing coffee?

Sunny: IVY BETTER BE BRINGING THE COFFEE FOR ACCOSTING US AT THIS UNGODLY HOUR.

Gabriel: I thought we already established that the hour was, in fact, extremely godly.

Me: I'm on the coffee. We're meeting in the Bat Cave.

Julia: Uh . . . it's Sunday.

Gabriel: Have we not gone over this?

Me: I copied the janitor's key in December. Meet me at the field by nine.

Julia: We'll be there!

Sunny: BUT ONLY IF THERE IS COFFEE.

Twenty minutes later, the four of us assemble next to the Sixth Avenue entrance of Sunset High. Gabriel slumps near the chain-link fence, his hands tucked into the pockets of his giant hoodie. The hood rests over his thick mop of hair, which already covers the top of his eyes so most of the time he resembles a sheepdog. Julia bounces up and down on the balls of her feet. She's dressed in a short-sleeved button-up shirt and the just-above-the-knee shorts every parent desperately wishes their teenage daughter would wear. Her notebook is out, along with a handful of different-colored pens. Sunny, the tiniest member on our staff, stands in an actual pink fuzzy robe with her arms firmly crossed. She's wearing sunglasses light enough to reveal her closed, pinched eyes. I round out the group with my usual ensemble of rumpled black jeans, Doc Martens, and some thrift store sweater LeVar Burton probably rocked in the eighties. The four of us look like Greta Gerwig's fever dream version of the Avengers.

"What the hell?" Sunny says as I join the circle.

"Sorry." I thrust the cardboard tray into the center. "Coffee took forever."

Everyone grabs their order and takes a sip. I march us over to the custodian door near the basketball court and usher the others inside. We creep down into the basement. Julia turns on the hoard of discarded holiday twinkle lights we got at a yard sale a few months ago, just after winter break. We thought it would cheer the place up considerably, but with all the computer towers humming and lights blinking . . . the twinkle lights overhead have the effect of making us feel like we're inside the bridge of a spaceship on *Star Trek*. Which isn't all bad, actually.

Gabriel and Julia sit at their usual spots. Sunny stands next to my desk and stares at me while I open my laptop.

"Hey, Sunny," I say as I sign in to my accounts. Her stare is so menacing that I mess up my password twice.

She flips her sunglasses up. "It's Sunday."

I look at her and smile. "You know, I think you're the third person to point that out."

"So, what's going on?" Julia asks. She and Gabriel have their spinning chairs twisted to face me. Sunny eventually backs into her own chair and plops down. She takes a huge swig of her coffee, and I make a mental note to get her another as soon as that one's empty.

I plug my laptop into the projector. Instantly, my home screen lights up the large screen hanging over the back wall. I click open the yearbook document.

"It's fucked," I say.

Gabriel chokes on his coffee. "What? Did the files become corrupted?"

"No, but . . ."

The next words get caught on my tongue. I've never really talked about my mom to anyone but Cam. I know how she comes off to other people when she's sending food back or commenting on someone's outfit or décor. It might seem easy to dismiss her criticisms as bitchy and move on. But my mom is the worst kind of bitchy. She's both bitchy *and* right, meaning it's all but impossible for me to ignore her.

I also, of course, haven't shared my Paris plans with anyone at school either. I feel like there's little point, seeing as my one real friend dumped me and there's not enough time to make good friends again before taking off. The yearbook crew and I are all about business. We get shit done and we do it well, and that's the foundation for whatever pseudo-friendship it is we have.

But the deadlines here are too much for me to vault on my own. We've been working on the yearbook throughout the school year. And now we have less than a month left to salvage it into a good portfolio before classes let out for the summer.

"There's . . . no story here," I say finally, despising how much I sound like Mom.

The others stare at me.

"I know," Sunny says slowly, "that you did *not* wake us all up at eight in the morning to come to school and talk about whether or not the yearbook is telling a story. So what are we doing here, Ivy?"

Gabriel and Julia look at Sunny, then turn again to me.

"Umm . . ." I stare up at the page layouts splashed over the wall across the room. I'm so used to seeing the entire yearbook crammed into my little laptop screen that, for a moment, the work really does look completely different. The old photos are so blurry and pixelated that seeing them blown up like this makes me cringe. Suddenly, the once invisible lines dividing the archival images from our own become stupidly obvious.

And that's all this is, I realize with horrendous, sinking clarity. It's old photos and new photos spliced together. It's the equivalent of the guy on the internet who holds up movie stills in front of the same film locations years later.

I'm the movie guy, I think miserably.

My mother's voice rings in my head: *I'm sure you have some nicely written paragraphs on something like the past and the present intermingling—*

That's exactly *what I had written*, I growl back.

There's nothing like seeing a pool of endless depth in your own work and then having someone else throw in a rock that just bounces off the surface to show how utterly shallow it all is. And yet . . .

I keep clicking through the page spreads.

There's this strange, tingling feeling I get every time I open these files. Even if Mom is right, even if what we have is shit . . . then why do I keep wanting to come back and look at it over and over? Maybe there really is a story here, and I haven't figured out what that story is. Maybe it's just not my story.

Or maybe it's not my story yet.

Gabriel makes a loud, obviously fake cough. I pause on the dedication page to Mr. Torres, the school's head janitor.

"Sorry," I say with a jolt. "I got lost in my head."

"Uh, no," Gabriel says. "I'm pretty sure you took us along with you."

"Who's the movie guy?" Julia asks, scanning her notebook. I look over and see that she already has a page filled in. "And what exactly did you write?" she adds, circling another line. "And why isn't it your story?"

"Damn it!" I slap my forehead. "Was I just talking out loud the whole time?"

"Not the whole time," Julia says, at the same moment Gabriel answers, "Yeah, pretty much."

Sunny gives a barely perceptible smile and takes another long sip of her coffee.

Julia points the end of a purple pen toward me. "Is this

a riddle? Or one of those fill-in-the-blank puzzles? Does the movie guy have a story you stole for the yearbook?"

I groan and turn toward the projector screen, where we've superimposed Mr. Torres dancing over a 1970s party along Castro Street. My eyes get lost in the blurry background. "No. I'm just realizing that my mission statement isn't what I . . ."

My eyes skim across the photo until they land on a partial flyer pasted over a building in the background:

My jaw goes slack. I forget how to breathe.

Holy shit.

I grab my laptop and roll the cursor over the screen. "What is this?" I ask.

"What's what?" Gabriel pushes his hair to one side.

"This," I say again. The cursor arrow is now flying in little circles as I highlight the specific words:

btwn 17th & 18th Streets

A GIANT BTWN STREETS. That had been the final clue in the treasure hunt. The one Cam and I never figured out. And the answer's been right here this whole time—cryptic "btwn" abbreviation and everything! I've had this image on my computer for months. I just never looked at it on a big screen until now.

"*This* is my story!" I say. I can already imagine the professors at the Paris College of Art opening up my portfolio and reading the title:

Foray into San Francisco's Past Turns Up Literal Gold

"All right," Sunny announces. "I've had about enough of this Ivy-flavored nervous breakdown, or whatever it is that's happening. Give us a reason to stay or I'm going back to bed."

"You already drank an entire cup of coffee," Julia says.

Sunny sniffs. "Bold of you to assume that was my first cup."

I whip around to face the others. "You want a reason to stay?" I ask Sunny. I march up to the projector screen and smack my palm over the flyer. "How about digging up an actual buried treasure?"

CHAPTER FIVE

When Cam first brought *Gay Treasures* to my house freshman year, we were, at that point, extremely amateur sleuths. The book itself is basically an introduction to gay rights told in the style of a fairy tale:

> *Once upon a time, not long after midnight, in a room crowded with smoke . . . four, two, one, and one knocked on the double doors of Greenwich Village's Stonewall Inn.*
>
> *"Open up! Police! We're taking the place!"*
>
> *In stormed the four officers in plainclothes suits.*
>
> *In stormed the two in uniform.*
>
> *In stormed the detective.*
>
> *In stormed the deputy.*
>
> *But they were not the only storm in the room that night. And despite the formal announcement of their intentions, in the early morning hours of the twenty-eighth of June, the Stonewall Inn would not be for their taking.*

Each chapter is another tale from the gay rights movement, set in places across the country, filled with different protagonists who each become, by the story's end, gay treasures in their own rights.

That's the obvious part of the book, at least. The hidden part, the part Cam and I were so focused on, was about the *other* gay treasures. Not the people themselves, but the actual treasures hidden in the ground in honor of each story's hero. Clues leading to those treasures were in the book too. But instead of being hidden in the stories, the clues were hidden in codes and ciphers peppered throughout the pages.

The night Cam first brought over *Gay Treasures*, we watched *National Treasure* together and took notes on all the ciphers featured in the movie. Then we went back through the book and circled anything that seemed like a potential clue or cipher. After that, we spent almost every day that summer poking around San Francisco.

"Copyright says 1983," Cam had said. "We shouldn't need to use modern technology to solve a riddle that was written forty years ago."

But if my yearbook crew has a specialty, it would be mixing modern technology with the past. Everything it took Cam and me months to figure out ends up taking Gabriel, Sunny, and Julia mere minutes to uncover, thanks to their internet-sleuthing skills.

"Okay," Sunny says as the Wiki page loads. She nurses the second round of coffee I went out and bought everyone immediately after announcing our new angle. A caffeinated Sunny is a happy Sunny, evidenced by the fact that her fuzzy robe and sunglasses are now discarded in a pile by the stairwell.

Sunny uses the find-in-page function and skims through the highlighted sections.

"*Gay Treasures*. Written and published by an anonymous BGR. Later revealed to be Gilbert Baker, inventor of the Pride rainbow flag."

"Why the BGR initials, then?" Julia asks, looking up from her notebook.

Sunny smirks. "Stands for 'Busty Gay Ross,' apparently." She keeps reading. "That was Gilbert's drag name, based on Betsy Ross, creator of the American flag."

"Ahh." Julia nods and scribbles more notes.

"Book's been out of print since its initial publication," Sunny reads off the bottom of the page. "No known copies in circulation. But two of the seven treasures have already been located."

"The treasures are based on specific people," I add.

Sunny nods and reads the next section out loud. "There were seven treasures buried for seven different gay icons. The Marsha P. Johnson treasure—an enamel vase painted with Marsha's portrait—was found in New York City twenty-five years ago. Then the Judy Garland treasure—a tennis bracelet made up of rainbow-colored gemstones—was found by accident in Grand Rapids, Minnesota, around nine years ago."

Gabriel looks over from his own computer and wrinkles his nose. "But Judy wasn't even gay."

"She was a *gay icon*," Julia counters. She reads from her own screen, "In the 1970s, you would check whether someone was gay by asking them, 'Are you a friend of Dorothy?' The question refers to Judy Garland's character Dorothy from the 1939 *The Wizard of Oz* film." Julia glances at Gabriel. "She's basically the OG ally for the queer community."

"Hmph," Gabriel says, turning away from us.

"So where are the other five treasures?" Sunny asks me.

I shrug. "I don't know. There are a lot of theories about the other icons and cities. But we do know that San Francisco is a pretty good bet."

Sunny swivels around in her chair. "Gilbert invented the rainbow flag when he lived here. You think he might've buried a treasure in honor of himself?"

"Nope!" Gabriel says before I have a chance to answer. He slides to one side and shows us his screen, where he's been cleaning up the background flyer from the yearbook dedication page. The flyer that's changed everything.

brate
vey's Birthday

sday, May 22nd
0 PM
Castro Street
btwn 17th & 18th Streets

"Whoa," Julia says.

The transformation is definitely impressive. Gabriel has dialed out the shadows and pumped up the contrast to get the words "brate," "vey's," and "Birthday" sharp enough to read. But all my focus is on the last line, which has been surprisingly clear from the beginning.

In the end, despite hundreds of hours combing through the book, Cam and I managed to solve only one cipher in *Gay Treasures*. The answer we came up with was *A GIANT BTWN STREETS*. Which, of course, is nonsense without any context. A giant could be anyone. "Between streets" could mean anything. Without the next step, we were lost. We needed the right clue for everything else to unlock.

"Vey's birthday," Julia says, her voice lilting as she tips her head to one side. "Who do we think is Vey?"

"It's cut off," Gabriel says. He types something into the search bar and grins as the results load. "Harvey Milk was born on May 22, 1930. He was famously known as the Mayor of Castro Street. That's pretty giant-like, if you ask me!"

I do a quick map search on my own computer.

"Oh my gosh," I say under my breath.

Julia's by my shoulder in an instant. "What is it?"

"Look at this," I say as Gabriel and Sunny cram next to Julia on either side. I point to a satellite map of the Castro neighborhood. "There's Seventeenth Street, and there's Eighteenth Street. See where they each intersect with Castro? Now, look right in the middle."

I draw my finger down the road, pausing at the exact midpoint between Seventeenth and Eighteenth. A tiny alley juts out from Castro Street and ends in a cluster of trees. If the Mayor of Castro Street is our giant . . . and there's a perfect hideaway just off Castro between Seventeenth and Eighteenth . . .

"The treasure has to be there," I say. The clues match up too well for this to be pure coincidence.

The verdict sets the team in motion, and in a moment everyone is scrambling madly around, grabbing their bags and shouting out directions for how we should get our asses over to Castro. But I linger on the map in front of me.

I don't want to admit it out loud . . . but it feels wrong, somehow, to be doing this next step without Cam. He's the one who always said Harvey Milk had to be the gay treasure of San Francisco. We even went to Harvey's old storefront, Castro Camera, a few times, as well as the GLBT—Gay, Lesbian, Bisexual, Transgender—Historical Society Museum on Castro and Eighteenth Street to look for clues.

I can't believe we were so close.

But even more than that, even if Cam had never figured out the Harvey Milk thing . . . he was the one who squeezed in through my window with the book. This was his hunt first.

No, a voice in my head pipes up.

This was *our* hunt. I was the one dragging Cam to museums and libraries. I was the one who wanted to talk about the gay rights movement. It shouldn't matter who found the book first. What matters now is that I've found the next clue. And it's not my responsibility to drag along someone who ghosted our friendship just to finish something we started so long ago.

In the end, Gabriel, Julia, Sunny, and I agree to grab the train over to Market Street and then ride it down to Castro. When we get on at Irving and Sixth, we can barely contain our excitement. Sunny keeps asking how much the treasure is worth and how we're going to split it four ways. Gabriel starts counting the trees in the satellite map so we'll know which one to look under. Julia wants to know what our cover should be if the cops show up. Everyone has their own ideas and questions, but overall we're collectively buzzing. An hour ago we were mere yearbook staff editors. And now we're like Benjamin freaking Gates heading down the mine shaft in Trinity Church. The intoxication of treasure hunting is *real*.

By the time we get off at Market and Castro, however, the vibe has shifted considerably.

"We didn't bring a shovel," Sunny says in a monotone as the train clangs on behind us. She looks around at the group. "We literally just hopped on the train to go dig up treasure, and we don't even have a *shovel*."

"We could buy a shovel," Gabriel offers.

Sunny narrows her eyes. "Where?"

"I don't know . . ." Gabriel gestures down Castro Street. "Maybe there's a hardware store around here."

"I have a clipboard," Julia says, pulling her backpack to her front. "That could make a decent shovel."

I hold up my hands. "Let's go check things out first," I suggest. "Make sure we're on the right track."

It's hard for me not to get too carried away, though, as we walk farther down the street. Every single light pole has a Pride flag waving underneath. Nearly every storefront is sporting some kind of rainbow. This has to be a sign. It's hard to believe, even two years later, how much I desperately want this all to be a sign.

But if Castro Street seems like a yellow brick road . . . the so-called secret path between Seventeenth and Eighteenth is no Emerald City. It's not even an Emerald Hamlet.

"It's just a parking lot," Julia says as we round the corner.

"Of course it is," Sunny mutters.

My shoulders sag as we stare down the alleyway. My brain is spinning out like a car caught in mud. I can feel the ignition kicking, can feel the wheels trying to get to another point. But all that work just goes in circles. *How could we have been wrong?* The flyer was too spot-on for us to be wrong.

Gabriel points over the parked cars. "There are a couple trees back there," he says.

We glance at each other and trade nods. We've come this far, after all.

We slip into the alley and hurry toward the parking lot. Julia clutches her backpack to her chest and runs. Gabriel hunches halfway over as he follows on her heels. Considering it's midmorning on a Sunday, we all probably look ridiculous.

Once we reach the end of the alley, we see firsthand how closely packed all the cars are together. Even the trees Gabriel pointed out are wedged between the asphalt and the vine-covered wall encircling the lot. I shimmy past the noses of two cars to stand next to one of the trees. There's not really any "shovel prospect," as Cam used to call it. Everything is way too crammed together to dig in, let alone bury a treasure. I lean in closer to check out the tree roots.

The second my hand touches the earth, a blaring alarm shatters the air to pieces.

CHAPTER SIX

The only sound louder than the car alarm is Sunny's scream as she essentially jumps out of her skin.

Julia dives behind the next car over. Gabriel clamps his huge hands right over his hood and pulls it down over his face. For my part, all I can do is look back over my own ass at the source of the alarm.

An old man with shock-white hair stands at the other end of the car I'm currently crouched in front of. He clicks his key fob again, and the alarm stops with a single chirp. Despite the over-the-top reactions from Sunny, Julia, and Gabriel, the man's focus is directed entirely at me.

I stand up straighter.

"I'm so sorry," I say quickly. I realize then that I sound like I'm saying sorry for trying to break into the man's car. I motion toward the tree. "I was actually looking for . . . I didn't mean to get close to . . ."

The man blinks at me. He walks around the car to my side.

"I know you," he says, his voice tipping into surprise. "You're that kid from the museum."

I consider responding that, actually, I'm seventeen, and there are tens of museums in this city that I've visited many times. I am simply not *that kid* from *the museum*.

But then I recognize him too. He's an Asian American man with perfectly arched eyebrows and rounded cheeks. He grins, revealing the same brilliant, boxy smile I remember from two years ago.

"You're the volunteer," I say, "at the GLBT Historical Society Museum."

The man points to his chest. "Mr. Wong."

"Mr. Wong," I echo. I motion toward the cluster of hunching teenagers. "I'm Ivy. This is Sunny, Julia, and Gabriel."

Mr. Wong looks at the group, then turns back to me. "Where's the other girl?"

"No," I snap impulsively.

My chest tightens. I never know how to react in situations like this. I haven't mastered the art of correcting someone in the kind of easy way where the conversation can move forward immediately after. I tend to face-plant right back into my own past, circling through the same unresolved feelings of stupidity and humiliation.

Despite everything that Cam's done to me . . . I still have this horrible lump of guilt for not realizing he was, of course, transgender all along. Not that Cam gave me much of a chance to support him. He came out a whole year after ending our friendship. Even so, I feel like such an idiot whenever

I have to address this. How could I not have seen? Why was I such a dumbass when it came to my own best friend? The questions begin to spiral like a whirlpool, and then I'm standing there, drowning in yet another internal crisis, while the other person looks on, utterly flabbergasted.

Which is about the way Mr. Wong looks at me right now.

"He wasn't a girl," I say finally.

Mr. Wong nods slowly. "I understand. My apologies. But I do remember you both. Very passionate. Very intelligent. Looking for some kind of clue from a book, if I remember correctly."

If Cam were here, we'd do the thing where Cam would raise his hand for "passionate" and I would raise my hand for "intelligent," because that's just how we tended to look at almost everything. We split the world in half, divvying every attribute between us.

But today I don't want to be Cam's other half. Today I'm with a whole team of people that doesn't include him. I get to be both passionate *and* intelligent this time.

"We're still looking for that clue," I tell Mr. Wong. I pull out my phone and open a screenshot of the flyer. Gabriel and the others gather around as Mr. Wong looks it over. "We found this in the background of an old photo," I say. "I think this might be what my—what Cam and I were looking for when we met you."

Mr. Wong leans in until he's only an inch or two away from my screen. He squints at the text. "Oh my," he says softly. "This is about Harvey."

"For his birthday, right?" I ask.

Mr. Wong hands the phone back to me. "It was for the first birthday after his death, actually."

Julia gasps. "He died?"

Gabriel looks over his shoulder at her. "He was born in 1930, Julia. Get a grip."

"He was only forty-eight when he died," Mr. Wong says. "Harvey was assassinated while in office as city supervisor."

"Everyone knows that," Sunny says, squinting hard at Julia and Gabriel.

"Not everyone." Mr. Wong gives a pained sort of smile. He points at my phone. "And a lot of people don't know about the party."

"Why not?" I ask.

Mr. Wong lets out a long, heavy sigh. "This is not a conversation for a parking lot," he says finally. He points toward Castro Street. "Walk with me."

We turn out of the alleyway and head south on Castro.

Mr. Wong gestures at the buildings around us. "Look around," he says. "Look at all the streetlights and walls and windows."

We do.

"Harvey's party never happened," Mr. Wong tells us as we walk. "At least, not in the way we had wanted. When you have the time, take another close look at that old photo you found—the one with Harvey's flyer. Right away, you'll know when that photo was taken."

"How will we know?" I ask. "And why didn't the party end

up happening? Why were people throwing a birthday party for Harvey after he died in the first place?"

Mr. Wong presses his mouth tight. He draws himself up with a breath, then turns to us.

"Do you know who killed Harvey?" he asks.

Julia and Gabriel glance uneasily at each other. Even Sunny doesn't answer. But I remember my research with Cam from two summers ago. "Wasn't it another member on the board of supervisors?"

"Dan White," Mr. Wong says. His teeth grate on the name. "The killer's name was Dan White. He jumped through a window into city hall to avoid security. He walked into Mayor Moscone's office and shot him point-blank. Then he turned for Harvey's office and did the same to him. That was in November of 1978. On May first, 1979, the case went to trial. There were a lot of people in the neighborhood who didn't know how to keep going—"

Mr. Wong chokes up for a moment.

"We were trying to wrap our heads around the grief. We didn't want Harvey's death to shake us from his mission. So the Gay Democratic Club planned a huge celebration to remember Harvey on his birthday: May twenty-second. We thought the trial would be over by then. We thought the verdict would come out, and the party would help us all move on. But then White's lawyer came up with some ridiculous argument about junk food . . ."

"The Twinkie defense," I say. For a moment I have that game-show rush of adrenaline from knowing the right answer.

But then I look over at Mr. Wong and realize—this isn't some fun fact or trivia. This is something real.

Mr. Wong shrugs. "That's what the media called it. I don't know what medical-sounding term they used in court. But the defense meant a long line of bogus experts, and the trial kept getting pushed out and out. Tension in the city was building. People were starting to worry about the timing of everything. The jury had been deliberating for days, and we didn't want the verdict to come out on Harvey's birthday."

"Did it?" Sunny asks.

Mr. Wong shakes his head. "It came out the day before. They found White not guilty of murder."

Gabriel's mouth falls open. "What? But the evidence—"

"Manslaughter," Mr. Wong says, nearly whispering. He clears his throat. "They found him guilty of manslaughter, which means the unlawful killing of a person without premediated thought."

"But he snuck into city hall to do it," I say. "He knew he couldn't get past security. That's all premeditated."

Mr. Wong raises his palms. "That verdict wasn't decided because of the facts," he says. "It came on the shoulders of bias and homophobia. Which we all well knew. So that night, we didn't hang streamers or set up games or prepare food for the potluck. That night we marched to city hall and battered it like it was a ship in a storm and we were the ocean. We crashed into storefronts and parks. We wrote on buildings. We shattered glass. We needed every scream to come with a mark so that the next morning, San Francisco would see the pain we all felt."

He sits at a bench and stares at one of the hanging rainbow flags.

"That's why I said to check your picture," Mr. Wong says quietly. "And you'll know whether it was taken before or after the White Night riots."

I look at the others. Suddenly, the treasure hunt seems so shallow within the wider context of Mr. Wong's story. People fought and bled on these streets. And here we are, looking for a silly treasure like little kids.

But then I think back to that summer with Cam. I remember the feeling we got as we read through *Gay Treasures*. Gilbert Baker made this book because he wanted people to remember gay history. He buried treasures and made a hunt based on real people because he wanted to make sure the truth itself wouldn't get buried. Maybe unearthing the treasure would mean unearthing all the stories like this behind it. We can make people pay attention to the past if we can show them how truly valuable it is.

"That's it," I whisper.

Julia looks at me. "What's it?"

"Our yearbook's mission statement," I say. I turn to the group. "The clues are based on important parts of gay history that have been largely forgotten—like Harvey's birthday party. We have to find this thing. We can't stop looking in a parking lot."

"Well, what are we supposed to do now?" Gabriel asks. "There's not a logical next step."

"No, there's not," I say. I pause a moment, thinking about all the number grids Cam and I found in the chapter, all the puzzles we never got around to solving. Suddenly the answer bursts into my head. It's a *key*! The flyer must be a cipher key for another puzzle in the book. I snap my fingers and turn to Mr. Wong. "We need to find the full version of the flyer. Would the GLBT Historical Society Archives have it?"

Mr. Wong winces. "Hmm. Not likely." He rubs his chin. "But there's a used bookstore not too far from here—Bolerium Books. They carry a lot of vintage political memorabilia. I've seen some of Harvey's old campaign signs there."

"Bolerium Books . . ." Gabriel types the words into his phone. He looks up. "It's eight blocks east. And there's a bus line on Eighteenth."

"Well? Let's go!" Sunny barks.

I look over at the bench. "Let's walk Mr. Wong back to his car first."

Mr. Wong shakes his head. "You go ahead," he says, waving us on. "I'd like to sit with my memories a while longer."

We each thank Mr. Wong. I glance back at him as we rush away toward the next bus stop. He's already staring off into nothing, clearly in some other place and time. His mouth twists into a strange shape that somehow looks both wistful and devastated. I know that combination of feelings all too well.

CHAPTER SEVEN

Cam's jolt of popularity at the start of junior year used to be a total mystery to me.

How could someone be a total loner for so long, I wondered, and then suddenly get star treatment? But the more time went on, the more I realized what other people saw in him.

Cam is the type of person who reminds you of a hero. Not a beefy superman hero. But like a Frodo Baggins–type hero. The underdog with the golden heart, who fights for things because he's determined and passionate. Who doesn't want to root for a person like that? Who doesn't hope he gets every last thing he's after?

But here's the thing about passion: Passion only makes sense when you actually understand what it is you're fighting for. That's why I put on *National Treasure* at the start of our treasure hunt. In the movie, Benjamin Franklin Gates is passionate about the hidden American treasure because he basically has a PhD in American history. Gates's passion rests on a foundation of knowledge. *Knowledge* is the real key.

I had to show Cam the movie first thing, before we took even one step forward as actual treasure hunters. Because it's important to see what a good treasure hunter looks like. Especially when Ben is compared to the movie's antagonist—Ian—who's essentially a British dumbbell only in the hunt for the money.

Of course, Cam didn't get the contrast at all.

"What a messed-up ending," he said as the fancy script end credits rolled.

I turned to him, shocked. "You think Ben and Riley should have taken a bigger cut of the treasure?"

"The other guy shouldn't have gone to jail!" Cam splayed his hands open. "The dude with the accent—"

"Ian," I supplied.

"Ian, whatever, he was the one who helped the main guy—"

"Ben."

"Right. He helped Ben get that first clue. Ben never would have gotten to the Declaration of Independence or seen the map if it weren't for Ian, and he just, what? Sends Ian to prison? And then buys some fancy house with his treasure money and lives happily ever after?"

"You're missing the entire point," I said. "Ben and Ian *were* working together, until Ben realized that Ian didn't actually care about American history at all. He just wanted the treasure."

Cam gave me the side-eye. "Um, they both definitely just wanted the treasure."

We stared each other down for a few moments, until it became clear that neither of us would give. Cam bounced off the bed and sat at my desk.

"Come on, no more movies. Let's get to the good stuff," he yelled out.

"You mean the treasure," I muttered, rolling my eyes.

That's when my suspicions started. Cam may have been the one to find the treasure book. It might have been sitting in his uncle's old trunk. But when push came to shove . . . Cam didn't really care about gay history at all. That had to be why he brought the hunt to me in the first place. I would play the part of the history nerd, and only once I found all the answers would Cam come swooping in, shovel in hand.

Such an Ian move.

"You need to ask him," Sunny says.

I shake my head and look at her. "Sorry, what?"

Sunny pokes the manila file in my arms. "You need to talk to Cam."

I groan and roll my head back. We're standing outside of Bolerium Books, triumphantly holding a scroll from the Library of Alexandria. Well, it may as well be an ancient scroll, considering the salesperson inside told us this was probably the last intact flyer from Harvey's 1979 birthday.

That wasn't the case back in the early 1980s, of course. Like Mr. Wong said, the Castro neighborhood and surrounding areas used to be plastered with this same flyer. Its ties with the White Night riots made it a symbol of the gay rights movement. No wonder Gilbert Baker decided to use it as a clue in his chapter on Harvey.

The downside of our trip to Bolerium is what I'm not holding.

Julia slumps outside the doors. "I can't believe they don't have a single record of *Gay Treasures*. They have everything! The book had to have come through their store at some point!"

"Except, obviously, it didn't," Gabriel says, shuffling after her. He nods toward the flyer. "If Ivy's right and this is a cipher key, that means it's completely useless without the actual puzzles left in the book."

"Yes," Sunny says. "Although . . . the book is just as useless without the key."

I sigh. "So what am I supposed to do?"

"Make a scan of the flyer," Gabriel suggests. "And trade it for Cam's book."

Sunny frowns at him. "Why the hell would Cam want to give up the book in place of the flyer that goes with the book?"

"Uhhhhh . . ." Gabriel blows a raspberry.

"Maybe I do the opposite," I say, thinking. "Maybe I try to downplay the treasure hunt as much as possible. Try to grab the book for another reason."

"For the yearbook!" Julia says.

"*Yes*," Sunny adds. "That's good. Say you want to take some scans of it. Hell, we can take a full scan of just the San Francisco chapter and then give the book right back."

Gabriel grins and nods. I can see the plan taking full form in front of me. And it's definitely not a bad plan. I daresay it's even more solid than Ben Gates stealing the Declaration of Independence. But I know Cam. He's much smarter than he lets on. Much smarter, and much more conniving. Exactly the way Ian was in *National Treasure* when he left Ben Gates marooned on a ship in the Arctic.

I shiver.

"I'll do it," I promise the others. "But just by myself, okay? Cam will know something's up if the four of us are asking."

We walk together all the way up to Market Street and grab the Judah line back for home. Julia jumps off early to hit up a bakery before going home. Then Gabriel. When Sunny gets off at Twelfth Avenue, she glares at me from the door.

"You won't mess up," she says. I can tell this is Sunny's way of being supportive, but it comes out a lot more like an order.

"Right," I say. "I won't."

I try to hold my head high as I march toward Cam's house, even though I'm pummeled with wave after wave of déjà vu along his block. That's the curb I crashed into on my bike five years ago, where Cam pulled off his jacket and held it against the bleeding. That's the tree branch where we saved a cat, who then promptly scratched both our faces off in apparent gratitude. I know every detail of this street so well that even the memories are painful. By the time I get to Cam's front door, I can barely breathe. I knock twice, but no one answers.

"V?"

I turn around, away from the door. Cam stops halfway up

the porch steps. A duffel bag is slung over one shoulder. Of course he would be at some sports practice.

I clear my throat. "Oh, hi, yeah. Heya."

Great start.

Cam leans against the railing. "What's up?"

My knuckles go slightly white around the file. I try to think of a good answer. My teeth skim over my bottom lip. "The yearbook needs some filler pages for our archive scans, and I remembered that old book you had—"

"*Gay Treasures?*" he says, eyebrows furrowed.

I nod as if I had completely forgotten the title. "Right! That one. And anyway, the others thought it could work, maybe. So I was wondering if, um, you might still have it hanging around so we could scan a few pages. For the yearbook."

Cam squints hard at me. "For the yearbook."

I pretend to be super interested in a spider scrambling up the wood siding. "That's what I said."

Cam sets his duffel down next to him. I can feel his demanding glare, but I'm determined not to look back. If I can just avoid eye contact for a couple more minutes—

"I thought we were done with the treasure hunt," Cam says. And suddenly it's extremely hard not to look at him, because for the first time in ages, his fake, carefree vibe is gone. For the first time in—maybe ever?—he looks truly and utterly pissed.

Fine, I think to myself angrily. The masks are off.

"*We* are done with the treasure hunt," I say in agreement.

"What's that?" Cam asks. He points to the file.

"Noth— Hey!"

The whole thing is suddenly yanked out of my hands. I watch as Cam pries it open and sees the flyer. His breath catches on the line that matches our clue. His eyes flit back to mine.

"When were you going to tell me about this?"

"Um, never? We're not friends anymore."

"This was our thing," Cam shouts. I cannot believe he is actually shouting. "You can't just go behind my back and keep working on it without me!"

"I can do whatever I want!" I yell back.

I'm so tired of Cam pinning me under his thumb. It's like he can't be happy unless he knows I'm nearby and miserable. But not this time. This time I'm winning our stupid game. I'm finding that treasure and getting the hell out of here.

I hold my hand out expectantly. "Give that back," I growl.

"So that's why you want the book?" Cam asks. "You're going to finish the hunt?"

I pause, then give a curt nod.

Cam looks down at his hands. "I see," he murmurs. He sets his jaw and raises the file halfway out to me. But just as I reach for the other end, Cam's eyes widen. It's like I can actually see the evil idea entering his brain.

"Don't you dare—" I start.

But before I can finish, Cam whirls around and sprints down the block, clutching my one and only copy of Harvey's birthday flyer.

That *fucking* Ian.

CHAPTER EIGHT

For a moment, I'm transfixed. My feet stay planted on the front doorstep. The pure outlandishness of what just happened clears away slowly, exhaust pluming after a car guns it. The tip of one finger stings, and as I look down and see a tiny bead of blood, I realize Cam jerked the file back so hard that it gave me a paper cut.

Cam.

What the hell is his problem anyway? He's acting like I'm the worst person in the world for not immediately including him in all this. But he's the one who walked away from the hunt—and *me*—in the first place.

"Dropped like a bad habit," Mom tutted as she stroked my hair that evening, the day I came home from the park with a puffy red face and tear tracks down my cheeks. It's probably the closest she's ever come to being maternal.

Even so, Mom was wrong. Dropping a bad habit is supposed to be hard. It takes time. Cam made forgetting me look easy.

He didn't drop me like a bad habit—he dropped me like I was a mistake.

I yank myself back into the moment and press my thumb pad over the small cut to stop the bleeding. My right leg sails over Cam's duffel bag as I leap off the steps. If Cam thinks he's going to get away with ghosting me a second time, not to mention outright theft, he's absolutely insane.

"CAM!" I scream out.

I race across the street to where he turned, trying not to fall as the sidewalk slopes downward. Cam and I used to joke that if we ever tripped on the way to school, our neighborhood is so steep that we'd tumble all the way into Golden Gate Park.

I get to the next avenue and see that Cam's already a tiny dot in the distance. Even with our tumbling jokes, he's never been afraid of leaning forward while running. While every normal person compensates for the sharp hills in San Francisco, tilting their shoulders back and tucking their butts in while walking down, Cam simply acts like gravity does not exist.

"Just let your legs do what they want to do!" he would yell out in middle school. As if my legs had any personal interest in buckling, getting completely tangled up, and making me eat shit off the sidewalk.

I try to hustle as much as I can while looking like an eighty-year-old being blown backward. Damn Cam for taking off with my flyer and then heading straight for the downhill, knowing I won't follow him at full speed. I gulp down more air and start to run, determined to snatch the file out of Cam's hands as quickly as he grabbed it from mine.

The next block spits me out into a sea of heavy traffic on

Nineteenth Avenue. Two cars are honking at each other on a left turn, a screaming match that won't find a compromise. I look across on Judah, but Cam's not there. I tip my head to the right, where Nineteenth runs south, then left, as it snakes north into Golden Gate Park. There is zero sign of him anywhere.

Shoot.

I wait for the jumble of cars in the intersection to clear out. Maybe he's pressed up against a street pole or crouched behind an A-frame sign, just waiting for me to run past. Two more light cycles go by, but nothing moves apart from the steady motion of traffic. My chest is heaving. My legs are on fire. I can't tell whether it's the running or the anger that's making my blood churn so hot and fast.

I'm going to have to give up, I realize. I'll have to tell Sunny, Gabriel, and Julia that not only did I not get the book, but actually, I lost the flyer too.

Great news. *Fantastic.*

I pull out my phone and stare at the lock screen, my brain suddenly going blank as I look down at my chosen wallpaper.

It's a photo of me, which, admittedly, sounds pretty self-absorbed. But I can't seem to change it, even when I get a really good shot of fog curling around the Golden Gate Bridge or the rare pic of Mount Sutro exposed against a robin's-egg blue sky.

I think the real reason I'll never change the current photo is because, secretly, it's another photo. And I'm the only one who can see both.

At first glance it's just me lying in the grass. Closing my

eyes and laughing. I had stretched out my arm to take a selfie, but I was laughing so hard when I clicked the button that the phone was already shaking. The resulting image is blurred and hazy. Looking at it is like climbing directly back into that laugh, hearing it vibrate in my belly, feeling the squeeze of tears in the corners of my eyes. The world gets drunk and tips to one side. At least, that's how it feels to me. Because the other side of the photo—the half I cropped out nearly two years ago—is the person who made me laugh so hard, the entire world shook.

I look at myself and I see him there too. His nose is only a few inches from mine. (It was a tricky crop job.) His mouth is open, mid-rant in whatever silly impression he was doing. His eyes are crinkled almost as much as mine, and you can tell from studying his face (not that I've ever done this) that I'm making him laugh as much as he's making me laugh—a weird symbiosis between us. Like he can't be funny if I'm not there to nearly pee my pants in reaction.

The long meadow grass in the background bows forward, hanging over my forehead. Every picture of us had nearly identical backgrounds back then. Always after another long day of poking around some park in the city. Always after collapsing on our backs and staring up at the clouds. Always nestled in greenery.

"Wait."

I look north again. Two blocks away, the old Breon Gate pillars stand on either side of the road as it swerves away from the urban landscape, suddenly disappearing into a sea of endless trees. Cam and I used to head into the park through one of the hidden stone entrances attached to each pillar. We said they were our secret doorways, leading into our own version of Golden Gate Park, where no one else could follow us.

I tuck my phone back into my pocket.

I know where Cam is.

The traffic ebbs with the next light, and I make my way down Nineteenth Avenue, slipping through one of the hidden doorways in the Breon pillars. If Cam thinks he can escape into some private dimension of the park, I'm onto him.

I dip west, leaving the main road and threading between the trees until I find the narrow footpath that cuts across the park. I walk between Mallard and Elk Glen, two tiny lakes that don't really have business calling themselves anything more than ponds, but whatever. I cross Hellman Hollow and watch the families sprawled out on blankets, passing around store-bought containers of fresh strawberries, or friend groups scattered across the field with baseball mitts, one person pointing a Wiffle bat to the sky. At the edge of the meadow, I see two people lying next to each other, staring into the tree branches as their fingertips brush. I look away quickly and swallow.

As I get closer to JFK Drive, I see the doorway rising out of the iridescent green water of Lloyd Lake—which, again, is another pond essentially wearing the title of "lake" like it's their dad's comically oversized dinner jacket. I cross the road and stand at the edge of the water, peering toward the white marble columns plunked in between the trees in the distance.

Portals of the Past.

Cam and I didn't name it that, although we totally would have, had it been our own secret place to christen. It's a Greek-architecture portico that used to be attached to a huge mansion in downtown San Francisco in the late 1800s. When the 1906 earthquake hit, this was apparently the only thing in the whole neighborhood that survived. A journalist took a super eerie photo of the earthquake's wreckage through the open, empty door.

The clean-cut view in the center between the columns now reveals a scraggly hill behind it, covered in tufts of long grass. I wait and watch until, after a minute or two, the toe of a sneaker quickly wags in and out of view.

"Got you," I say to myself.

I hopscotch over the stepping stones next to the burbling waterfall and make my way around the perimeter of Lloyd Lake. As I get closer to the portal, the path opens into a wide clearing, something the city probably did to make room for all the wedding ceremonies I've seen here. I step onto the marble porch and lean against the inner right column.

"Knock, knock."

I hear Cam suck in his breath.

"Dude, I know you're here," I say. "Just give me the flyer back and we'll call it a freaking wash of a day."

"I don't have it."

I step through the stone entrance and see a cluster of trees at the base of the hill, where Cam's draped himself over his favorite tree branch like a bobcat. This used to be our main meeting place in Golden Gate Park.

"What do you mean, you don't have it?"

He shrugs, his fingers lazily entwined over his stomach. "I stashed it."

"You did *not*," I growl. "I may not be Sha'Carri Richardson, but I followed you out here fast enough."

"That so?" Cam lifts an eyebrow and smiles, but I immediately notice it's another Cheshire Cat smile. I have to tread carefully.

I walk over to the tree, subtly scanning the area.

"It's not stashed here," Cam says in singsong. I want to climb the tree and throttle him.

"I'll go back to your house and take the book."

"What makes you think my mom will let you in?" he asks.

"Your mom loves me."

"Loved."

The past tense pierces my heart so sharply that I almost gasp. I try not to let it show.

"I'll go grab your duffel bag, then," I call up to him. "I'll swipe your backpack the moment you set it down at school. I'll take things off your desk every single day. I swear to God, you will not have one sharpened pencil in class for the rest of your LIFE!"

But I can tell none of this lands. Cam closes his eyes like he's in a hammock on the beach. He starts to hum some random tune until it becomes the theme song from the old San Francisco–based sitcom *Full House.*

Everywhere you look, everywhere you go . . .

"What do you want?" I ask.

"Whaddya mean?"

"For the flyer. What. Do. You. Want."

The humming stops. He angles himself away from me. "I'm keeping the flyer," he says over his shoulder. "Because that's what I want."

"To do the hunt, or just to keep me from doing it?"

He shrugs again. "Haven't decided."

I'm nearly frothing at the mouth with unfiltered rage until I freeze, a sudden realization dawning on me. Cam's hiding himself on purpose. The closed eyes. The scrambling up our tree. He's only pretending to be above all this.

I hop back onto the marble riser.

"I'll just go get another flyer," I announce with false bravado. "And then I'm getting another copy of that book, and you'd better believe that I'm going to dig up the treasure myself. Completely without you."

Cam goes stiff on the branch. He pushes himself onto his elbows and twists to look at me. "Guess I'd better find it first, then."

It's true that, in this moment, he has everything and I have nothing. The book, his. The flyer, now also his. The odds are hopelessly in his favor.

But it's also true that right now, for whatever reason, Cam looks completely and uncharacteristically terrified. Which means that even with a score of two to zero, I have a fighting chance of winning this thing for real.

"Good luck with that," I say, walking back through the columns.

The words come out like a warning.

CHAPTER NINE

From the second I step out from the Portals of the Past, it's like a stopwatch instantly goes off in my head.

If I had an ounce of athleticism, I would be running back toward my house. As it is, I'm already gassed from chasing Cam this far into the park in the first place.

He stashed the flyer, I tell myself for the umpteenth time. He stashed it somewhere on the way here, and so far he hasn't scrambled out of his tree and raced past me to get to it. He's playing it cool. I can play it cool too. There's time. It's not a sprint.

The mental stopwatch keeps ticking.

My phone buzzes in my pocket. I take it out and look at the screen. Texts are coming in from Julia and Sunny.

Julia: Heeeeeey, how did it go with Cam? Everything okay

Sunny: Did you get the book or not.

I wince and click out of the thread. There's this strange feeling in my belly, a total clash between what's happening in my personal world and what's happening all around me. People keep playing baseball and stretching out under the sun. Dogs are pulling leashes taut as their owners laugh and fish out treats from their pockets. It doesn't make any sense for everyone to be this calm.

I steal a glance behind me every so often, but there's no sign of Cam. I try to think about where he put the flyer on his way over.

I'm actually really good at finding things, in a general sense. The trick, I've learned, is to be logical. If you're missing an AirPod and you start to look in every place an AirPod could possibly be, you're in grave danger of having to search forever. Instead, you have to be strategic. *When do I last remember taking the AirPod out? Where are my usual listening spots?* And then, instead of doing a half-assed job tearing your whole house apart, you home in on the two or three most likely places for it to be and search meticulously.

I try this technique with the flyer. Of course, the entire path from Cam's porch to the Portals is full of places a flyer *could* be. But where would Cam specifically think to put it?

I lost him at the intersection on Judah and Nineteenth. Maybe he dipped into a shop and bribed an employee to hold on to the flyer for an hour. Maybe he found a bulletin board and tacked up Harvey's birthday announcement, camouflaging it among all the other notices for book clubs, CrossFit gyms, and pet sitter ads.

No. I shake my head. Both those options are way too dangerous—if you let go of the flyer once, you could lose it completely. And maybe Cam doesn't want me to do this treasure hunt, but I don't think he wants to destroy it either. That hunt was everything to him a few years ago. Which means . . .

I pause on the sidewalk. "Damn it," I mutter.

It's with him.

It has to be with him. He must've rolled it up and stuck it into a knothole in the tree trunk. Actually, knowing Cam, he probably just stuck it straight into his waistband. If I had really wanted to get the flyer back, I would have had to climb the tree and goose him.

Just the idea of doing that sends a tingly, unpleasant shock wave over my whole body. I take out my phone and pull up the group thread before I lose the nerve.

> **Me:** No book. Flyer's gone. Cam swiped it and took off.

Sunny immediately starts typing.

> **Sunny:** WTF?!?!?! REPORT HIM!

> **Me:** To who, the treasure police? He knew exactly what we were up to.

Before I can answer, text dots appear next to Julia's name. They blink and disappear, blink and disappear again. I hold my breath for almost two minutes. It seems like she's writing us a manifesto. Except, when she finally does hit send, the text isn't a manifesto at all. She simply writes:

Despite Sunny, Gabriel, and I piling on Julia in a barrage of messages, Julia refuses to clarify what a smiley face could possibly mean in this context. She tells us to get every school assignment we know of out of the way tonight and to meet her in the Bat Cave tomorrow at four p.m. After Sunny threatens to burn all of Julia's completed assignments if she doesn't explain herself *TODAY*, Julia finally relents that she might have thought up a plan B for our mission.

Whatever that means.

I end up blowing the rest of the evening fantasizing about scenarios wherein I break into Cam's room and steal both the book and the flyer while he's sleeping.

I can't imagine that he's already working on the hunt. Or maybe the real problem is that I *can* imagine it. It feels insane to have to sit and wait around when he's probably already out somewhere digging with a shovel. I keep creeping back onto the local news website, refreshing the headlines over and over in case one particular title comes up:

ANNOYINGLY CHARISMATIC BLOND TEEN FINDS LOCAL TREASURE

Even the specter of the words is enough to haunt me all night long.

"Woof," Sunny says when she sees me after school the next day. "Did you join a raccoon posse last night?"

I scowl and rub my eyes. "It's called a gaze."

"What?"

"A group of raccoons," I say impatiently, "is called a gaze."

"I didn't know raccoons were queer!" Gabriel strides up to my locker, both his thumbs hooked in his backpack straps.

" 'Gaze' like the look," I say.

"Oh, gays *love* the look," he says, wiggling his eyebrows. Sunny smirks.

I let out an aggravated sigh. "Has anyone seen Julia yet?" I ask impatiently.

"HI!"

I crash backward into my locker as Julia hops seemingly from NOWHERE into the middle of our circle.

"What. The. Heck!" I choke out. I grab on to the locker door and hoist myself up.

Gabriel folds his arms. "Treasure is waiting, Julia. Why couldn't we meet this morning?"

"Because Sunny's not a morning person," Julia replies, like this is a perfectly acceptable reason.

"Ah, but little did you know," Sunny says, "I'm not an afternoon person either."

Gabriel raises his eyebrows. "Evening? Nighttime?"

"Witching hour only," she says with a sniff.

I roll my eyes and turn to Julia. "So, what's the plan B? We figure out how to steal the book and flyer from Cam?"

Who's looked suspiciously smug all day, I think to myself bitterly. If I were remotely religious, I'd probably be off crafting and passing out strings of prayer beads to every student at school as if the strands were friendship bracelets, each one with the same beaded letters:

HE-WONT-FIND-IT

HE-WONT-FIND-IT

HE-WONT-FIND-IT

Julia waves off my suggestion as she turns down the hall. "We don't need the flyer. Now, come on. To the Bat Cave!"

She dips out of view into the stairwell. Gabriel grins and points a finger in the air. "To the Bat Cave!" he echoes. He runs down the hall after Julia, his backpack thumping with each stride.

Sunny and I trade looks, then shuffle behind them. By the time we reach the basement lab, Julia already has our machines logged in and whirring. She pops the projector cable into her laptop and queues up the front screen. As the screen warms up, Julia does a drumroll on her lap.

"Bum bada dum . . . Ta-da!"

Harvey Milk

There, filling the entire back wall, is the complete flyer from Harvey's birthday party in 1979.

I let out a gasp. Sunny makes a tiny squeak.

Gabriel speaks first. "How did you . . . ?"

"I took a photo at Bolerium," Julia said. "*After* we bought it, of course. I saw the ABSOLUTELY NO PHOTOS sign. Okay, maybe I took it while we were checking out, but Ivy was already handing the money over! It was fine!"

Sunny tuts and smiles at Julia. "You broke the rules. You're a rule breaker."

"I am *not*!" Julia says, face turning red. "We were buying it."

"*Ivy* was buying it."

"And I should have taken a photo first thing," I say, standing. I seriously do not know what's come over me as I cross in front of Sunny and Gabriel's chairs and wrap Julia into something that must be the equivalent of a hug.

"Thank you," I say into Julia's hair, though her hair muffles the words so much that it probably sounds like I'm whispering, which is weird. Actually, everything about this is weird. I gently press myself away. "Thank you," I say again, at a normal volume this time.

"You're welcome," Julia says, grinning. She's not acting like the hug was weird at all, bless her. I'm going to make all the prayer beads/friendship bracelets for this girl. She looks over at the others.

"So. No book, but we still have the flyer." Julia glances at me nervously. "Is Cam looking for the treasure now too?"

"Maybe. Probably. Yeah, I'm pretty sure he is."

"Well, *that* escalated fast," Sunny says.

She presses her feet into the thin gray carpet, then wheels herself over to her computer. She clicks open a link in her web browser and starts typing.

"Guess that means we'd better get this damn book."

CHAPTER TEN

Gabriel nods like Sunny's given him an order. He pushes over to his own computer.

"AbeBooks and ThriftBooks," Sunny mutters.

"Etsy and eBay," Gabriel replies.

This is Yearbook Club convention. If there's a big task that needs to be done, a school activity to write up, or an event from the archives to research, we all call out what we're doing so we won't overlap.

Julia sets her laptop aside and parks herself at her usual desktop computer.

"Title and author search on Google?" she asks me, eyebrows tilting.

"Go into 'Images' for results," I suggest. "We don't have to find the whole book if we can find digital scans. Do a deep dive; go in twenty or so pages."

Julia nods. I sit down at my own computer and pull open the browser.

"Reddit and Quora," I call out. Gabriel looks at me questioningly for a moment but quickly disappears back into his own monitor's results.

Personally, I think finding a whole copy of *Gay Treasures* for sale is almost impossible at this point. I'd never heard of it before Cam squirreled the book into my room. I haven't heard of it from any other place since. Even Bolerium Books has never seen a copy. If we're really going to find this thing, we'll have to pick up clues wherever we can.

Obscure book from the 1980s, I type.

The screen pulls up page after page of completely mainstream books. Of course, the internet is the exact kind of place you wander into asking about a book no one's heard of, and then everyone immediately shouts, *How about* The Handmaid's Tale *by Margaret Atwood?*

I try again.

Obscure "gay treasure hunt" book from the 1980s.

The cursor blinks a moment as the results load. My eyes scan through each listing, then stop on a Reddit thread near the bottom of the page. I click the link.

"Bingo," I murmur.

A little over ten years ago, a user by the name of u/DyslexicStoner240 wrote into a subreddit forum called r/tipofmytongue, a community where members can ask for help finding something they almost—but not quite—recall.

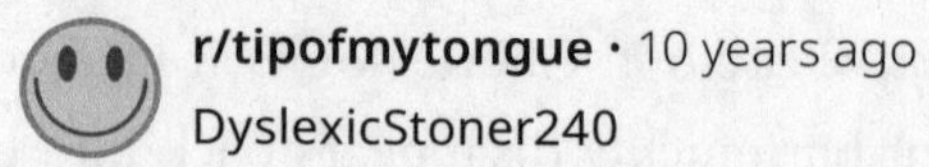

[TOMT] [BOOK] PLEASE HELP! NINETIES TREASURE BOOK I FOUND AT A GARAGE SALE AS A KID. IT HAS BEEN DRIVING ME CRAZY EVER SINCE.

Locked: OP Not Responding

Hey, guys, appreciate anyone reading this. When I was a kid in the 90s, my mom used to drag me to estate sales around the greater Minneapolis area every Saturday. We definitely went to other towns a lot, so I'm not sure where exactly this was. But I remember hanging out in the backyard of one estate sale where the family had put the cheaper things on foldout tables like a garage sale. There was a giant, beat-up beanbag chair in the corner of the yard, and I dragged a box of old comic books over to it while my mom looked at the jewelry inside the house.

In the box there were a bunch of issues of Gay Comix, which I hadn't heard of before, but maybe it's going to be important for figuring out whatever this book was. Anyway, I pull out a random comic book issue, and this tiny little book drops out from between the pages. I swear it was called *Gay Treasure Hunting* or *Hunting for Gay Gold* or something about being gay and finding treasure, but I opened it up, and it was like I could tell that this was legit. All these words were crammed together, but you just knew that if you squinted real hard, you would find a treasure map in the words or something. Like in those Magic Eye books.

I wanted to buy it, or at least try to steal it (dumbass ten-year-old-boy brain), but I didn't hear my mom come outside, telling me it was time to leave. She walked right up to me surrounded by all the Gay Comix and had this crazy meltdown and stormed us both out of there. Then we had to read a bunch of passages from the Bible that night and do, like, a bajillion Hail Marys. (Raised Catholic FTL.) So I never got to go back . . . and then I was sort of scared that it really was this Satanic cult pamphlet like she said. And since then I haven't been able to find anything about it online.

PLEASE help me end this awful scratching at the back of my head. Like, WHAT WAS THAT BOOK, AND WAS I ALMOST A REAL-LIFE GOONIE?!

I immediately notice a little gray bubble below the title. *Locked: OP Not Responding.*

"Uh-oh," I murmur. I'm guessing it's about to get real nasty in the replies.

Sure enough, most users popped in only to tell u/DyslexicStoner240 that this so-called memory was more likely his way of dealing with coming out of the closet. He probably concocted the book because he was reading a bunch of gay comics and realized he was gay too.

The real treasure's in owning your truth, bro, wrote u/Colonel_Panic, which, actually, is sort of nice, I guess. But everyone crashed on DyslexicStoner240 hard, saying he probably made the story up. I feel like I'm hitting another dead end just by reading this guy hit his.

I click on the username. He's been inactive on Reddit for almost ten years, basically since he made the post. Probably had to get another username or something, poor dude. I scroll down his profile and click on his last recorded comment.

It looks like the comment is from a small thread about a totally different subject. Dyslexic Stoner replies and then gets a reply from another user directly to him. The other user has the screen name u/BusTRoss.

I pause and stare at the screen.

Bus T. Ross.

As in . . . Busty Ross?

I click into another window and type out Gilbert Baker's info. *Died 2017.* One year after this exchange. *It can't be the same person, though,* I tell myself. Just because Gilbert's drag name was Busty Gay Ross doesn't mean he made that user profile on Reddit.

But whoever did probably knew about BGR and the treasure hunt.

I open the conversation.

u/BusTRoss: scarecrow, lion, or tin man?

u/DyslexicStoner240: . . . huh?

u/BusTRoss: friend of Dorothy, right?

u/BusTRoss: are you a scarecrow, a lion, or a tin man?

u/DyslexicStoner240: Oh.

And that's it. But the last phrase, "over the rainbow," is hyperlinked. I paste it over into a new tab and land in an absolutely ancient-looking web forum. Like, clearly this was one of the first websites to ever be designed for public use.

An incredibly garish *Gay4Treasure* icon blinks at the center of the website heading. It's in an old rainbow WordArt font that I've seen used in countless internet memes. There's a subheading underneath that reads *Gay Treasure Icon: Judy Garland*.

Of course, I think, palming my forehead.

Busty asked if Dyslexic Stoner was a friend of Dorothy. He meant "Dorothy" as in Judy Garland's character Dorothy. It's all making sense. But, wait a second . . .

Didn't Julia say that's how people used to ask if someone was gay? *Are you a friend of Dorothy?* I click back to the conversation on Reddit. Busty didn't ask about the treasure hunt itself. They asked if Stoner was a friend of Dorothy. Why? Did Stoner have to say yes, to confirm that he was gay, before Busty could send over the link? Are only true insiders allowed to find this treasure?

I measure this conundrum against the only other treasure hunt story I really know. Ben Gates would never have been able to solve the hunt in *National Treasure* without knowing a ton about American history. But also, at the end of the day, Ben was an American with a deep-cut American legacy. Whereas Ian—the bad guy—was British. He was an outsider.

Is there something to that?

What does Busty's question really mean, I wonder, for the hunt in general? Does everyone who's interested in *Gay Treasures* have to be gay? Are they not allowed to go looking for the treasure otherwise? And if they do have to be gay, do they have to be a specific type of gay? Busty gave Stoner three choices: the Lion, the Tin Man, and the Scarecrow . . . Why was only one of those choices correct?

I shove the questions crowding my head to one side and click open the top thread, which is titled "SOLVED: Grand Rapids." It's posted by none other than former Redditor DyslexicStoner240, same username and all.

Good for him, I think. Screw those haters on Reddit.

As the thread loads, my eyeballs nearly pop out of my head. Photocopied images directly from the book show up, pixel by pixel, on the screen.

"Hey! I found something!" I call out.

The three rolling chairs Sunny, Julia, and Gabriel were sitting in suddenly whoosh backward. Gabriel's even clatters to the floor. They all slam into my sides and crowd around the screen.

"You got the book?" Julia asks.

"Some of it," I say. "These are scanned pages from the original. Well . . . maybe not scanned. Maybe photocopied or . . ."

"Or photographed with the world's first phone camera in dim lighting?" Sunny supplies. Still, I catch her failing to tamp down a grin as she grabs my mouse and scrolls through the page. "Oh, we can totally handle this."

"I don't know if it's worth cleaning up these specific pages, though," I say. I point to the first image. "This is for the Judy Garland treasure. That's in a different chapter of the book."

"Not our chapter, then," Gabriel says. "I'll look through the website." He copies the URL onto his phone and nearly sprints back to his own computer.

"There's a thread here on Harvey Milk!" he calls out a few moments later. "Should I look through it?"

"Obviously!" Sunny says, nostrils flaring. She doesn't let go of my mouse. She's scrolling down the Judy Garland page messages, rolling further and further back in time until she reaches the earliest message, posted by a user named EggBert in June 1999.

"Found this weird book at Quatrefoil Library," Sunny reads aloud. "It was being used to prop up a table. Apparently it's a treasure map?"

She opens a side tab and Googles *Quatrefoil Library*. "This is a queer library. I think Gilbert Baker planted copies of *Gay Treasures*. I don't think the book was ever widely circulated at all. That's why we can't find it anywhere."

Just in specific gay communities, I think to myself.

I remember sitting next to Cam in my room, how uncomfortable he seemed when I asked if his uncle Brian was gay. I wonder what Cam would think of the whole "friend of Dorothy" question. I wonder if he would feel included in this particular lens of the old-school queer community. Then again, I think about what it must have been like in the 1960s and '70s and '80s, when the old-school queer community was *everything*. It was all queer people had. And even then, so many people weren't able to be a part of that community at all.

I motion for Sunny to scroll to the top of the page.

"The Wiki said the Grand Rapids treasure was found by accident, but clearly it wasn't," I say. "These people have done all the work, step by step."

"But they wanted to stay anonymous for some reason," Sunny adds.

"Yeah. For some reason."

I picture Dyslexic Stoner as a little boy, repeating Hail Marys over and over as his mother loomed next to him. The thought makes me unbearably sad.

CHAPTER ELEVEN

"I've got more page scans!" Gabriel calls.

Julia, Sunny, and I migrate from my station to Gabriel's. He's pasted the images from the website over into Adobe Photoshop and is already fiddling with the contrast and brightness features.

"Is this the right chapter?" Gabriel asks me. He stands to one side and offers me his chair.

I sit down and squint at the pages crammed with the familiar hurried, slanted writing. Maybe Dyslexic Stoner was onto something about there being a picture hidden within the words. But no matter how much I try to blur my vision, nothing really comes together. *This isn't a Magic Eye kids' book*, I remind myself. It's supposed to be a remembrance of gay history. That's why it pointed to Harvey's birthday flyer as a clue. Solving this thing means uncovering something important, something real.

For whatever reason, this only makes tackling the next piece of the puzzle seem a million times harder. I sigh and turn my attention over to the one feature in the book Cam and I fixated on when we started the hunt: the endless tiny grids filled with numbers.

"There," I say, my finger tapping the last page. "This is definitely Harvey's chapter."

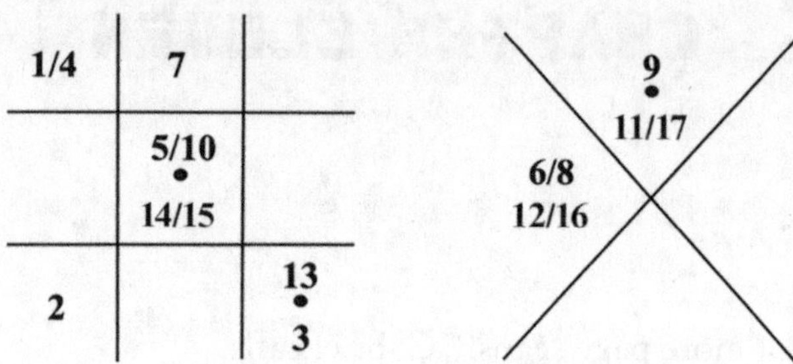

I'm pointing to a tiny tic-tac-toe grid and an X grid set into the bottom right corner of the third and final page spread. There are several numbers jumbled inside the grids, with two or more numbers sharing the same spot. Other spots, notably, are blank.

Actually, it was Cam who first noticed the blank areas when we pored through the book years ago.

"What's that about?" he had asked.

I was still trying to figure out the words themselves—if there was a larger riddle within them. I lost my place in one sentence. "What's what about?"

"The blanks here," he said. He opened a drawer in his desk and dug around, random items clanking like cartoon sound effects until—"Aha!"—he pulled out a chipped magnifying glass and hovered it over the grids.

"There's something to this."

I rolled my eyes. "There's something to everything, Cam. That's the entire point."

"No, I mean these numbers are different from the rest. The way they're stacked in some places and missing in others. And look here . . . there's a dot next to two of the numbers."

He cut the air in half with a tiny gasp. "It's a pigpen cipher."

I didn't have to ask what that was. We had been making a master list of ciphers ever since we'd watched *National Treasure*. Book ciphers, Playfair ciphers, Caesar ciphers—we knew them all.

A pigpen cipher splits up all the letters of the alphabet into four grids: two tic-tac-toe grids and two X grids, one of each type with dots in the spaces.

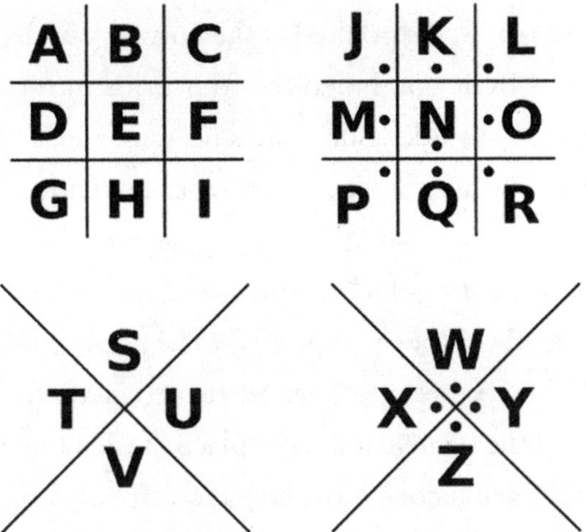

A letter goes into every space, and you figure out that letter's symbol from where it sits in the grid and if it has a dot or not. Meaning most messages coded in pigpen look like a sort of alien language.

for "gay."

for "treasure."

You're supposed to read the symbol and then find the corresponding place in the grid where the correct letter goes. Simple enough. But the grids in *Gay Treasures*, the ones Cam was indicating, seemed anything but simple. One tic-tac-toe grid and one X grid, with only numbers inside. No letters. No alien symbols. And no encrypted pigpen message anywhere else in the book.

"How is it a pigpen cipher?" I asked incredulously.

"Well, look." Cam pointed at the numbers with dots underneath them. "BGR combined the four grids into two."

"Okay . . ." I said. "But there's no message."

"There is!" Cam was really getting excited now. He grabbed a pencil and started writing something on a piece of scrap paper. No, he wasn't writing. He was drawing. He made the four pigpen grids exactly as they're supposed to be drawn and filled them with all the correct letters. Then he turned again to the grids in the book and the strange numbers placed inside them.

Cam touched a corner of the page softly, his fingertip balanced on the edge. I remember seeing it, his finger pressing into the paper, and feeling the strangest touch on my lower back. Like my skin was suddenly the book, and he was reading it. I turned away and stared at the wall.

He cleared his throat. "One and four," he said, lassoing my

attention back to the cipher. "They're both in the place where *A* goes in the pigpen grid." He looked at me. "What do you want to bet that *A* is the first and fourth letter in the message?"

I didn't say anything. Didn't bet anything against it. Which turned out to be pretty wise, since a few minutes later, Cam's idea gave way to an entire decoded sentence:

A GIANT BTWN STREETS

As I look at the corner with the pigpen cipher now, the solution seems glaringly obvious. But isn't that the way it always goes with riddles and codes? Hindsight's twenty-twenty, and foresight is double cataracts with melted sunscreen running into your eyes.

Not for Cam, I think miserably. Cam understood the puzzle right away. So why wouldn't he understand the rest of this too?

With the weight of Gabriel, Sunny, and Julia's presence sitting heavy on my shoulders, I'm suddenly overcome with an intense wave of imposter syndrome. I didn't even help solve the one cipher we managed to crack from the book. Cam's going to unlock this entire thing while we hang out in a basement, fiddling around on web archives.

"You haven't taken a breath in, like, two minutes," Sunny murmurs.

I make a "Pah!" sound, mostly to annoy Sunny, and blink the pages back into focus.

The pigpen cipher seems easy now, but not just because Cam solved it. It was the only grid of its kind in the entire book. None of the other numbers in this chapter are in pigpen grids. Out of six pages, the other five contain three-dimensional-looking Rubik's Cubes, each filled with random numbers. The last Rubik's Cube is partially covered, but that's the only clue we get about what they could mean. They don't have any blanks. None of the numbers are doubles. There are no dots, or *X*'s, or anything like that. It looks like a bunch of sudoku games completed by someone who has no idea how to actually play sudoku.

I feel like I'm on a Slip 'n Slide covered with baby oil as my brain scrambles to make sense of all this. I try flattening the information into math terms. Six pages in the chapter. Five Rubik's Cubes, plus a pigpen cipher. Three sides are visible on four of the cubes. Then just a side and a half are visible on the fifth. Nine numbers per side. So nine . . . times three . . . times four . . . plus nine and six equals . . .

Shit.

Everything I'm saying is complete nonsense. I literally have no idea what any of these numbers mean.

I shove my head into my arms. "What if I'm not gay enough for this?" I groan.

"Excuse me, what now?" Gabriel prods my elbow.

I look up. "There was this weird conversation online. It's how I found the website in the first place. Basically, one person asked if another person was gay—or, no, if they were a 'friend of Dorothy,' but that's basically the same thing—and when the other person hinted that, yes, they were gay, the first person said, 'Right answer,' and sent them the link."

The others only stare at me, bewildered.

"So?" Sunny asks after a moment.

"So," I say, "maybe you have to be super gay to figure this whole stupid thing out!"

"Aren't you supposed to be, like, the gayest person at this school?" Sunny asks.

Yes, I want to snap. *Obviously*. But a weird knot catches in my stomach. I'm the co-chair of GSA. I came out by myself as a sophomore. If Benjamin Gates was the ideal headstrong American, then I should absolutely be the ideal nerdy gay teen. I'm basically the Benjamin Gates of gaying!

Except . . . sometimes it feels like I'm not really the gay queen everyone at school thinks I am. When I first came out as a sophomore, it was as a lesbian. I made a whole poster board presentation on why the acronym LGBTQ+ starts with the letter *L*. I love the specific history of lesbians in the gay rights movement. How, as a group, they've stood up for all identities under the queer umbrella. How Anne Kronenberg, Harvey Milk's campaign manager, was a lesbian. Lesbians are so completely badass. They use their privilege the way it's meant to be used to help and protect others. They've been fearless when they've had so much to lose. Being a part of that group, considering myself in line with heroic lesbian trailblazers, felt so validating and powerful during my sophomore year.

Cam's face suddenly blooms in my memory. The way he looked when he came into school junior year with his short hair. The way he grinned as he told everyone he was trans. My stomach flops. I feel so completely lost about everything.

"Well, I'm sort of gay too, if that counts," Gabriel says. "So we can add up my gay to your gay."

We all turn to him.

"Is this some kind of gay superhero team-up?" I ask. God, maybe we really *are* Greta Gerwig's version of the Avengers.

Gabriel splays his hands. "You're the one who said that maybe you weren't gay enough! I don't know!" He pauses, looking at each of us in our silence.

"I haven't done anything," he adds quietly. "With anyone. I just feel like I *could* be swayed by a really hot guy. Like if Nico Hiraga ever slid into my DMs . . ."

"Anyone with a brain would hook up with Nico Hiraga if he slid into their DMs," Sunny says. She clamps a hand on Gabriel's shoulder and gives it a tight squeeze. "You don't have to have done anything with anyone to justify your sexuality," she states firmly. Sunny sniffs and turns her nose up at the group. "And I don't feel a need to comment on my sexuality one way or another."

"Wait. That's not what this is." I offer my hands in surrender.

I didn't mean to pressure anyone to come out. Unlike what Gabriel might think, I highly doubt we get to combine our gayness for ultimate treasure-finding power.

"I have my own reasons, though," Sunny adds after a moment, "for doing the hunt."

"That's great," I say quickly. "We don't have to talk about about—"

"The thing is, I'm tired of seeing Harvey Milk's name thrown literally everywhere in San Francisco but with almost no real context," Sunny explains. "He has an airport wing named after him, and a bunch of gift shops and streets, and yet . . . none of us knew about the White Night riots. We didn't know about the first birthday party after Harvey's murder. And that's messed up! History should be something deep enough that we can actually explore it. It shouldn't be oversimplified to a street sign or a single line in a book."

I'm stunned into silence.

I turn and check the number cubes again. Threes. All the numbers come in threes . . .

Julia picks up her notebook and starts scribbling. She mumbles as she writes. "History shouldn't be oversimplified to a street sign or a single line in a book." Julia reads it over to herself and grins. "That's great, Sunny. We should put this in the yearbook. Can I quote you?"

Sunny shrugs. "Sure. Whatever."

I lean so close to Gabriel's computer that my nose is nearly touching the screen. The cubes are so tiny. But the numbers have to be here for a reason. Sunny's words keep echoing in my head.

A line in a book.

A line.

*In a **book**.*

"There's no message," I had told Cam about the pigpen cipher. But I was wrong. Gilbert Baker had hidden a message in those grids through the numbers.

And he hid one in these grids too.

CHAPTER TWELVE

I pull back from the screen.

"We have to make these bigger!"

Gabriel leans over. "Which pages? What's going on?"

"All of them," I say. "Well, not the whole page, but the number cubes." My index finger hovers under one of the images. "See the numbers in there? We need to know exactly what they say. We have to be able to read all of this for the next step."

"Which is . . . ?" Sunny prompts.

"It's—"

Complicated. Uncertain. Possible I'm completely wrong about everything.

I shake the responses off. "We just need to see these first," I say. "Then it'll be easier to explain." I go into the view function and start zooming in. Almost immediately the image shatters into a jumble of boxy pixels.

"Yeah . . ." Gabriel runs a hand through his hair. "The scans were already pretty low quality to begin with."

I stand up from his chair. "No, I get it. You did a great job in Adobe. Let me try something else."

Before I can let the idea marinate, I've whisked my backpack off the floor and fled into the hallway. Julia follows me at a half trot. "What's going on?"

I pull up to the vending machines and dig around the very bottom of my pack, scratching the unholy, crusted surface.

"I need money," I say breathlessly.

Julia lifts her palms. "For what?"

"For—" I nod to the machine again, like it isn't completely obvious. "We need a bottled water."

"There's a fountain right there."

"To use as a MAGNIYFING GLASS," I spit out. Sheesh. Sometimes it really does seem like I am the only person in the entire universe who's watched *National Treasure*.

In a pivotal scene that follows the main characters buying some clothes at an Urban Outfitters (which admittedly is about as random as it sounds), one of the characters rushes in with the next clue, except it's missing something—a specific time. Just as everyone is stumped, Benjamin freaking Gates whips out a hundred-dollar bill and a nearby water bottle. He frames the bottle over his already ginormous eyeball until—*BAM!*—lo and behold, it becomes a magnifying glass and reveals there's actually a clock on the back of the bill with the exact time they need to get to the next step.

It's genius! It's inspired! It's . . . maybe a little too conspiracy-theory driven, but I don't have time for that TED

Talk. Either way, it's the kind of energy I'm trying to channel in this moment. I have a plan. I'm going to get us all to the next step of this hunt.

I just need a goddamned Dasani to get us there.

Julia watches me scrounge around for another minute as I turn my backpack inside out. Now that I've spoken the plan aloud, the stupidity of it seems to be slowly oozing from it, like a cracked egg on the floor between us. My amazing idea is . . . a water bottle? I feel like a person could use a flashlight and squint and it would be a better strategy than looking through a water bottle. I might as well be out here looking through a Fanta Orange for how far that's going to get us.

Julia's eyes remain trained carefully on my pack. Finally, she clears her throat.

"I don't think you have any money in there."

My shoulders sag. "I don't. And the water bottle idea is—"

"Is *fine*," Julia says, her voice straining up an octave. She shrugs. "It might be a little impractical, though."

"Yeah," I say, grateful she's sparing my dignity from total impalement. "I . . . Yeah. Oh, wait!"

I run down the hallway toward the locker bays. 505 . . . 506 . . .

"507," I say out loud.

"What are you doing now?" Julia asks. "This isn't even your locker."

"It was—" I stop myself before I sound like a complete idiot and say this used to be halfway mine. Cam and I were assigned lockers on either side of the school. We used to split both of them so each of us could stash books in them for the nearest classrooms. But the locker was never actually mine. It's always been Cam's.

"Cam keeps a magnifying glass in his locker," I say. At least, he used to.

The metal door squeaks as it opens. I'm not prepared for the sudden smell of Cam—sandalwood and Old Spice. It makes my head dizzy and my knees inexplicably weak.

At first glance, the contents inside his locker look relatively normal. There's a messy stack of notebooks, binders, and a few textbooks trying to hold on to their peeling spines. No magnifying glass. I sigh, ready to close the locker door again. But then I notice a piece of paper poking up from one of the binders with a message written on the top.

A GIANT BTWN STREETS

I pull the page the rest of the way out. Underneath the line, I see that Cam's been trying to unscramble the letters, as if the message were an anagram.

SWAN BETTERING STAT
ENTREATS BATT WINGS
WATERGATE INT BTNSS

I smile at the last line, then reach into my backpack and pull out a pencil and my own scrap of paper. On the paper I write down:

Watergate Internal Business

Then I stuff my note, along with Cam's, back into his binder.

"What was that about?" Julia asks as I shut his locker door.

"Just planting a fake clue," I say. "Maybe Cam will come across it and think he's onto something with Watergate. Or at least the coincidence will throw him off."

Julia laughs and shakes her head. "Come on." She leads me back down the hall and up to the next floor, then strides to the science classrooms and tries one of the doors. The handle sticks at a quarter turn. "You still have the custodian keys, right?"

I lift my key ring from the front pocket of my backpack and hand her the set. "It's the brass one," I tell her. Julia slides the key in and opens the door. She goes immediately for a cabinet in the central island. "What are you getting?"

"A magnifying glass," Julia says calmly. "We used them for worm dissection last year. I remember because I didn't want to be at my station when my partner was cutting the worm open, so I spent fifteen minutes pretending to look for a magnifying glass."

We both laugh. She pulls the glass out, not nearly as old and mysterious-looking as Cam's magnifying glass but just as effective. And undoubtedly a hell of a lot more effective than a Dasani.

Julia pauses, the thick, rounded glass balanced in her hand. "Do you want to know?" she asks.

I raise my eyebrows. "Do I want to know what?"

"Why I'm doing this," she says quietly.

At first I think she's talking about the whole magnifying glass thing, and the question doesn't make any sense. *Um. Because I'm an idiot?* Then I realize she's referring to the conversation from the basement. About being gay.

My skin suddenly goes clammy. I didn't mean to corner anyone into talking about this. It doesn't matter if Julia's gay or straight. It doesn't matter if she's queer, or questioning, or asexual, or aromantic. Heck, it doesn't even matter if her great-great-great-grandmother was a pirate and now Julia has to dig a hole in the ground every five years to live up to her family name. She can have any reason she wants to work on the hunt. I should have kept my darn mouth shut.

"Well, you've always been ridiculously committed to yearbook," I say jokingly.

Julia shakes her head. "That's not it."

The silence opens up between us. I can't tell if it's a hole I'm going to step into or a doorway she wants to walk through. But before Julia has a chance to make a move either way, the actual door behind me swings wide open.

"Um, hello?" Sunny yells. "Gabriel was able to print the pages at 110-percent zoom. We've been calling your names for the last five minutes!"

"Sorry!"

Julia bumps the cabinet door closed with her hip and whisks past me into the hall. Just like that, the conversation's gone.

I lock the door to the lab behind us, then catch up with Sunny and Julia at the bottom of the stairs. Gabriel is already hunched over our worktable, which is now covered with the printouts from online. He's lifting his glasses and squinting hard at the pages. He stands when he sees us come in, then points at the magnifying glass in Julia's hand.

"Nice!" he says. "That will help."

He steps off to one side, and Julia offers me the magnifying glass. I hold it gingerly by the handle and approach the table. No one says anything. *They're waiting for me*, I realize. This is my theory. Cam might have been the one to lead us through the pigpen cipher, but this time I'm on my own.

I take a deep breath and lean over the corner of the first page. Slowly, I bring the magnifying glass down until it hovers over the Rubik's Cube.

The cube expands, a bubble widening under the thick glass lens. In an instant, the tiny, crammed picture becomes a set of actual numbers we can study.

And there is definitely something . . . *off* about these numbers. This isn't just a bad sudoku game. It's like what Cam said when he first noticed the pigpen cipher—something's here. It's another message. I stare at one face of the cube.

524

213

912

"Let's try something." I nudge Harvey's birthday flyer toward Sunny.

"Fifth line," I tell her. Sunny blinks back at me, profoundly confused, until understanding takes hold and she jerks to life. Her finger moves down the lines of the page.

One, two, three, four, five.

Sunny looks up and nods. I check the number grid again: 5-2-4.

"Second word," I tell her. "Fourth letter."

"*T,*" Sunny reads aloud.

I pause. This could be nothing. I could be dragging us all toward a dead end in a labyrinth. Then again . . . only hindsight offers clear vision. Everything is cataracts until you're looking at it from the other side.

"Can you write that down?" I ask Julia. "Please."

I hear her pen scratching in her notebook.

"*T*," Julia echoes.

I go on. "Second line . . . first word . . . third letter."

Sunny picks up her role as translator. "*R.*"

My chest goes tight, a rubber band stretching farther and farther. I'm waiting for the *G* or *J* or *Q*. I'm waiting to reach a random letter that makes this whole idea fall apart.

But it doesn't come.

"*E*," Sunny dictates to Julia. Gabriel points to the next grid of numbers on the cube. I shift the magnifying glass, and we keep going.

"*A. S. U. R . . .*"

We've nearly finished the third side when Gabriel starts giggling like a small child. "Holy shit," he says, shaking his head. "Gay power for the win."

Before we can ask what he means, he takes Julia's notebook and writes in the eighth letter himself, then turns and shows the rest of us.

TREASURE

CHAPTER THIRTEEN

Thirty minutes and five decoded number cubes later, we're all standing around Julia's open notebook, staring at the six lines scrawled on the page:

TREASURE

ISLAND

BUILDER

READS

ARCHITECTURE

723

At first I think that no one's saying anything because no one *can* say anything—we're all in too much awe, too inwardly thrilled by this secret message we've brought to life, to be able to talk. It's like we're staring down at the invisible map on the back of the Declaration of Independence. The air is weighted with reverence. Some nonexistent movie camera lens dials in on me for the close-up.

Then Sunny breaks the silence.

"What the hell even is this?"

The beautiful soundtrack in my head featuring a particularly uplifting French horn is cut short. I sigh and look at her. "I told you two minutes ago—it's a book cipher."

A book cipher is pretty clear-cut. You use a series of three numbers and a book or piece of writing as the key. The first number points to the line in the key. The second number points to the word in that line. And the third number points to the letter in that word.

"I think, technically, this one's a flyer cipher," Julia says.

Sunny rolls her eyes. "What I mean is, we just decoded a whole treasure map, and instead of it telling us where to go dig, we get a random list of words that looks more like a fourth-grade spelling test!"

"I don't know," Gabriel says. "I feel like 'architecture' is sixth-grade spelling material, easily."

Sunny glares at him.

"It's okay!" I say quickly. "It's not a spelling test! It's a clue."

"Another clue," Sunny says, shaking her head. "Which leads to another clue, which leads to another—"

I wag my finger. "Watch it, Patrick Gates."

"Patrick who?"

"Ugh. You guys really need to watch *National Treasure.*" I hold Julia's notebook out to the others. "This message may look random and vague, but I promise you, it's not as bad as 'a giant between streets.' Figuring out *that* phrase was like finding a needle in a haystack. Only people who already knew about Harvey's party and the White Night riots would get it."

"Except we figured it out," Julia says. "Because we're total badasses."

Gabriel raises an eyebrow. "Whoa—the Girl Scout curses."

Julia's eyes flash for a moment, and I look at her curiously. There's something she's not saying. Suddenly, I want to be back upstairs in the science lab. I want her to tell me why she's really working on this puzzle. But before I can say anything, Julia shrugs and smiles.

"I only curse on special occasions," she says. She nods to me to keep going.

"The point is," I say, "this message isn't actually random. It's just *disguised* as something random."

Sunny massages her forehead. "I think I literally hate you right now."

"You go right ahead." I hand over Julia's notebook and log off my computer.

"Where are you going?" Julia asks.

I stop at the door. "*We* are going on a field trip. Pack up the hate in a to-go box, Sunny. We're heading to the library."

To everyone's blank stares, I add, "Unless anyone here has a copy of *Treasure Island*."

Gabriel and Julia shake their heads. Sunny continues to glower. But all three grab their bags and follow me out of the Bat Cave.

The Sunset neighborhood library holds court on the intersection of Irving Street and Eighteenth Avenue. It's not actually any taller than the other town houses and apartment buildings surrounding it—but there's something about the wide, heavy stones on the façade, the three giant arches over the front door, and the words etched into the architrave that give it a regal appearance.

SUNSET BRANCH SAN FRANCISCO PUBLIC LIBRARY

"Check out the doorway," Gabriel says as we walk up to the front.

We look up at the stone frieze carved above the central door. It's of an open book flanked by scrolls on either side. Above the book, a globe spins as though in motion. The meaning seems clear enough: Through books, you can explore the world.

"Treasure, island, builder, reads." Gabriel flings his arms toward the door. "*Reads!* And it's a book!"

"Yeah, because it's a carving over the doorway to a *library*," Sunny says dully.

"It's a pediment," I murmur.

Julia nudges me. "What?"

"A pediment. It's the triangle above a doorway. This one's a broken pediment—see how the frame at the top doesn't connect all the way? It's a stylistic thing." I pull the door open. "My mom's an architect."

Gabriel grins at me as he walks past, into the library. "*Architecture, seven two three!*'" he whispers, like I'm just as much of a clue as the carving above the door.

And I mean, I get it. Once you're in the mindset of solving riddles, everything seems connected. I remember that feeling washing over me two summers ago as I chased shadows with Cam and felt like the entire world was one big challenge for the two of us to solve. Everything we did seemed to have another deeper, secret meaning. It felt like together we were stumbling upon something huge and weighty and . . . and it's probably for the best that I don't think like that now. Most things, after all, are just coincidence. And the real skill in tracking down a treasure is figuring out what's real life and what, at the end of the day, only exists in your head.

The warm cherrywood shelves sit under the giant arched windows and welcome us inside. I love the smell of libraries. It's not even the same as bookstores. The paper here has a distinctive scent. There must be something about being passed around a community that changes a book at its DNA level. Shared stories just hit different.

"I think we should check out the reference desk," Sunny says.

I make a face. "We're looking for one of the most popular fiction novels in existence. We already know it was written by Robert Louis Stevenson. I think we'll be good on our own."

Gabriel raises his hand. "I'm with Sunny. What if there's another clue we're missing?"

Julia stands between us, notebook held out in front of her. She chews her lip.

"Go with them," I say, waving her off. "I'll grab the book and find you guys after."

I turn and snake my way through the fiction shelves, heading over to the section marked R–T.

Stevenson. Stevenson. S . . . St . . .

I become vaguely aware that someone's shadowing me down the aisle. Except they're not behind me. They're in the next aisle over, the top of their head peeking above the book spines. I stop walking suddenly. The figure also stops, then leans over to peer through the shelves.

"What are you doing here?" I ask, glaring.

Cam's eyebrows go up. "Oh, whoops. Is this another place where überdudes aren't allowed?"

I march around the endcap and into his aisle. Cam steps back, surprised.

"Are you following me?"

"Actually"—Cam folds his arms over his chest—"I watched you and your group come in here. Which means, technically, *you* would be the ones following *me*."

I grit my teeth and look at the book spines behind Cam. To my horror, I realize the exact book I want, *Treasure Island*, is tucked on the shelf just beyond his left elbow.

"How's the hunt going?" I ask.

"Fine." His eyes slip for a second as he glances to the left. *Oh God, does he know about the* Treasure Island *clue?* "How's it going for you?"

"Also fine," I say. "Very fine. Probably even more than fine." And then, just for good measure, I look directly at *Treasure Island* and back at him.

I'm trying to put on a convincing bravado that says, *Okay, so maybe we both know about the book. But I am still doing so well that I am entirely unbothered by this possibility. I'm going to find the treasure first anyway and make you regret the day you decided to walk off that damn field two years ago.*

But that is a lot to communicate with a single smolder, which, admittedly, is probably less of a smolder and more of a stink eye. I have been informed by my mother that most of my pointed looks come across as a stink eye.

Julia bounds down the aisle. "Ivy! Ivy! We found—" She stops short as she sees Cam standing next to me.

"Mm?" Cam asks. He perks up.

I turn to Julia, suddenly remembering the note I left in Cam's locker.

"Watergate?" I murmur.

Julia looks at me, bewildered.

Remember? The fake clue? I'm trying to say telepathically. Although, again, this is probably all coming across as a stink eye.

"Watergate?" Cam asks.

"We have to go. Bye!" I press Julia out of the aisle, resisting the urge to look over my shoulder and take in Cam's full reaction.

"That was great!" I say once we're safely a few rows away. "He totally bought the Watergate thing. Now we'll just wait until he leaves, and I'll go back and grab the copy of *Treasure Island*."

"Unnecessary!" Sunny calls from the next row over.

Julia and I look up as Sunny and Gabriel march over to us. I notice that Gabriel is holding a different book at his side.

"Did you find another edition?" I ask.

Julia shakes her head. "We don't think Stevenson's book is the clue."

"Um . . ." I make a face. "We just solved a cipher with the phrase 'Treasure Island,' and you don't think we're supposed to look into *Treasure Island*?"

"We do," Sunny says, grinning. "Just a different Treasure Island, that's all."

Gabriel holds up the book so I can see its cover.

Images of America: San Francisco's Treasure Island.

CHAPTER FOURTEEN

A wave of total embarrassment washes over me. We're look-ing for a treasure buried in 1980s San Francisco, not 1880s Britain.

In San Francisco, we have a real Treasure Island. Well, as real as a Treasure Island can get, I guess. It's a man-made is-land northeast of the city. I actually have no idea what it was originally made for. Some kind of world's fair or exposition, I think. Or maybe it was just an airplane hangar. I do know it got used a lot in World War II, but to be honest, I haven't really paid that much attention to military history. I feel like there's plenty enough history right here, in the neighborhood under my feet.

"So, what are we thinking?" I ask as I start paging through the book.

"Not sure yet," Sunny says. "Maybe we figure out who built Treasure Island? Or one of the buildings on Treasure Island? Since our riddle is about the Treasure Island builder."

I nod. "Okay, that's a good plan. There are lots of buildings there." I turn another page and frown. "But this book doesn't have any information about who built what. There are only pictures, no captions."

Not to mention, we still have no idea what the "seven two three" part of the clue means, which is tricky. I feel like whatever our decoded message points to, it should be pretty obvious once we've found it. Exactly the way it was obvious when we first came across Harvey's flyer.

I startle a little.

"Harvey!" I say, looking up.

Julia does a full three-sixty turn. "Where?"

"No," I say. I hold the book up. "Treasure Island doesn't have anything to do with Harvey Milk. At least, not on the surface. But the whole point of *Gay Treasures* is to get to know the actual gay treasures who made this community. The *people*. So we need to know what Harvey Milk did on Treasure Island. Maybe *he* built something."

"Let's see." Sunny taps on her phone and scrolls down. "Hmm. Doesn't look like he did anything there." She sighs. "But they do have a statue and a boat named after him. See, this is the kind of superficial stuff I'm talking about."

Gabriel holds up a finger, like he's pushing the pause button on our conversation. He's reading something off his phone too.

"It might be superficial, and it might not," he says mysteriously.

I stand on my tiptoes, trying to read over his shoulder. "What do you know?"

"Nothing yet. But there's a way to find out exactly who

did what on Treasure Island. I think we need to visit the main library."

"What's in the main library?" Julia asks.

"The San Francisco History Center," Gabriel says. "Sixth floor. We can request all the city archives that have anything to do with Treasure Island. Maybe we'll find out how this all connects to Harvey."

"Well, what are we waiting for?" I say. I slip the *Images of America* book into the return box near the front desk. "Let's go!"

Julia's pocket begins to buzz. Her eyes widen. "Shoot!"

She pulls out her phone. "Shoot," she says again. Her screen is filled with text messages. Julia scans through them and winces. "My mom's super mad. I was supposed to be home for dinner an hour ago."

I check my phone. It's already seven p.m. I'm lucky my own mom doesn't care when I get home.

"Should we go tomorrow?" I ask. I'm trying hard to sound diplomatic. If it were just me, I'd be catching the Judah train out to the main library this second. But then Gabriel shakes his head and says something that makes the entire situation ten times worse.

"The history center collection is open by appointment only, for viewing on Tuesdays and Thursdays from noon to four."

"Tomorrow's Tuesday," I point out impatiently.

"Yeah," he says in the same tone, "and we have school until four."

I throw my arms up. "So? What else are we supposed to do? We have to get there!"

"Shhhhhhhhh!"

The four of us turn in unison to the librarian sitting behind the front desk.

"Sorry!" Julia stage-whispers. She hooks her arm around mine and ushers us to the door. We head down the front steps.

"I wasn't done," Gabriel says when we're all outside. We cross the street together. "The collection is also open on Saturdays from ten to noon. I can make us an appointment."

Saturday?! I look around the group, but it's clear that I'm the only one who seems to be freaking out over sitting on our hands for five entire days. And all the while, the information we need to solve this thing could be waiting in an archives box for us to find it. Why can't we skip school tomorrow afternoon and go then? Why can't we go there and sneak in right now?

"What's up?" Sunny asks.

"I . . ." My voice dies out. How do they not get how important this whole thing is?

"What about Cam?" I ask finally. "I think he solved the book cipher too. I saw him near Stevenson's *Treasure Island* at the library."

Sunny smiles faintly. "Good," she says. "That means he's making the same mistake you did. Maybe that will keep him busy through Saturday."

With that, the others nod their goodbyes and take off in separate directions. Sunny hangs back for a moment. She pinches the cuff of my sleeve.

"Seriously," she says. "Don't worry so much about it."

Right, I think. There's clearly nothing to worry about in

this situation. We're definitely not trying to uncover an actual treasure buried in the ground. All while racing someone else to get to it.

"Thanks for the advice," I mutter.

Sunny gives me a strange look. She waves and walks up Irving.

I'm left there on the corner, staring out into traffic. I don't get why I seem to be the only person in this entire world who's taking the hunt seriously. Well . . . at least one of the only people. I glance at the library across the street just as Cam is coming out.

His silhouette is framed under the broken pediment of the front doors, the stone-carved world frozen over his head. He's clutching a stack of library books in his arms.

For a moment, I vaguely wonder what the books are. Does he have Stevenson's *Treasure Island*? The *Images of America* Treasure Island? Was I convincing enough to make him check out a bunch of books on Watergate? But then my eyes travel back up to Cam's face, and my mind moves on from the mystery of the treasure hunt over to the perpetual mystery of Cam the person.

He's so tiny from this distance—like a miniature doll version of himself. I squint my eyes, but I can't read his expression. He could be scowling at me. He could be smiling. Confused or confident. Lost or laughing. It's impossible to see the details from here.

Does he miss me even a little? I wonder. *Does he wish it were the two of us working on this together instead of against each other?* I always thought, if Cam and I split up as friends, that he would be the one leading a group to eventually find the treasure. I would be the person standing alone in the doorway.

I contemplate walking across the street. Saying something, anything, to him. But just as I start to take the first step forward, Cam shakes his head. The momentary spell between us is broken. He rushes down the stairs and toward his house.

Our separate worlds go on spinning again.

CHAPTER FIFTEEN

It's dark outside by the time I climb up our steep stairway and let myself into the apartment. Mom's done her usual thing where she's turned off all the overhead ceiling lights and flipped on the small lamps in the corners of the living room. I think it's her way of signaling that it's quiet time, which is actually pretty funny, considering that we're probably already the two quietest cohabitators in all of San Francisco.

I find her lounging in her favorite chaise in the corner, staring down at her phone screen. A mostly empty wineglass sits on the side table next to her.

"Ivy," she says distantly, without looking up.

I'm already on my way past her, heading toward my room down the hall. I'll need to look up the number 723 in every possible context. The history center may have lots of information on Treasure Island and whoever built it, but that number has to mean something specific.

Mom sighs behind me. "Please tell me you're not still sulking."

I stop in the hallway, then turn again toward the living room. "Sulking about what?"

She swipes something on her phone. "Your project. The yearbook thing. I haven't seen you since you barreled out of lunch on Saturday."

I walk back to her, puzzled. Of course she hasn't seen me since Saturday. That is the entire point of our living arrangement. We barely see each other at all. It's not sulking; it's *courtesy.*

"I'm fine," I tell her. "I've been . . ." The word catches in my mouth, a bubble of laughter I swallow down. "Busy."

Understatement of the century.

"Well, that's good. And you know, art school isn't the be-all, end-all. I switched my major from fine arts to architecture my first year in college and never looked back. It's so much better to be practical than conceptual, yes? I think you're like that too."

The topic of art school gives me momentary mental whiplash. That's right—two days ago, all I could think about was Paris. It's crazy how much has changed since then. And yet . . .

Better to be practical than conceptual.

Mom's words tug on my skin uncomfortably. Suddenly I'm back on Castro Street, talking to Mr. Wong and internally divvying every personality trait there is between me and Cam. And I'm doing it again right now with Mom. *I'm* the practical one. *He's* the conceptual one.

Being practical is a good thing, I want to say. Practical people get things done. We don't drag shovels around and poke under trees dreamily. We make connections, solve clues, go deep-sea internet diving when we don't get answers handed straight to us. But I know my mother well enough to recognize when a jab is carefully hidden in a compliment. I'm not conceptual enough for art school—that's what she's really saying.

"So you weren't good enough for art school either," I say. I'm trying to turn the pointed thing she's aimed at me around on her again. But she just laughs.

"Naturally. I'm an architect, not an artist."

I pause. I don't understand why Mom has to see everything as some kind of hierarchy. Why some forms of art have to be better than others. But right now, in this moment, my mind catches on one specific word:

"*Architect.*"

I can picture Gabriel whispering the word "architecture" at me outside the library. As if anything, everything, might be a clue to help solve this riddle. I come closer to Mom's chair.

"Do you happen to know anything about the buildings on Treasure Island?"

Mom looks up from her phone. "Why are you asking?"

I shrug. "My yearbook thing."

"Oh." She takes a final sip of the wine and purses her lips, thoughtful. "No, I don't know about the buildings. I know the island was built during the beginning of the Moderne style. Not my taste, of course, personally. Leans too brutalist for San Francisco, even with the occasional rounded corner. San Francisco is a city of ornament. It's too fine for that kind of look."

"The island was a military base at some point," I say, remembering.

She peers at me. "Any building can be pretty," she says seriously. "Even ones that house weapons."

I sigh and shake my head. "Okay. Thanks for that. Good night."

"Wait," she calls.

I pop my head back into the living room. "Yeah?"

"You're not still applying to Paris, are you?"

I pause. Mom swallows, nervous, like even the idea of her daughter submitting a subpar application would be the most horrendously embarrassing thing to happen to her. Or maybe she's just already imagining the scenario where I get rejected from art school and give her further confirmation that our family line just doesn't have what it takes to be proper artists.

"I might be," I say.

"Are you using what you showed me?" she asks carefully.

I picture Harvey's flyer hiding in the background of the yearbook dedication page.

"Parts of it," I say, smiling. Then I bound into my room before I have to see her suffer any further secondhand embarrassment.

As expected, Saturday takes ages to get to. Tuesday and Thursday are especially rough, knowing the history center is open across town. Throughout those days, I catch myself daydreaming about cutting class and jetting off to the main library, before remembering that I am now working with a team and it would be super rude to go off by myself, and also, I have never cut class in my entire life.

The only thing that keeps me from going off the deep end is the knowledge that my fake clue absolutely worked, and Cam is safely a few steps behind us at least. On Wednesday, I see him quickly stash a copy of *The Watergate Girl* into his locker. On Thursday, I see him holding another book on Watergate before he spots me coming and jumps behind a large tree. On Friday, there's a third book hidden behind his math textbook in class. Waiting for fame and glory is agony, but it's a bit less agony when your closest competition is unknowingly heading in the wrong direction.

Finally it's Saturday, and I'm waiting bright and early outside of San Francisco's main public library. The wind absolutely wrecks my hair as I pace back and forth outside the three sets of front doors. Whenever I get tired of pacing, I stop and re-count the flags whipping in the wind across the street at the Civic Center Plaza.

"Are you crazy?" Gabriel asks as he and Julia walk over from Grove Street.

Gabriel has one of our nice yearbook cameras around his neck. Julia's carrying a tray of to-go coffee cups all bearing the logo *UN Café*. I grab the cup marked "IV" and gratefully take a sip.

"Thank you," I say to Julia. "You're seriously a lifesaver."

She nods and gives me that same guarded smile from Monday. I make a mental note to pull her aside later today so we can finish our conversation from the science lab. But it will have to wait until after the history center appointment.

Maybe we'll even already have the treasure in hand, and she can explain why she joined the hunt to the reporter interviewing all of us.

Gabriel gives me a once-over. "You've been here for hours, haven't you?"

"What are you talking about?"

"Well, for one, your hair looks like you've been electrocuted."

My free hand immediately clamps down on my head. "Excuse you. Maybe I did it this way on purpose."

Sunny jogs up to us and grabs the last coffee from the tray. "So sorry I'm late," she says, breathing heavily.

I cock my head at her, surprised. I don't think I've ever heard the words "so sorry" come out of Sunny's mouth. Ever.

"Actually"—Gabriel checks his phone and looks pointedly at me—"we're all early."

"By two minutes," I snap. I chug the rest of my coffee and push it into a nearby trash can, then take the empty tray from Julia. "We need a plan for the second they unlock those doors. Julia, do you mind taking notes?"

"Oh! Of course!" Julia pulls out her notebook, flustered as she turns to a new page. "I didn't think anyone actually cared about my notes," she murmurs as she clicks open her pen.

"Are you kidding?" I say. "If we find this thing—*when* we find this thing—your notes are going to be famous documents! You're taking down history right now."

Julia's cheeks turn pink as she writes the date and location at the top of the page.

"Well, I already asked the center to pull their records on

Treasure Island," Gabriel says. "They said it would be a couple boxes' worth of stuff."

"Great," I say. "We need to pay special attention to anything we find about the buildings. And especially keep a lookout for any mention of Harvey. Or the number combination seven two three."

"We got it," Sunny says. Again, her sincerity is throwing me. Maybe she's like a reverse coffee person, and coffee only restores her to her usual grumpy self.

A lock clicks behind us. One of the librarians pops a door open by a few inches, clearly testing it to make sure it's unlocked. She jumps a little when she sees us standing outside. I'm guessing the library doesn't normally have teenagers lined up and waiting like die-hard groupies.

Gabriel starts to head through the door.

"Wait," I say.

He gives me a look. "Now who's wasting time?"

"It's just . . ." Mom's words from Monday come back to me. What if I am being too practical right now? What if Baker meant for the treasure to be found by someone more like Cam, someone who thrives on ideas over details? What if we end up overlooking the answer entirely because I don't know how to see the bigger picture?

"Let's not only pay attention to the clues we know," I say, "but try to listen to our feelings too."

"Our . . . feelings?" Julia asks, looking up from her notebook.

"Well, our gut instincts. Like if we have a *feeling* that

something's important. Or if we sense a story," I add. "If Treasure Island is telling us a story, we should be listening to it."

Sunny blinks. "No offense, Ivy, but you sound completely unhinged right now."

"Yeah, I know." I shrug and wave them inside. "Forget it. Let's just go."

Mom's right: It's way easier for me to be practical than conceptual. But I'm sure as hell going to do my best to be both anyway.

CHAPTER SIXTEEN

We merge into a single-file line up the stairs and to the sixth floor. Gabriel checks us into the San Francisco History Center, and the librarian on duty brings us over to one of the rows of long, narrow tables that stretch across the room end to end. Two cardboard boxes sit in the middle of our assigned table.

"This is it," Gabriel says. He reaches for one of the lids.

"Ahem." The librarian slides a much smaller open box toward us. Inside is a stack of white cloth gloves.

"To protect the documents," they say. Julia starts writing this down. "Also, no pens."

Julia looks up, startled. "No pens?"

The librarian points again at the box. I move the gloves to one side and find a set of stubby yellow pencils, the same kind the library puts out on reference desks for taking down call numbers.

"Here." I hand Julia one of the stubs. She narrows her eyes at it as though I've handed her a used cigarette from a parking lot. Then she lets out a deep, unappreciative sigh and finishes the line in her notebook with the pencil.

"You can photograph whatever you'd like," the librarian tells us, eyeing Gabriel's camera. "And if you need any full-resolution scans, I can send you downstairs to collect them at the end of your appointment."

"Thank you," I say.

The librarian leaves, and Gabriel puts on the first pair of gloves. He places a hand on either box and takes off both lids with a flourish.

"Ta-da!" he says. We all lean over to peer inside.

Julia gasps.

Sunny shakes her head. "Holy hell."

I don't know what I was expecting—maybe a collection of labeled files we could sort through the way I've seen people do at law offices. We'd find everything written about the island, sorted out year by year. Maybe there would even be a file labeled *Harvey Milk*, and we'd start there.

In reality, the boxes are less like the inside of a filing cabinet and more like the box someone brings home from work right after they've been fired on the spot. Piles of photos tip over in every direction, crushed alongside county fair ribbons, a tiny bowling trophy, and random wrinkled pages that probably haven't seen the inside of a folder in their entire existence. A few of the papers look way too much like empty hamburger wrappers for my liking.

"Welcome to city archives." The four of us look over at the front desk. The librarian gives us a tight smile. "Good luck."

Gabriel winces. "Glad I'm wearing gloves for this."

I take a deep breath.

"Okay," I say. "This is salvageable. Gabriel and Julia, you two take the first box. Sunny and I will take this one. Try to divvy up the contents as best you can."

"What about those?" Sunny asks, tipping her chin at one of the suspiciously garbage-looking bundles.

I roll my eyes. "I'll take those. Let's just get started."

Load by load, we slowly empty the contents of both boxes in front of us. Things get easier as we sort. Photos from certain events and time periods start coinciding. Most of the loose papers turn out to be government forms, and we stack the same types of forms together until our own filing system emerges.

"They should be paying us for this," Sunny murmurs next to me.

The first hour flies by as we sort and organize, searching for clues. Every time I check the clock over the librarian's desk, my heart starts racing. It's entirely possible we're going to reach our appointment time limit, and then what? We book another appointment? I'm not waiting a full week to come back here.

Luckily, not long after hitting our halfway point, Sunny triumphantly holds up a sheet of paper.

"I found the architects of two buildings on Treasure Island," she says. She reads off the page in front of her: "Court of Honor and Court of the East."

I drop my pile of ceremonial-tree-planting photos. "Amazing! So, who are they?"

Sunny shrugs. "Just some random dudes," she says, and hands me the page to look over.

Two black-and-white photos of buildings have been Xe-roxed side by side, with a typewriter-style caption underneath listing the three names of the architects. I frown. I had hoped that the right answer would jump out at us the moment we found it. That I would naturally know just from looking what the next step should be. I pass the sheet over to Julia so she can copy down the names.

"I've got the architect for the Court of Pacifica," Gabriel adds a few minutes later.

We make a master list of all buildings on the island, with Julia taking notes on every name attached. Three architects. Then four. Then seven. My stomach starts to sink. The only strategy I can think of is to research the hell out of every indi-vidual name we find. But what if, by the end of the day, we have twenty architects on the list? What if we have fifty? Our break-through clue is starting to look more like broken glass, with the cracks in my plan spider-webbing out farther and farther.

Then, with only twenty minutes left in our appointment, Julia finds an article that changes everything.

"Um . . . guys?"

I look up from an ancient parking citation issued in the 1950s. "Another building architect?" I ask absently.

"No," Julia says. She's blinking over and over, her eyes scanning back and forth across a clipped newspaper article. She runs a gloved finger over the title. "Listen to this heading: 'The Lost Boys of Treasure Island: How Discharged Naval Sail-ors Built a Homosexual Hub in San Francisco.'"

Immediately, we abandon our stacks and crowd in next to Julia.

"What does the article say?" I ask.

Julia adjusts her glasses. "Well, we knew that Treasure Island was a naval base for World War II, right? It turns out that, afterward, in the late 1940s and '50s, sailors from all over the country—if they either came out or were discovered as gay—got sent here."

Gabriel scoffs. "That was the navy's genius plan to squash homosexuality? To round up all the gays together?"

"Why did they send them here?" Sunny asks.

Julia points farther down the page. "Treasure Island was a port," she says. "They didn't make the sailors stick around or anything; this was just where they were told they were getting kicked out of the navy. But tons of sailors stayed behind. They started living in the same neighborhoods in San Francisco, going to the same shops and stuff. They went from a bunch of scattered individuals to a group, a community."

I catch one of the final lines of the article and read it out loud: "In many ways, Treasure Island laid the foundation for the beginning of gay culture in America."

I pause. I'd never really thought about why San Francisco has such a rich history in the queer community. It's always kind of been a chicken-or-egg scenario in my head. Did gay people come here because San Francisco was so accepting, or was San Francisco so accepting because so many gay people came here?

According to this article . . . the gay community *made* San Francisco accepting. They forged their own home here, together.

"Ooh!" Sunny stands and points a finger into the air. She holds up another article. "Harvey Milk used to be in the navy!"

"I thought you said he didn't do anything on Treasure Island," I say.

Sunny shrugs. "He didn't. He served before he ever moved to San Francisco. But now naming a naval ship after him makes sense."

I pull Julia's notebook toward me. "Okay, we can put this all together. I still think we're looking for an architect. But if Harvey is the key to this puzzle, then we should be looking for an architect of a *naval* building on Treasure Island, yeah? Any idea which one that could be?"

Gabriel raises his hand. "I think I have the answer to that."

He reads a caption from a large eight-by-ten photograph in front of him. "Administration Building, also called Building 1, was the primary headquarters of the command naval base in San Francisco. In World War II, the building was known as Naval Station Treasure Island."

"Any architects listed for that building?" I ask tentatively.

"Two names," Gabriel says. He flips through a couple more photos, then stops, frozen in place. He turns to the Naval Station photo again, then back to a new mystery photo.

"No freaking way," he whispers.

"What?" I say, leaning over now. "What is it?"

Gabriel blinks and looks at the rest of us. "I'm pretty sure the second architect on the naval building is our guy." He holds up the photo, covering the front dramatically with his giant gloved hand. Underneath, we see a single name scrawled across in delicate script.

George W. Kelham.

"Okay . . ." I'm already confused. This is just another

name, exactly like all the ones already on Julia's list. "Why this architect? Was he gay or something?"

"I don't know," Gabriel says. "But I *do* know that he happened to design another really important building in San Francisco. One that fits our clue perfectly."

"What building?" I ask.

Gabriel slowly lifts his hand from the mystery photo and shows us.

CHAPTER SEVENTEEN

We pack up all the forms, ribbons, and photos back into the boxes. Gabriel goes to the front desk and signs us out.

"Did you find what you were after?" the librarian asks.

They must ask everyone this. That's why people come to a city history center, right? To find some specific piece of history that fits an assignment, or research paper, or whatever. Even so, just the librarian's question has the four of us vibrating with excitement.

"Oh yeah," Gabriel answers. "I'm pretty sure we found exactly what we were looking for."

The moment we're out of the city history room and in the hallway, we implode into the softest collective scream we can manage.

Here, I think to myself. *We're already here.*

TREASURE ISLAND BUILDER READS ARCHITEC-TURE 723

The Treasure Island builder who reads architecture has

to be George W. Kelham, the architect who designed both Naval Station Treasure Island *and* the San Francisco Main Public Library. As in, the library we're currently standing in.

"So 'seven two three' is all that's left," Julia says, studying the cipher solution in her notebook.

"No," Sunny cuts in, "'*Architecture* seven two three.'"

"But George is the architect," Julia counters. "He's a builder who reads architecture . . . That was the clue to him being an architect."

Gabriel clears his throat. "I thought the word 'reads' was pointing to the main library."

TREASURE ISLAND BUILDER READS.

"Stop," I say suddenly.

The others jerk toward me. "We're not actually fighting," Gabriel says.

"No, no." I shake my head. "I meant 'stop' as in 'period.' I think you need to put in a period to figure out the clue. 'Treasure Island builder reads.' We know who the builder is: George W. Kelham—and we know what he designed: the navy building on Treasure Island and *here*. We're in his library, right? So if that's the next step, and all that's left in the clue is 'architecture seven two three . . .'"

Sunny snaps. "It's a call number! It's a freaking call number!"

We rush down the stairs to the main collection. Right there, laminated in all its rainbow glory, is an old-school Dewey decimal system poster. Sunny points to the seven hundreds.

"Arts and Recreation," she reads. "Seven hundreds—Fine Art. Seven tens—Landscaping. Seven twenties—"

She looks back at us. "Architecture."

"Holy shit," Gabriel squeals. "This is so legit."

I gaze around the room, trying to figure out which direction the call numbers are heading. Finally, I see a cluster of shelves marked as five hundreds. As the numbers tick up, the shelves get smaller and smaller in the distance, to the point where they almost seem to disappear into the recesses of the far wing.

"This way," I tell the others.

And even though we're not underground beneath Trinity Church or sneaking into caves behind Mount Rushmore, I feel exactly like Ben Gates reaching the final step of the puzzle.

We creep past the sea of shelves until we reach the seven hundreds. As I get ready to turn down the next aisle, my chest swells. I don't know what we're about to see, but I know it has to be important. I take a deep breath and peer around the corner, and . . .

It looks exactly the same as any other row of books.

The shelves are the same nondescript metal shelves as the ones in the rest of the library. The books look like the ones in every other row. The floor's the same gray tile—no one square slightly out of place. There's not a nearby lamp switch leading to a back room, or a mysterious framed picture of Harvey Milk or George W. Kelham. There's not even an old letter stuck to the underside of a shelf ledge.

"Do you see anything?" Gabriel asks from the back of the line.

I inch my way in, holding on to my breath like I can swallow back the disappointment. The clues in *Gay Treasures* are hidden. They're *really* hidden. They have to be, or else Gilbert's treasure hunt wouldn't have survived for more than a week. I follow the call numbers until I reach the section marked seven twenty-three. There are at least a hundred books spanning down the row starting with that same number. I poke my head over the top of the books and look behind them. I shove the spines back and look underneath them. I pick up an older-looking vintage book and leaf through it. Nothing. There's nothing.

"Well," Sunny says behind me, "this is definitely the architecture section, at least."

I've gone numb. I missed something, skipped some important piece of the puzzle. But *how* did I miss something? We found the gay history behind Treasure Island. We made the connection to Harvey. We know the name of the builder who reads. I've taken all the right steps to get to this point.

Or have I?

My mind instantly goes to Cam. Would he have sifted through all that crap upstairs? He never does the "boring research work," as he called it that summer. If he were on this team, he would have led us all straight to the real Treasure Island, I bet, where there's probably a secret, hidden library in the Naval Station building. And that secret library is probably filled with colorful jewelry and the ghosts of every fabulous gay naval sailor in history, chilling in the afterlife like a haunted Studio 54.

Meanwhile, I've followed the boring research route, and now I'm surrounded by a bunch of books on building codes and blueprints. I'm too practical—I've always been too practical. How could someone like me ever find a buried treasure?

A tear has already escaped before I can stop it. I become suddenly very interested in the floor.

A hand gently lands on my shoulder.

"Ivy?" Julia's voice sounds so far away.

I can't do this. Not here. And for the love of God, not in front of anyone else.

"Sorry," I huff.

I beeline down the rest of the aisle and make a hard turn toward the back of the library. More tears are spilling out. I press my sleeves into my cheeks as I walk. Farther. Farther. I see a corner where the overhead light has gone out, and I sink onto the floor underneath it, my back to the wall, grateful for this pocket of shadow. I pull my legs up to my chest.

After a minute or so, someone else approaches. A thick sweater slides down the wall. I feel a tiny elbow knock into mine.

"I don't want to talk," I say into my knees.

"Is it okay if I do?" Julia asks. "Not about you, I mean. But what I was trying to talk about before."

In an instant I forget how stupid I look, and I lift my head. Julia's crouched next to me, not a notebook or yellow pencil stub in sight. She must've left her backpack behind in the aisle.

"Remember how Gabriel called me a Girl Scout?" Julia asks. "And you saw how it pissed me off?"

I nod.

"I actually was a Girl Scout when I was a kid," Julia says.

"And I really loved it. I wanted to be a Girl Scout for the rest of my life. I kind of remember thinking that when I graduated, all my badges would transfer into police badges or something. And then I could go be a sheriff somewhere."

I laugh a little. "You thought Girl Scouts were like police officers?"

"Hey!" Julia nudges me and smiles. "You know that if all police officers were former Girl Scouts, the world would be a much better place."

"Okay, yeah. True." I bob my head. "So . . . what does this have to do with the treasure hunt?"

Julia pulls her knees closer and sighs. "Well, I was a kid at the time, right? So everything—fairy tales and real life—was all weirdly conflated in my head. It didn't make sense that adults said magic wasn't real but then told so many stories where magic existed anyway. And getting mysterious gifts from Santa and the Easter bunny sure didn't help. It just made everything more"—she shakes her head—"confusing.

"Anyway, when it was time to leave the Daisy level in Girl Scouts and go into Brownies, my mom told me the bridging ceremony would happen in an enchanted forest. And on the day of the ceremony, the whole troop met out in Golden Gate Park, but in a part of the park I had never been in before. It was really mystical and quiet. Our troop leaders laid down a mirror in the long grass and told us it was a silver pond. They said there was a magic elf that would help take us from one side to the other. I still remember standing there, feeling cold and nervous, wondering when the elf would come out."

I shift over so I can see Julia better. "What happened?"

Julia's eyebrows furrow. "I was called first. My mom brought me up in front of the group. The leaders read a poem about how magic was all around us. And the thing is, I could *feel* it. I knew the magic was real. They spun me around three times and had me look into the silver pond and call for the elf. There was a rhyme, and I was supposed to say the last word.

'*Twist me and turn me and show me the elf,*

'*I looked in the water and saw . . .*'

"And the answer is obvious, right?" Julia says. "We were looking in a freaking mirror. But at the time, I was completely focused on finding that elf. I was so frustrated. I started crying and saying that I couldn't see the elf, and I remember—"

She sighs.

"I remember that everyone, the troop leaders, the other Daisies, even my mom, started laughing at me."

I put my hand over hers. "Oh, Julia."

"And they weren't even trying to get me to laugh with them." She presses the heel of her other palm into her cheek. "They were just laughing at how stupid I was. That I was dumb enough to believe that elves and magic mirrors could really exist."

For a moment, I picture Julia as a kid, off in some quiet area of Golden Gate Park. I can imagine me and Cam just on the other side of a nearby tree, scaling up its winding branches, pretending we were lost in the enchanted woods. Cam and I believed in magic then too. We believed in magic for a long time. Until one day . . . we just didn't.

"You must've felt lonely," I say, staring off into the distance.

"Yeah—I ended up quitting. Sunny once mentioned being a Girl Scout Brownie, and I didn't say anything at the time, but, gosh, on the inside, I was so angry. I couldn't believe that *Sunny* of all people outlasted *me* in Girl Scouts."

She lets out a halfway laugh.

"But, anyway, that's why I'm doing the treasure hunt now," Julia says. She blinks and looks directly at me. "Because fuck my troop."

My eyes bug out. "Excuse me, did you just say the f-word?"

Julia raises her chin. "You shouldn't laugh at people who believe in things. Sometimes, even in the real world, magic can exist. Sometimes fairy tales can be real."

"Yeah, well." I sniff and stare off into the distance. "Sorry it didn't turn out that way for us this time."

Julia pushes herself from the wall. "Ivy, what are you talking about? We're doing amazing. This, already, *is* magic."

I roll my eyes. "Yeah, all those books on how to design support beams and retaining walls looked super magical back there. What a treasure trove."

"Stop it," Julia says seriously. She pauses, contemplative. "You know, the reason I wanted to tell you this story earlier was because there was this ugly voice in my head saying you guys would all laugh at me and then kick me out of the group. And I wanted to get that over with before I got too involved."

I give her a look. "Why would we have kicked you out?"

"I don't know." She flaps her hands. "Because you three are cool, and I'm just this nerd trying to do vengeance for my eight-year-old Girl Scout self?"

I laugh. "Are you kidding me? Girl Scout vengeance is probably the best motivation I've ever heard of."

Julia laughs and stands. "So my mean internal voice was wrong," she says. "I wonder if yours is too." She offers me her arm.

I take Julia's hand and stand up after her, then surprise myself by not immediately letting go.

"I feel like I'm going to give you another hug right now," I say, in the same way a kid informs everyone in a car that he's about to vomit. Which roughly describes how I feel about hugging.

But Julia doesn't seem to mind. "Of course you are," she says cheerfully, and pulls me in, technically beating me to the punch.

The crush of her sweater against my jacket feels strange, and I think boobs should really be strategically placed in a hug to not squeeze the life out of anyone. Still, it's not bad. For a second I even relax into Julia's shoulder as she squeezes mine.

We separate and look down the shadowy aisle of the library.

"We're going to figure this out, aren't we?" I ask.

"Yes." Julia flashes a playful, unreserved smile. I can almost see her kid self shining directly through it. "We really are."

We walk back to the others.

CHAPTER EIGHTEEN

We find Sunny and Gabriel in the same aisle, although at this point it doesn't look the same at all. Every book marked with the call number 723 has been swept off the shelf and is now sitting in one of several extremely tall stacks along the floor.

"Okay," Julia says as we goose-step over the shortest pile. "This is either an insanely elaborate game of Jenga or the most creative cityscape model I've ever seen."

Sunny huffs as she pulls a book down from the top of the tallest stack, which currently ends at her waist. The books are sticking out in every direction, precariously holding together while they pull a slow-going Leaning Tower of Pisa. But the pile near Gabriel, I notice, is meticulously stacked.

Sunny and Gabriel are sorting the books.

"It might be a third option," I offer.

Julia shakes her head. "Nope. No . . . only those two. Jenga or cityscape."

"Oh! 1979," Sunny reads from the inside jacket.

Gabriel holds out a hand. "Give it here." He carries the book to his pile.

"You're pulling all the titles that were published before *Gay Treasures*," I say.

Sunny already has her nose in the next book. "Ding ding ding."

"Dang." Julia snaps her fingers. "Ivy wins."

I walk over to the pile near Gabriel. "Anything interesting?"

"Sadly, no," Gabriel says. He makes a frame with his thumbs and index fingers. "But I'm still waiting for a pattern to spring out at me."

"And we're not done," Sunny calls. She nods at the rest of the books over her shoulder. Julia dutifully pulls the next book down and checks the copyright year.

I tilt my head sideways to look at the titles in Gabriel's stack. An unpleasant feeling is gnawing at my belly. There's an unspoken agreement here, I think. If you're playing a game, you assume the game is fair. If you're answering a riddle, that means the riddle must have a proper answer. Doing a treasure hunt is like the extreme version of that. It's the ultimate trust fall. There has to be some kind of stability to the clues, because otherwise, the entire concept disintegrates in your hands.

"Let's pause a second," I say uneasily.

Sunny glares at me. "Says the person who literally got here one second ago."

"Okay, fair! Yes, I just got here. But hear me out: I am seeing a pattern."

Gabriel whips his head around. He looks again at his stack of books. "What's the pattern?"

"The pattern is, books circulate between library branches," I say. "And I'm pretty sure they always have, even in the 1980s. So it would be a terrible idea for Gilbert Baker to put a clue in a single book, even if it did manage to stay in circulation until now."

"So, what?" Sunny says icily. "You're saying this is all useless?"

"No." I shake my head. "I'm not saying that. Nothing you're doing is useless. I was the one who walked away and made Julia go after me. And the whole time, both of you were working your asses off. No one has acted useless in this group except me."

Sunny snorts. "Say it louder for the people in the back."

"I'm useless!" I call out in the loudest stage whisper I can manage. I mean, we're still in a library, after all.

"All right." Sunny sets her book down. "So what do we do now?"

I look around at the shelves. "Julia, can you get your notebook out? I want to see the history center notes again."

Julia hops over a stack of books to her backpack at the far end of the aisle. She pauses a moment, staring down into the open compartment.

"Did one of you open my backpack?" Julia asks.

Sunny and Gabriel shake their heads. The three of us zigzag around the maze of books and stand next to Julia. She carefully extracts her notebook, which now has some kind of laminated page peeking out over the top.

"I didn't put this in here," she says quietly.

I hold out my hands, and Julia passes the notebook over. I open it to the insert, which turns out to be three different brochures stacked on top of one another. But they're not actually brochures. They're more like . . . *Oh no.*

I take a sharp breath.

Gabriel reads the titles of each empty book jacket over my shoulder. "*The Watergate Girl. The Truth About Watergate. Watergate: A New History.* What's all this? Is Watergate a clue or something?"

Julia's eyes slide over to mine. There's a small note on top of the book jackets. It's the same note I left in Cam's locker.

Watergate Internal Business

Except now there's an additional line in Cam's handwriting, just below mine.

NICE TRY! ☺

"Damn it!" I say, slightly too loud for library-speaking levels. "Damn it," I say again in a whisper.

This is bad. This is extremely bad. I think about the past week of watching Cam hide his books on Watergate and how smug I felt, knowing he was behind us. And now I know that the entire time *I* was feeling smug, *he* was feeling twice as smug!

I look up at Julia. "When did you put your backpack down?"

"Like five minutes ago! Right after you stomped off." Julia swallows and checks over her shoulder.

"Someone please tell me what the hell is going on," Sunny says.

I lean out from our aisle and peer down either direction before turning back to the group. "Cam's here. He's here, and he knows I planted a fake clue in his locker, and wherever we're supposed to be looking right now, like wherever the clue 'architecture seven two three' actually leads, he's probably already there."

Sunny's eyes widen. "Damn it!"

"Exactly!" I say. "So we'd better start thinking fast."

I start pacing back and forth down the aisle.

"*Treasure Island builder reads. Architecture seven two three.* Builder. Architecture. George W. Kelham. The Naval Station Treasure Island. The main library. Builder. *Builder.*"

"Are you, like, a shitty AI program?" Gabriel asks. "Where we feed you a list of random words and you spit out an awful slam poem?"

My head snaps up. "Wait a second. The clue isn't leading us to one book! It's to a whole section!"

"You already said that," Julia murmurs, clearly a little embarrassed for me.

"Yes," I say, "but now I might actually have an idea of what's going on."

I look down at the gleaming ivory tile, then up at the glazed porcelain wall. The outer rim of the wall curves slightly as it twists toward the central circle in the main foyer. Overhead, the windows mimic a golden spiral. The lines are all clean and modern. This isn't Art Deco architecture. It's not Moderne style. It's not even brutalist.

"What year did the library first open?" I ask Gabriel.

He turns on the yearbook camera and looks down at the most recent photo. "The archival note said . . . 1917."

He zooms in on the image so I can see what he's reading. It's the handwritten caption on the original photo we found in the history center.

"Can you zoom back out?" I ask. I stare at the front façade of the building. "I don't remember columns above the front doors."

Gabriel squints. "It's the same building, Ivy. Maybe they just took the columns off sometime after it opened."

"Yeah, maybe." But suddenly I have to go look again. Right now. I dip into the next aisle and pull an empty return cart over, then grab an armload of books off the floor. "Come on. Let's put these away and go outside and look."

"Are you serious?" Sunny asks. "We're just going to walk away from all this work? With Cam lurking around somewhere?"

"I just want to look!" I hiss.

After a few minutes, we've loaded the cart and walked back through the front doors. I signal everyone across the street over to Civic Center Plaza so we can see the building properly. The three front doors of the main library match up with Gabriel's photo. So do the five overhead windows and the wings on either side. Gabriel is right—this does look like the same building. But something *feels* wrong. Why would they take the front columns away? And why is the shape of the windows suddenly different?

Sunny leans against my arm as she looks at the photo. I

feel her head tip up and down as she goes through the same checklist.

"So your theory," she says slowly, "is that we're in the wrong library?"

"Maybe. I didn't say that exactly," I say. "I'm just trying to figure out what's going on."

Julia comes to my other side and looks at the photo. I half expect to see her chin bob up and down like Sunny's did. But instead of looking up at the library and back down, Julia cocks her head to the left, then back at the photo. Left, and photo. I follow her gaze to another large concrete building farther down the block.

"What is it?" I ask her.

Julia points. "I came that way this morning," she says. "I got lost looking for the coffee place. I sort of think . . . the building in the photo might be . . ."

She trails off and starts walking down the sidewalk. Sunny, Gabriel, and I all glance at each other. We turn and head after her. The three of us have barely crossed to the other side of Civic Center Plaza when Julia suddenly whoops triumphantly a few yards ahead.

"This is it!" she shouts.

She waves us over until we're standing directly across from the building literally next door to the place we just were. Gabriel opens the camera again, but we don't even need to see the old photo side by side to know, immediately, that Julia is right. This is the library from the photo—the one that George W. Kelham designed and built in 1917. But it's not the main library anymore. Now it's—

"The Asian Art Museum," Julia reads off the building's stone inscription.

ASIAN ART MUSEUM

CHONG-MOON LEE CENTER FOR ASIAN ART AND CULTURE

"Wow." Sunny looks impressed. "My people! This is, like . . . the coolest form of gentrification."

I look over at her. "I think, technically, gentrification is when wealthy people take advantage of cheap property in poorer areas. So I don't know if a library turning into an art museum counts as gentrification."

Sunny nods. "Okay, Asianification, then."

"But that's not really a thing—"

Gabriel stops me. "Shhhh. Let her have this," he says.

We stare at the building.

"So, what do we do now?" Julia asks.

I take a deep breath and close my eyes to think. I've been in this situation before—watched buildings' signs change, seen their insides gutted, seen new personalities take over old bodies like it was no big deal. Nothing in San Francisco ever stays the same.

Nothing ever stays the same.

My arms feel uncomfortably warm. I open my eyes. "I guess . . . we go inside anyway," I say finally. "And see how much things have changed. Who knows, maybe Gilbert Baker's clue is still in there."

Julia links arms with me. "Let's go, then, Dorothy."

"Hell no," Sunny says. "I'm the Dorothy in this scenario."

151

I shrug. "That's fine. You can be Dorothy." I'm trying hard not to sound as completely defeated as I feel.

"Lion!" Julia calls, raising her hand.

Gabriel throws back his shoulders and links his arm with my free one. "As long as it's agreed that the Scarecrow was actually smart the whole time—because he *was*—I'll be the Scarecrow."

"You can be the Tin Man," Sunny tells me. "Come on, everyone. For a home!" she says, marching us ahead.

"For bravery!" Julia shouts.

"For a diploma!" Gabriel adds.

I turn over my shoulder and spare one last glance at the new library. I think about Cam inside, stalking up and down the gleaming aisles, searching for the next clue. Something aches deep in my chest.

"For a heart," I say softly.

CHAPTER NINETEEN

Before Cam stole the flyer and ran.

Before I confessed to him under the trees.

Before he first tumbled into my room with *Gay Treasures*.

We were friends.

Friends friends. The kind of friends who are supposed to stick together, no matter what. In a city where buildings are changing hands and names faster than a seasonal menu at a fancy restaurant, it's people we depend on to be constant. People are the ones we count on not to turn from exposed brick to faux shiplap overnight.

I still remember the way Cam's hand brushed over my shoulder the morning we discovered that we'd lost Damascus Bread & Pastry to yet another Starbucks. Starbucks was doing the thing it had been doing all around the city: trying hard to pretend like it wasn't a giant corporation taking over another mom-and-pop storefront. Every new opening was like watching a wolf wear a sheepskin onesie.

As we surveyed the wreckage—the hasty paint job, the unfamiliar employees, the faint smell of cardamom that felt like a scream in the distance—Cam reached over and gave me a strange half hug. His palm skated over my sleeve, pressing solidness into me when I needed it most. But then his hand settled on my arm, pressed fabric turning into pressed skin, and everything inside my chest that he had just smoothed down suddenly sprang back up, wild and untethered. He was supposed to anchor me, and instead, unexpectedly, he had set me buoyant. I probably would have floated right into the ugly shiplap ceiling if I hadn't been wearing my Doc Martens.

I knew then. Even before he took off a year later, I realized the friendship was unraveling. Things were changing between us—his skin on mine like crisp, new wallpaper.

The building we'd made was turning into something else.

We walk through the main doors of the Chong-Moon Lee Center. Almost immediately, time seems to fold back, to soften into the texture and warmth of porous stone and incandescent lightbulbs. Both the floors and walls have the same pattern of marble, like a swirl of milk just stirred into coffee. Two alcoves are stamped into the hallway with scallop-shell archways. An intricate honeycomb design blooms over the arched golden ceiling.

"Well," Julia says as we let the front doors close behind us. "This definitely feels a lot older."

"And a lot more like a place to hide treasure," Gabriel says, rubbing his palms together.

Sunny is too eager to say anything. She spots the front desk and beelines for it, already pulling out her wallet.

The young Asian American woman sitting behind the desk waves her off.

"First Saturday of the month," she says. "Free admission. Donation only."

"Oh." Sunny pauses. "Can you take donation by card?"

"Of course!" The girl beams, her cheeks tinged pink like apples in early fall. She scooches the register slightly closer to Sunny.

Sunny taps her card and presses a button, then shoots us a look over her shoulder. I scramble to pull out my own wallet.

"Right! Yes! I want to donate."

"Me too," Julia adds quickly.

Gabriel beats both of us with mobile pay. "I love donating!"

The girl at the desk smiles politely at the rest of us as we tap our cards and phones. She hands us each an "I donated!" sticker, then holds out a QR code.

"Your digital visitor guide," she explains as we scan it. "The last page has a map of the full museum. Our permanent collection is on the top two floors. The second floor has the Japan and Korea wings. The China wing is split between floors two and three on the north end. South and Southeast Asian art is on the third floor, south end."

"Thank you," we all say.

She stares at Sunny for an extra moment before turning

back to her computer. I check over my shoulder to see if Sunny noticed, but she already has the digital guide open on her screen. I open mine too and quickly find the map.

"Should we have asked about the architecture section?" Julia whispers.

Sunny looks up from her phone. "From the old library? How the hell would she know where it used to be?"

"Maybe we should have asked someone at the new library," Gabriel says. He pauses on a step, as if we might turn around and head back out.

"Let's scope this place out first," I say. "Maybe we'll see something obvious."

"Obvious like what?" Sunny asks.

"I don't know yet. But there had to be a reason Gilbert Baker chose this place, right?"

We reach the second floor.

Sunny raises her hand. "Well, my dad's family is from Japan, so I'm taking the Japan wing."

"I'll take Korea," Julia says.

Gabriel points across the hall. "China!"

I look back and forth. "I'll take Japan with Sunny," I say with a sigh. "Let's meet back here in thirty minutes and report, then head up to the third floor together."

Julia nods and darts into the first gallery room of the Korea wing. Gabriel weaves around the open staircase toward the China wing. Sunny eyes me warily, then walks into a room with the heading *Tateuchi Japanese Galleries*. I walk inside after her.

"What was that?" I ask.

"What was what?" Sunny says, not turning around.

"That look you gave me."

"I didn't give you a look."

"Sunny, please. You're *always* giving a look."

Sunny whirls on me. "Maybe I just don't understand why you decided that *I'm* the one who needs a babysitter," she snaps.

I extend both arms. "Okay, you three called out all the wings in, like, two seconds! And Japan's the largest one on this floor! I'm not babysitting you. I'm trying to help."

Sunny snorts and turns away from me again. She does a full three-sixty turn around the first room, then crosses into the adjoining gallery. I glance around at the smooth, painted walls before following her. So far everything looks exactly like a standard art museum. I try to fight off the rising dread that whatever was here in Gilbert's time is now long gone.

I catch up to Sunny. "You're being weird," I say. "And not your usual weird either. Is it something about the museum?"

Sunny sighs in front of a giant painting of cranes and trees leaning over a riverbank.

"It's not the museum," she says. She pauses a moment. "Well, yeah, it is, but not for the reason you probably think."

"Okay . . ."

"Do you remember how we passed the museum on Castro?" Sunny asks. "With Mr. Wong?"

I nod. "The GLBT Historical Society Museum? Yeah."

"Well, like, this is my other big problem with Harvey

Milk's name on everything in this city. Just seeing all the post-
ers on the outside of the GLBT building with only white people standing in the front felt . . . shitty. Sometimes the whole
San Francisco gay history thing feels so predominantly white.
Like all the people of color are footnotes. And then we come
here, and it's traditional Asian art, and that's great—I really
appreciate seeing an entire museum of this—but then it's like,
where are the gay people? They exist, of course, but they're
footnotes again, right? Intersectionalism feels like constantly
being a footnote in everyone else's history. No matter where
you go."

My heart sinks with this realization. Sunny's completely
right.

"And I may or may not be gay—that's not the point," she
goes on. "But the point is that it feels impossible for gay people of color to have their own spaces and communities. Ask
Gabriel about how it feels to be a queer Latino. It's the same
thing."

"I'm sure it is," I say.

Sunny prods me. "But *you're* the one who was so disappointed when we got here and saw that the library had turned
into this."

I look up, startled. "I'm not disappointed it's an Asian art
museum."

"It sure felt like that," Sunny whispers, "when you saw
the name on the building."

The strain in her voice finally gives. I can see the exhaus-
tion in her. I see how tired she is from trying so hard to look

like she doesn't care, like she's only mildly annoyed by most things instead of emotionally drained by everything.

And I'm part of it. Maybe not me personally, but I am a part of the notion that San Francisco gay culture has been spearheaded by white people. I run the GSA at our school with another white person. I've made Being Gay my entire thing the way that only white people can, because I'm not reconciling multiple marginalized identities.

I was freaking out earlier over Gilbert gatekeeping the treasure hunt from outsiders, but the truth is . . . people with intersectional identities are treated like outsiders all the time.

"I hear you," I say quietly. "I hear you, and I'm so sorry. You're right, Sunny. It was dumb to talk about not being gay enough before. I wasn't even thinking about other people's experiences; I was being selfish. And I did act like an asshole when I realized the library had changed. It doesn't actually matter if we're inside a library or an art museum; these clues are just as fragile. If the treasure hunt falls apart with this next step, it's not the museum's fault. Sometimes things just . . . break."

We wind through two more gallery rooms before Sunny's face lights up.

"Hey. Come look at this." She walks over to a softly lit glass case with several displays of golden-painted pottery.

"It's kintsugi," Sunny says.

I step closer and peer at a pale blue serving bowl. I've seen pottery like this before, but I had always assumed the gold lines were painted over the top. Up close, it's clear that the pieces of the bowl aren't quite perfect. They're aligned, but not exactly. The gold isn't just a decoration, I realize—it's what's making the whole thing function.

"Is it soldered together?" I ask.

Sunny shakes her head. "No, it's an incredibly strong lacquer made from tree resin. And then it's gilded with gold leaf after, to make the cracks pretty. It's part of sabiru, or wabi-sabi. About celebrating imperfection."

She turns to me. "Japanese tradition tells us that we're supposed to look at bowls like this one and imagine the cracks as signs of aging, which is nice. But sometimes I see the cracks, and I just think of me and all the times I've felt broken or messed up. And the gold reminds me that even though I'm not perfect, there is so much beauty in survival."

She shrugs. "I don't know. That's probably stupid."

"No, it's not," I say quickly. "It's not stupid at all. I get it."

I look at the gold spider-webbing across the ceramic. For a moment it's like I can see hands holding the original bowl, cradling it across a room, stumbling, and letting it slip through their fingers. I can feel the impact of the ground, the way a whole thing instantly becomes a fraction. I know the heartache of it, the feeling of brokenness Sunny's talking about. But then, just like she said, I can see the beauty in it too. The hands gathering up the pieces. The artist lining each section back together like a puzzle. The brush dipped in gold, marking each repaired crack like it's an achievement. Because it's not nothing, to fall apart and come back together. The pieces *matter*. Survival *matters*.

We're not stepping back into a time machine with this hunt. We can't see it the way Gilbert Baker did when he hid the pieces. But we're stitching it together through our lens. The library is an Asian art museum. The book *Gay Treasures* came out so long ago that it's old enough to have a midlife crisis. And it's okay. The only way forward is to celebrate the cracks.

I look away from the bowl and smile at Sunny.

"Thank you for sharing this with me. All of this."

CHAPTER TWENTY

Sunny steps back from the kintsugi display and glances around the room. "Well, I haven't seen anything out of the ordinary around here."

"Yeah," I say. I gaze at the glass cases lining the walls. "Me neither."

We walk out of the Japan wing and into a strong afternoon light. We're adjacent to a large, open hall with windows that go from floor to ceiling. The windows are lined in an intricate checkered pattern. Marble columns with rolling spirals at the top mark each corner of the room. Julia and Gabriel walk through doors on the opposite side.

"This is cool," Gabriel says appraisingly. He tilts his head back and points his camera at the ceiling, which has the same honeycomb pattern as the foyer. I stand next to Gabriel and study the carvings along the crown molding.

"Into Architecture?" Sunny asks.

I snort. "For our current visit? Obviously."

"No." Sunny holds out her phone. "I just found this page in our digital guide."

INTO ARCHITECTURE?

She reads to us directly from the screen:

"Take a tour through the past of our beloved 1917 Beaux-Arts home, which was designed as the city's original main library. Highlights include both the Wilbur Grand Staircase and the dramatic, intricately styled Samsung Hall, which held the main library's catalogue until 1996."

Sunny looks up. "This is it. This is the room where all the books were kept."

"Hey, check this out," Julia says. She's looking at something framed near the doors Sunny and I walked through.

It's an old sepia photo of a large, empty room. Rows of long tables with matching sleek chairs stretch from the foreground and into the distance. Every wall around the tables is filled with built-in wooden bookshelves, which are stacked, top to bottom, with books. The small metal plaque under the framed photo reads *Interior of Main Library—Reading Room, 1917.*

I step closer to the picture.

If the visitor guide is right and this room held all the books in the main library, then that means Gilbert Baker's clue might have been connected to one of those built-in bookshelves. I look around me at the marble walls and giant floor-to-ceiling windows. The bookshelves are clearly no longer here.

But there's something else going on. As I study the photograph, I recognize the windows next to us are the same windows from 1917. Intricate checkered patterns and all. Only, the windows don't go all the way from the floor to the ceiling in the photo, the way they do now. They ran from the ceiling and stopped halfway down the wall, where the built-in bookshelves took over. I pull out the map of the museum again.

"I think . . . I think they cut this room in half," I say.

Sunny scratches her head. "That's weird. It doesn't look like it's a half room." She glances back toward the Japan wing. "Where's the other half?"

"It's below us." I read from the guide. "The Osher Foundation Gallery on the first floor. They cut the room in half *horizontally!*"

"What?" Sunny walks over to me and Julia. "Why would they do that?"

"Well, look how open it was." I point to the framed photo. "No one needs ceilings *that* high, especially when you can use the extra space for something else. Come on. We need to go see if the shelves are still down there."

Gabriel snaps a picture of the photo and its caption on the fancy camera, then we all take the side staircase down. The stairwell ends on the first floor, directly across from the entrance to the Osher Foundation Gallery. I pause outside the entryway. We've figured out the mystery of the old library. This—this room right in front of us—is where Gilbert wanted his treasure hunters to look. And whatever he put there, if it's gone, then that's it. The San Francisco mystery will go unsolved forever.

"Now or never," Gabriel says next to me. He offers a reassuring smile.

We head through the doorway.

Julia takes a deep, sharp inhale as soon as we step inside. "This is *huge*," she whispers.

She's right. Samsung Hall, the room right above us, felt towering and grandiose, but that was sort of the point. The room in front of us now is dark and expansive, more like a labyrinth or a cave. It seems nearly endless.

My heart swells as I look around, because, apart from the lack of windows, there's another reason this room is so dark. The original mahogany built-in bookshelves cover every single wall.

"The treasure's still here," I say out loud.

It has to be.

It takes a few moments for my eyes to adjust from the bright windows upstairs to the cool, cozy feeling of spotlights scattered throughout the room. A few other people mill around in the shadows, reading the description cards and considering the works of art. I glance at the security guard in the corner, then gather Sunny, Gabriel, and Julia close.

"We have to check all the shelves," I whisper. "Can you show me the photo again?" I ask Gabriel. "The one from upstairs?"

He nods and passes the camera over. I match up the doors we just came through with the main entrance in the photograph. There's a built-in reference desk next to the doors in the photo. I look up. The desk is gone now. But maybe I can use this as a starting place. The Dewey decimal system poster from the library had call numbers from zero all the way up to a thousand. I remember that the first set of numbers were reference materials. Wouldn't that section start behind a reference desk?

"Zero to a hundred," I whisper, pointing to the section of shelves next to the doors, where the reference desk used to be. I point to the next section over. "One hundred to two hundred. Two hundred to three. Three to four."

I pivot with each section, my finger sweeping over slices of the room like a clock hand.

Five to six, six to seven . . .

"Seven to eight hundred."

I'm pointing at a random section of shelves across the room from us. "I think that's where the architecture section used to be."

Gabriel squints across the room, then looks back down at the photograph on his camera.

"What's that?" he asks.

In the photo, just above Gabriel's finger, there's a small, round pipe sticking out below the shelves. Exactly where a person would find the books marked 723.

I look up at the gallery in front of us and see something metallic glinting near the floor.

"I'm going to check it out," I say. "Cover me."

I stride past all the exhibits on display. The object poking out from the wall gets closer and closer. At the very last second, I pull a bobby pin from my hair and toss it onto the floor.

I drop down onto my hands and knees, pretending to look for the pin. I crawl over to the base of the wall, and there it is: a round brass pipe that sticks out maybe three or four inches below the bottom shelf. There's a cover over the end of the pipe, with several words embossed on top. I lean closer and peer at the writing.

My breath hitches. I feel like I should stand up and grab the others. But one person crawling on the ground in an art museum is already conspicuous. I can't pull three more people down here with me.

I reach out tentatively and touch the brass cover on the pipe. My fingers find a latch on one side. I pull gently until the lid releases with a small click and falls into my hand. The hollow space within the pipe seems dark and empty.

I reach inside.

Oh . . . my . . . God.

At the exact moment my hand connects with the edge of a smooth wooden box, I hear a set of footsteps cross over the floor. Someone kneels down directly next to me, and my heart plummets. I recognize his breathing, can smell the mix of citrus and Old Spice deodorant on his clothing, before I even look at him.

"Hey, V," Cam murmurs over my shoulder. "Ex marks the spot, huh?"

CHAPTER TWENTY-ONE

A million scenarios rush through my head at once. Ideally, I was going to pull the wooden box out, slip it into my jacket, then grab Gabriel, Julia, and Sunny and get the heck out of here. Ideally, I wasn't going to see Cam at school until Monday, where I would casually mention that, oh, yeah, I found the treasure from *Gay Treasures*. Ideally, the whole city would already be in the middle of celebrating me. I could see the headline in the *San Francisco Chronicle* as I waved the paper in Cam's face:

SURPRISINGLY ARTISTIC-MINDED TEEN FINDS LOCAL TREASURE

But Cam's current presence, his hand mere inches from mine, has forced me back to the drawing board.

I could scream. But then, of course, I would probably have to deal with everyone in the room looking at me. And the security guard coming over and asking why the heck my hand is halfway inside a pipe on the wall. Plus, I feel like a screaming person almost always leads to an ambulance, no matter what they're screaming about. And I just cannot be responsible for wasting a bunch of EMTs' time and then being charged hundreds of dollars a few weeks later.

So that's out.

I could just take the box and run. I know running isn't allowed in museums, but I'm pretty sure if you do run, the consequence is that you have to leave. And I would already be on my way out! Unfortunately, I do know that Cam is a way faster runner than I am. And at this point, he's already proven that he doesn't mind yanking something directly out of my hands.

Think think think.

Cam plays dirty. He's a total Ian. So, what would Ben Gates do?

Someone kneels against my other side.

"I'm open," Sunny murmurs.

The meaning registers, and immediately I pass the box over to her. She rises and speed walks toward the central gallery entrance.

Cam stands after her. "Hey!" he calls out.

The security guard looks over at us, but Cam hardly seems to notice. He takes off after Sunny. I place the cover back on the end of the pipe and follow him.

"Wait!" I say. "Cam, stop!" I am not even attempting a museum-level volume.

Other people in the gallery, including Gabriel and Julia, all turn away from the exhibits to gawk at us. Gabriel opens his hands in a question. But I don't have time to stop and explain myself right now. By the time I reach the front entrance, I see Cam in a full-out sprint across the plaza toward the new library.

Fan-fucking-tastic.

Luckily, Sunny is so far ahead that I don't even see her. She must've already gone inside. I pause a moment, thinking. Sunny's a sitting duck in the library. We have to find a way out of this. I turn around and see the museum gift shop behind me. There, in a case over the main counter, is a collection of fancy pens placed in narrow brown boxes.

Another plan B.

"Do the boxes come with those pens?" I ask the person at the register.

They nod, and I grab my bank card from where I jabbed it into my back pocket after donating at the front desk. "Great. I'll take two."

I run smack into Gabriel and Julia in the lobby.

"Were you just shopping?!" Gabriel asks incredulously.

"No time!" I yell. "We've got to find Sunny. She's running from Cam."

"And again," Gabriel says, "you thought now would be the perfect time to browse for a little keepsake."

I hold out one of the two slender boxes to Julia. "Here, take this."

The box I hand her is made of cardboard, not wood like

the one hidden inside the Osher Foundation Gallery. Still, the color and shape of the boxes are nearly the same. As long as Cam doesn't look too close.

Julia takes the box gingerly. "What do I do with it?"

I explain the plan: We have to get back to the new library. If Julia runs into Cam, she has to make sure he catches a glimpse of the gift shop box, then immediately tuck it away and run in the opposite direction. Or if she runs into Sunny first, Julia will trade boxes.

Same plan goes for me.

"What about me?" Gabriel asks.

"You can't run," I say. I point to the expensive camera hanging from his neck. "Not with this. Your job is to watch our backs. Try not to let Cam sneak up on any of us."

We burst through the front doors and jog over to the new library.

"You would think," Julia says between gasps, "that Sunny would have just gone home."

"Oh, right," I say, "and wait fifteen minutes at the Civic Center Plaza for the next bus to come? What was she supposed to do, run all the way across the city?"

"Good point," Julia murmurs as we slip inside the library.

The building is way too big for us to divide and call out sections the way we normally would. So instead, Julia simply turns right into the shelves of books. I keep left, heading up the stairs and hoping I run into Sunny before I run into Cam.

Now that I'm back in this building, it seems strange that I ever imagined Gilbert Baker hiding something here in the

1980s. This building is so crisp and new. It's all wrong for a treasure hunt. I creep behind the sleek silver-toned railing and squirm around the smooth, giant columns.

"*Psst.*"

I turn my head. "Huh?"

I'm looking into the children's book room. Giant cardboard cutouts of classic characters are scattered throughout, posted at the ends of every shelf and reading table. I turn from Corduroy, to Paddington Bear, to Clifford the Big Red Dog. Elephant and Piggie look suspiciously still next to the checkout desk.

"*Psst!*"

The sound is clearly coming from behind the White Rabbit from *Alice's Adventures in Wonderland* in the chapter book section. I tiptoe over to the taller shelves. Sunny and I will have to make the switch fast.

But when I turn into the aisle, I don't find Sunny at all.

Cam motions for me to be quiet. As I rear back toward the reading tables, he reaches out for my arm. We both freeze with him holding on to me.

"You were about to trip," he explains.

I pull out the pen box from the gift shop. I remember plan B so suddenly that my body goes into reflex mode before my brain has time to make sense of what I'm doing. I wave the decoy box back and forth in front of Cam's face, then stow it under my jacket.

Cam scrunches his forehead. "Um . . . What was that about?"

Now I run. Run! I think. The plan was to show Cam the

box and then run away. But I can already tell we're off course. For one, he doesn't seem remotely interested in what I'm holding. And two, he's not supposed to be after me in the first place. He's supposed to be after Sunny.

What's going on?

"I have the box," I whisper.

"Okay," he says, but I can tell he doesn't believe me.

I look around. "Where's Sunny?"

Cam shrugs. "I don't know. I was waiting for you."

"No, you weren't!" I say. "You ran out of the museum after *Sunny.*"

Cam rolls his eyes. "I needed to get *you* out of the museum so we could talk."

I glare at him. "Well, you're not getting the box from us. And you still owe me my flyer. I bought that!"

His face softens a little, and he slides down the book spines until he's sitting on the carpet. I don't want to leer over him, so I have no choice but to sit down too. Our knees brush at first, and I jerk my legs back. I wish, so badly, that being close to Cam didn't affect me anymore. It shouldn't affect me. After a year of silence, things between us should be beyond stale.

"I'll give you the flyer," Cam says, picking at the carpet. He looks up at me. "But I want back in on the hunt."

"No way," I say, shifting against the opposite shelf. "You haven't done a single thing to merit joining the group. Plus, we don't need the flyer anymore."

"You need the book, though."

I shake my head. "We don't, actually. We found scans of

the chapter online. We solved the book cipher all on our own. Treasure Island builder reads—”

“Architecture seven two three.” Cam nods. “I know. But I can still help you.”

“Like you helped me earlier with your stupid Watergate books charade?”

“Hey, you were the one who planted that fake clue in the first place!” Cam says. He raises his eyebrows and smiles, like the idea of planting fake clues and stealing real clues and general sabotage is all just good fun. *He does not really care about this hunt*, I remind myself. *He is only in this to win in his stupid game over me.*

“No.” I start to get up. Cam crawls over and reaches for my hand.

“Please, V. Please. Hear me out. That box you have? It needs a key. I have the key.”

I open my hand like I’m supposed to find it there in my palm. Instead, all I see is Cam’s fingers interlocked with mine. I untwist myself from him.

“Then give it to us,” I say.

“Put me on your team.”

“Whose team?” Gabriel asks as he and Julia swing around the corner.

Julia sees Cam and gasps. She holds up her decoy box, then turns and runs headfirst into a life-sized Cat in the Hat.

“Run!” Julia cries, kicking the Cat in the Hat away.

“He doesn’t want the box,” I tell her. I look over at Cam. “He . . . wants to help us.”

Julia stands the cardboard cutout back up. She turns to

Cam and mashes her hands on her hips. "Help? Now? A lot of help he was when he stole our flyer!"

Cam bows his head and stares at his shoes. I don't think I've ever seen him properly ashamed like this. It should be nice. I should be reveling in it. But for some reason, the moment feels awkward and imbalanced. No one is on his side right now. Cam is supposed to be the guy surrounded by friends all the time. Instead, here he is, begging to work with us.

There has to be a catch, I remind myself. *With Cam, there's always a catch.*

But even as I think this, my body begins to disassociate from my brain the way it did when I waved the box around in Cam's face. Something sharp pokes my heart, and though I'm groaning and muttering inside, I know what I'm going to do anyway. He does have the key we need, after all.

Supposedly.

I tug on Cam's arm so that he stands up next to me, then shift the both of us toward Julia and Gabriel.

"He's working with us," I say. "At least until we get to the next step. Now, let's go find Sunny."

CHAPTER TWENTY-TWO

After searching the entire second floor for Sunny, we head upstairs to the third level of the library and creep into an empty circular room across from the elevator. Everyone scatters, checking behind tables and chairs, whispering Sunny's name.

"Hey, Ivy. Look at this." Gabriel calls me over to an open space in the middle of the room. The whole thing looks sort of like a flying saucer, with recessed lights along the outer edge and a dim concave arch at its center.

"Ho-ly," I murmur as we step under the circle of lights. We tilt our heads back and stare toward the gently arched ceiling at one of the wildest murals I've ever seen.

The center of the sepia-toned mural opens into a swirling, ephemeral sky, where a waterfall of books tumbles down onto a group of builders. They lift posts and hoist blocks and carve and chisel at a wall along the perimeter of the mural. On the wall itself are names, hundreds of names. I recognize a lot of them—Virginia Woolf, James Baldwin, Cole

Porter—because they're famous gay writers. Several figures in the painting proudly wave Pride flags at the top of the wall. One man pushes all his weight against a giant globe, trying to get it to budge.

"Is this the gay Sistine Chapel?" Gabriel asks.

It may as well be.

This is one of those paintings that makes you feel like you've been given a glimpse into something so much bigger than you'll ever be able to wrap your head around. The beginning of the universe. The start of mankind. But it's also not that exactly, because it's clear that this is a very specific world we're looking at. In the Sistine Chapel, God touches Adam's hand, and the world begins. There doesn't seem to be one God figure in this painting. No one to jump-start this particular world into being. Instead, it's the people who are hard at work creating this space for themselves. The only sign of heavenly intervention is the collection of books raining down, penned by the people who used to be on the ground working.

Cam leans close to me.

"V, you're crying."

"No, I'm not," I snap, wiping my eyes anyway.

Cam looks at me and smiles that same impish smile from when we were younger. He steadies my shoulder. "I think it's cool to cry at something like this."

I sniff. "Not crying," I mumble.

"I've been staring at it forever," a voice croaks from the floor.

Julia screams. Gabriel whoops and leaps into the air. I

jerk to my left, which unfortunately lands me directly into Cam's chest. His arms come down over me on instinct, tight and protective. The physical contact gives my heart a second jump scare.

Sunny pokes her head out from under a reading table.

"Hey," she says.

Gabriel clutches the collar of his hoodie. "Maybe start with that when you first see us next time? Why didn't you come out earlier?"

Sunny crawls from underneath the table and stands, brushing herself off. I tap Cam's forearm gently, and he lets go of me. We take an awkward, wide step apart.

"Because," Sunny says, "I was worried Ian over here had you hostage or something."

"Ian?" Cam scrunches his eyebrows in confusion. His eyes widen as understanding takes hold. "You showed them *National Treasure*?"

I hold up a hand in defense. "No, I merely *told* them about *National Treasure*."

"I watched it," Sunny says, and both Cam and I turn to her.

"You did?" I ask. "When?"

Sunny shrugs. "Earlier this week."

"Because of me?"

"Because you called me Patrick Gates on Monday," Sunny says crisply, folding her arms. "And I wanted to know if I was being insulted. For the record, I think Patrick had the right idea all along. It was stupid to squeeze lemons onto the freaking

Declaration of Independence and then scorch it with a blow-dryer. Treasure map or no treasure map, that old paper would have disintegrated in five seconds in real life."

Cam looks at me. "You said I was Ian?"

"Um . . . not exactly," I explain. "I *might* have said I was like Benjamin Gates. And, really, you're the one who stole our flyer and refused to give it back. So if anyone set up that parallel, it was you."

Cam sighs. "You've been treating me like an Ian way before I took your flyer. Basically from the beginning."

"No, I haven't!"

"Excuse me?" Sunny cuts in. "But what exactly is Mr. Ian-not-Ian doing here anyway?"

"He has the key," I say, "for the box. We need his help to open it."

Sunny pulls a face. She side-eyes Cam.

"You are such a liar."

"I'm not lying," Cam says. But he doesn't seem particularly surprised by Sunny's reaction. Almost like he knew it was coming.

I step across the raised floor and stand next to Sunny. "What's going on? Why do you think he's lying?"

"Because of this."

Sunny digs into her bag and pulls out the box from the Osher Foundation Gallery. I can't help gasping when I first see it. The wood is pale and damp, maybe aspen or pine—that's Mom's favorite choice for flooring. There's an elaborate inlaid design on the latched lid. No wonder Cam didn't care when I waved the pen box around. You can't really mistake anything for this.

As I look over it now, details and all, I see what Sunny's referring to.

"It doesn't have a lock," I say. I turn to Cam angrily. "You tricked me!"

But he still has that same calm expression. He points at the box.

"According to the book, there's a message in there. It's coded with a simple substitution cipher. I have the key to read it."

I shake my head. "There's not a clue or cipher in here. This is the treasure. We solved the clues and found the treasure. This is *it*."

"Okay." Cam shrugs dramatically. "I mean, you can go tell Gilbert Baker's estate that, I guess. The book said you need a key word, and I have the key word. So why don't you open it and find out what's inside?"

I look over at Sunny. She gives me a tiny nod.

I turn to Gabriel and Julia. "You think we should?"

Julia smiles. "Hey, it's not every day you get the chance to open something from a forty-year-old treasure hunt."

"I say we open it too," Gabriel says. He motions toward Cam. "Then we'll know if our Ian can pull his weight in this group or not."

"I'm not an Ian!" Cam yells.

Sunny shushes him and sits right there on the floor. I sit next to her, then Julia, Gabriel, and Cam sit on Sunny's other side. The five of us come together in the middle of the room, right under the epicenter of the gay heavenly clouds. We form our own little incantation circle. Sunny carefully hands me the box.

I hold it closed for a moment, as if the lid will pop open and ruin the surprise for me.

Julia tilts her head. "What is it, Ivy?"

"What if . . ." I pause. "What if whatever's inside here doesn't split four ways?"

"*Five.*" Cam coughs conspicuously.

Sunny holds up a finger. "Absolutely not," she says in warning. "If anything, you've only slowed us down thus far."

Cam scowls at her. He draws his knees toward himself and hugs them as he gazes across the circle.

"I say we split bragging rights," Gabriel offers. "All four of our names in the papers. Or a group name. Sunset Yearbook? Yearbook Crew?"

"I mean, it's better than Dyslexic Stoner," Julia says, chuckling.

"Who?" Cam asks.

"I'll explain later," I say, waving him off. I hold up the box. "Okay, we split bragging rights. But what about this?"

Gabriel shares a look with Sunny, then Julia, in turn.

"You should keep it," Sunny says to me. "You're the one who spotted Harvey's flyer. You told us about the hunt in the first place. You deserve it."

My ears feel warm. I close my eyes, too nervous to chance making eye contact with Cam. I can still picture the way he somersaulted into my room through the window two years ago. His hair wild and staticky, like he had just touched something electric. How he placed *Gay Treasures* in my lap like it was a precious gift.

I open my eyes, and the memory of the book transforms into the slim wooden box in my lap now. I trace my finger over one edge, thinking of everything that could be inside.

Sunny leans over my shoulder.

"But maybe at least open the damn treasure chest in front of us," she says.

"Right," I say, snapping out of it. "Of course. Right."

I unlatch the clasp and press my thumbs into either side of the lid. The hinges creak in protest, then seem to exhale as they give way.

The box swings open.

CHAPTER TWENTY-THREE

"Treasure," Cam had said.

"Treasure," I'd echoed dreamily.

"*Buried* treasure."

"Right." I laughed. "Buried treasure. Which is somehow different, because . . ."

"It's not different, exactly," Cam said. He shifted in the grass and turned over to look at me, cheek resting on his arm like a pillow. Cam had a way of making even the largest open meadow feel like a tiny rectangle around only the two of us. "But being buried is important."

"What do you mean?"

He shifted closer.

"I mean that we could be over it right now. We're not just going out and looking for treasure, V. Looking's not enough. We have to dig for it. We have to figure out exactly where BGR put it, and *then* the real work comes."

I squinted at him. "You're only saying that because I'm in

charge of research and you're in charge of digging. I have the real job. You're just muscle."

Cam smiled and flexed the arm under his cheek. My stomach did a small, strange flip.

"Okay," he said gently.

I had to tilt my head in to hear. "Okay, what?"

"Okay, we'll see," Cam said, still smiling. "You do your job, and I'll do mine. And then we'll figure out which one was more work."

I felt his breath, even and light, on my cheek. We weren't touching, but the grass was warmer next to him, like he was this tiny slice of the sun, and the rest of the meadow knew it.

Our eyes met, and I felt something in me catch.

Buried treasure, I thought.

I wondered how it would feel, once I had this thing solved and the two of us were staring at a plot in the ground. It could be the very plot underneath us. And then it would be Cam's turn to take over. But how far down would it be buried? How hard would it be to find the actual treasure in the ground?

"Fine," I said. "I guess we'll see."

"Treasure!" Gabriel gasps.

I pull a long golden chain out from the box. An oval pendant and old-fashioned key, both in gold, hang from the chain. I recognize the key as a skeleton key, with its longer, smooth shank and a single tooth at the end. Mom brings home skeleton keys a lot when she takes on a new building renovation project. They're called skeletons because of how they're made. The middle teeth along the key are all shaved down, leaving only the "bone" behind. The last tooth at the end turns it into a master key, able to open a series of doors rather than just one.

The key in front of me now is a lot smaller than a real skeleton key, though. It looks more like the key to a diary than to a real door.

The pendant next to it is only slightly larger. There are no stones embedded in it or colors painted over the top—just a crude engraving of a stick figure posing with one arm on its hip and the other pointing out to the side.

I pass the necklace over to Julia and Sunny, who stare at it appraisingly, each in turn.

Sunny blinks. "You think . . . you think that's really it?" she asks me finally.

"What's really it?" I ask.

"That this is the treasure," Sunny says. I detect a trace of disappointment in her voice.

She holds up the necklace so the pendant and key dangle

in front of me. No rainbow-colored diamonds. No elaborate portrait of Harvey Milk. The edges of the pendant are already fading into a pale green patina. I sigh as I think of the Marsha P. Johnson vase and the Judy Garland bracelet. If this really is our treasure, it looks a lot more . . . well, boring, than I hoped it would.

"I'm not sure," I answer.

Cam points at the box. "There's more in there," he says, and I can tell he's restraining himself from leaping up and picking through the contents himself.

I reach back into the box and pull out a scroll tied with a small piece of twine. Carefully, I slip the twine off. The brittle paper bends and crackles as I unroll it.

"Ooh," Gabriel says, leaning over. "What's that?"

Cam has silently made his way across the circle, where he now presses against my arm to see the page in front of us.

I'm holding the top and bottom taut, like I'm about to read out the names of everyone invited to Prince Charming's royal ball. But there are no names in front of me. There are no words at all.

Instead, it's absolutely crowded over with various pictures. They're all drawn in ballpoint pen and convey the same feeling as the illustrations in the *Gay Treasures* book. Every line seems eager to pull together an image as fast as possible.

It would be easy to write off the picture as a collection of doodles on a page. A clock here. A woman there. An octopus in one corner. It's the same trick as with the book, I realize—it looks unimportant if you're not looking closely. But the pictures are so specifically layered, each piece fitting so cohesively together, that right away I know the image has been planned out.

I can feel Cam's breath on my skin. He points to one side of the page, at a drawing of two boys wearing triangular hats. The hats look stiff and strange, like a paper sailboat perched on each one's head.

"Golden Gate Bridge," Cam murmurs. He slopes his finger without touching the paper, tracing the outline of the overlapping hats.

As soon as he points out the shape, it becomes obvious. The paper hats form the exact shape, the exact curves, of the Golden Gate Bridge.

I turn to Cam, and his face is still so close to mine that our noses brush as he looks back at me. For some reason, the touch isn't enough to push us away. We lock in on each other.

"It's a map," Cam says.

I don't know if he whispers it, or mouths it, or even sends the words over to me through telepathy, but I hear them. I hear them because they're the same words in my head.

We're looking at a map of San Francisco.

This doesn't make any sense, though. We're supposed to be at the end of BGR's hunt. I remember reading all about the treasure found in New York. According to the articles online, the person who found the New York treasure went through four main steps:

They figured out that the first clue in the New York chapter in *Gay Treasures*—"the minded middle of Stonewall"—

referred to the middle name of Marsha P. Johnson, one of the most crucial figures in the Stonewall riots.

Marsha's middle initial, *P*, famously stands for the phrase "Pay it no mind." This phrase ended up being the key for a Playfair cipher in the chapter.

The decoded message to the Playfair cipher read:

NO FISH. NO PLAY. ONLY FOUND FAMIL-A.

The finder ended up digging in front of the first *A* at the Hamilton Fish Play Center sign in Manhattan, where Marsha P. Johnson founded and ran STAR House, a home for displaced young queer people. That's where they dug up the vase with Marsha's portrait.

I'm running through the steps of our own hunt in my head:

1. Figure out the gay icon—the giant between streets, Harvey Milk.
2. Locate the key to a cipher—Harvey's "btwn streets" birthday party flyer.
3. Solve the decoded message—
4. "TREASURE ISLAND BUILDER READS ARCHITECTURE 723."
5. Find the treasure.

So what the heck are we now doing with a random necklace and a treasure map?

"There's something else in the box," Gabriel says. "I think it's a clue."

"Another clue?" Sunny groans. "I don't even care if I sound like Patrick Gates anymore. This is ridiculous."

I let Cam hold on to the map as I pull out a final piece of paper, which isn't rolled and tied neatly but folded into quarters and pressed into the bottom of the box.

The paper is just as brittle as the drawing. I pry it open and smooth it out as best I can into the center of our circle.

"Are you kidding me?" Sunny cries as she sees what's on it.

The page is filled with random, nonsensical words. I study it a moment, then sit back on my haunches and turn to Cam. "What's the key?"

He looks up from the map. "Huh?"

I gesture to the note. "It's a substitution cipher, just like you said it would be. So, what's the key?"

Cam bites one corner of his lower lip. I see him chewing over his next thought, trying to disguise his worry. It's like he's in the tree behind Portals of the Past again, and I'm standing on the ground, staring up at him. If he gives this away, we don't need him anymore. We can go back to racing him to the end. He could lose everything.

"You promised," I remind him.

He blinks out of the trance and clears his throat.

"Harvey," he says quietly. " 'Harvey' is the key."

Julia pulls out her notebook. "How do you do a substitution cipher?" she asks me.

"Here."

I hold out my hand for the pen and turn to a fresh page in her notebook, then write out the alphabet over the top row.

Underneath, I write the word "HARVEY," followed by the rest of the alphabet—minus all the letters in the key word.

```
A B C D E F G H I J K L M N O P Q R S T U V W X Y Z
H A R V E Y B C D F G I J K L M N O P Q S T U W X Z
```

"Now you write the message again," I tell Julia. "But you replace every *A* with an *H*, every *B* with an *A*, every *C* with an *R* . . ."

"I get it," Julia says, pulling the notebook back. She flips back and forth between the pages, decoding the message letter by letter until we're left with a poem:

Congratulations! You have found
The San Francisco Bonus Round
For of my treasures, far and wide
My home imbues the deepest pride
No added ciphers, codes to break
Ground yourself for what's at stake
Read the map, find the point
Grab the shovel to anoint
If you seek the lock and key
You will have to dig down deep

CHAPTER TWENTY-FOUR

Julia's voice carries an eerie echo as she finishes reading the poem aloud. The five of us sit in silence, quiet and contemplative. Finally, after a minute or two, Gabriel speaks up.

"So . . . this definitely isn't the treasure, then?"

I look over at the necklace hanging limply in Sunny's hands and sigh.

"No," I say. "I guess it's not."

Sunny shakes her head and mutters something under her breath.

"What do we do?" Julia asks.

Cam clears his throat awkwardly. "Well, I think we should—"

"No." Sunny whips her head toward him. "*You* are not a part of group decisions right now. In fact . . ." She turns to the rest of us. "I think Cam should be out."

Cam's jaw falls open. "What?"

"We only let you open the box with us because of the key," Sunny says. "Now you're out again."

Gabriel sucks in air through an awkward, full-tooth grimace.

"Um." Julia leans into Sunny. "Maybe now's not the time to throw anyone out."

"But he's not a part of this!" Sunny stands in the middle of the circle. "Ivy, back me up here."

"I . . . I think . . . we should . . ."

I can't put the words together. *Things are complicated*, I want to explain. I feel like I'm caught between two different treasure hunts. If we were in any other *Gay Treasures* city, we would have found the treasure by now. And all thanks to the yearbook crew. Sunny was the one who first found that photo for the yearbook dedication page. Julia snapped a picture of Harvey's birthday party flyer before Cam stole it. Gabriel made every fuzzy internet document readable so we could decipher it. We all went through the archives, followed the changes in the city, found a single spot from some vague words and a number. When I look back at how far we've come, I see Sunny's point—Cam's not a part of it.

I think of the photo on my phone background.

It's strange and infuriating . . . but I can't get away from seeing Cam, from knowing that even if he's right outside the frame, he's still a part of the bigger picture. He's the unspoken subtext. The origin story buried underneath it all.

"Maybe we need a break," Julia says quietly. "All of us," she adds.

Sunny looks at her. "What do you mean?"

Julia sighs and scans the decrypted poem in her notebook.

"This is . . . a lot. And we're already running on fumes

from the earlier clues. Let's just take photos of everything and lock it up until Monday. We can meet after school and discuss what to do next. If anyone has an idea, great. If not, we'll get started together. Or . . . mostly together, if it's what the group decides." She can't quite make eye contact with Cam as she says this last part. "But at least until Monday afternoon, we're all in."

Cam swallows and nods solemnly.

"Who's keeping the box?" he asks.

"Obviously not you," Sunny says. "We already decided it's Ivy's. I don't think that's changed."

Sunny sets the necklace down into the box and closes the lid. My cheeks are warm as she passes the box over to me.

"Wait," Gabriel says. He turns his camera on. "I need to take photos of that."

"Oh. Right."

We lay everything out on the floor between us. The coded poem. The scroll of pictures. The pendant necklace and tiny skeleton key. Gabriel twists the zoom lens, resetting it each time.

Click. Click. Click.

I fold the note and slip it carefully back inside the box, then lay the scroll and necklace on top—exactly as we found it. We filter back down the library stairs and wait at the Civic Center Station. Sunny pointedly avoids eye contact with Cam, even though we've all agreed to Julia's suggestion. It's strange, because just one week ago, I would have thought that no one could possibly despise Cam as openly as I do. To not be his biggest enemy in this moment feels, well—unexpected, to say the least.

We sit side by side by side on the train, with Gabriel, Julia, and me cushioning the space between Sunny and Cam. My knee bumps lightly into Cam's every time the driver makes a hard turn. But then we dip inside the Sunset Tunnel, and in the darkness I notice that Cam keeps his knee pressed into mine until we emerge on the eastern edge of Golden Gate Park.

Sunny, Gabriel, and Julia get off the train at their usual stops. Sunny narrows her eyes at Cam before she heads down the steps.

He holds up his palms in surrender. "I'm not even doing anything!"

As Julia steps off, she nudges my shoe. "You coming?" she asks.

I shake my head. Cam looks at me but doesn't say anything. Julia just shrugs and hops down onto the pavement. I take a deep breath as the door closes behind her.

The train rolls down the next three streets, then stops again. Cam stands up.

"Here?" he asks. We're now two stops past my place and one stop early for his place. But I stand up after him. He knows exactly what I'm thinking.

"Yeah," I say. "Here."

We walk out into the usual gust of wind. Mount Sutro is smocked in a gown of clouds. Without a word, Cam turns and strolls onto Sixteenth Avenue. I lean into the wind and follow him up the next block to the first set of mosaic steps and then a few blocks farther to another set that leads to Grandview Park.

This was a spot where we liked to sit and think, especially when we were stuck during the hunt two summers ago. Cam's a lot faster on stairs than I am—he's always been faster. But he waits patiently every few steps, making sure I'm still close behind him, before heading forward. We twist down the last block of houses and climb up the final rickety wooden stairs to the top of the park.

Technically, this isn't really a park. There are no fields or play structures. It's more of a national park—preserved land. Grandview is one of the last few untouched sand dunes in the Bay Area. Before San Francisco was here, the whole area was made up entirely of sand dunes. Now they're all covered with houses and roads.

Cam sits at the viewing bench perched on the very top of the dune. He motions for me to join him. We look across the wide rectangle of Golden Gate Park, over Strawberry Hill, to the Golden Gate Bridge at the far end of the city. Cam extends his arm, finger pointing out to the horizon. He draws two invisible slopes in the sky.

"Thinking of the map?" I ask.

Cam sighs. "I was hoping the hats in the picture would line up with our view of the bridge at this angle. They don't, though."

"Ah."

Cam's hand drops back into his lap.

"You really want me out of the group?" he asks quietly.

"No," I say, surprising myself. We look across the bench at each other. Cam holds the gaze until I give up first and look away. "I'm not sure I want you in this group either, though. Looking for treasure with you is so much more . . ."

"Different," Cam supplies, "than looking with them."

I nod.

"V, I mean this in the nicest way possible—"

"Of course you do," I mutter.

"—but maybe things *need* to be different now," he goes on, "to finish this. You and Sunny and Julia and Gabriel have done great. But I don't think the rest of this puzzle is going to be solved on a computer screen."

I feel some of Sunny's rage seeping into me. "What is that supposed to mean?"

"It means we need to go back to the way we were before."

My eyebrows shoot up. "What?"

"With exploring the city," Cam says quickly. "We didn't have that map before, when you and I went out looking. But now we do. And I don't think the majority of markers on it are going to be as easy to spot as the freaking Golden Gate Bridge. I think we have to get outside—boots-on-the-ground style—and start looking around."

All the memories of us outside before, of circling trees, knocking on bricks, lying in the grass under the afternoon sun, curl around me like a warm towel straight out of the dryer. But there's something dangerous mixed in too. I've worked so hard to shape that summer of my life into a bruise that doesn't ache at the touch. It's a good memory because it's a distant memory, a fuzzy one, ambiguous and open-ended. I can't just *go back* to working with Cam the way I did before. The only way, for us, has to be forward.

"What about the agreement?" I ask, drawing myself up straighter.

"What agreement?"

"No treasure hunting until Monday," I say. "We're taking a break."

Cam holds up his index finger. "As a *group*," he says. "Julia said that if anyone had any ideas, we could share them on Monday after school. Well, maybe by then you and I will have an idea. Maybe we'll have an exact place to look. Maybe . . ."

"Don't say it," I warn him.

"Maybe we'll even have a treasure."

I rise off the bench, suddenly hot and itchy. "That would be cheating."

Cam laughs. "Cheating? On who?"

"Not on a person," I say, feeling hotter by the second. "On the hunt, I mean. We all agreed on it."

"Okay. Okay." Cam stands and ushers me back down onto the bench next to him. His arm stays wrapped around my shoulder, and I'm extremely aware of the fact that I'm sitting much closer to him this time. *But not so close that it would mean anything*, I remind myself.

I've fallen into that trap before.

"No treasure," Cam says, assuring me. "But some more clues. We could have the whole map figured out for the group. Maybe Sunny would even start to like me."

I roll my eyes. "Why do you care what Sunny thinks?"

"I don't care what *she* thinks," Cam says. He falters for a moment. "You're— The four of you are all— It would be nice to not have anyone wanting to bite my head off."

He pulls his arm back and shifts away from me. "Well? Is it a deal?"

"Fine," I say. I hold out a hand. "But only if you bring me the flyer *and* the book."

Cam furrows his brow. "Why the book?"

"It had the key to the substitution cipher, right? Maybe it will have some other clue we need too."

My hand hovers between us. Cam stares down at it.

"Unless you don't want to," I add. I start to pull my hand back. But he catches it, his fingers clasping tight over mine.

"We'll start tomorrow," he says. "Union Square. Nine a.m. You bring the box. I'll bring the book and flyer."

"No shovels," I warn him.

Cam flashes me his wide, boyish grin. "No shovels," he says.

He offers my hand an extra squeeze before letting go. My heart throbs for a moment, tight and unsure. Being alone with Cam like this, looking for the treasure again, feels risky. There's too much history between us. Our past is practically a minefield.

It's only a bruise, I tell myself. *A mostly healed bruise.*

But as I look at Cam, I can't escape the feeling that, even without shovels, we're about to dig into something neither of us signed up for.

CHAPTER TWENTY-FIVE

I creep onto the Judah line the next morning like a cartoon detective, back pressed to the brick town house on the corner. I can't imagine why any of the other yearbook crew members would be here on a Sunday morning, but still . . . just the thought of being seen alone with Cam makes me nervous.

Once I'm safely on the train, I look around, expecting to see him in one of the seats. But the entire section is empty save for an older woman surrounded by three crates of recycled plastic bottles. I glance at my phone and sigh. The next train doesn't come for another fifteen minutes. I'll have to wait around Union Square for him.

Except, as the train pulls to the stop at Union, I see that *Cam* is already waiting for *me*.

"Good morning," Cam says cheerily.

"You're too early."

"Wowza. Didn't realize that was a crime."

I squint at him. "How long have you been here?"

Cam hitches his thumb over his shoulder. "Not long. I just did a little exploring around the neighborhood."

My eyes widen. "Excuse me—'a little exploring'? Why not explore the entire city without me? What the heck am I doing here, Cam?"

"Relax, Goldilocks," he says, even though he's the one with springy blond hair and I probably look like Wednesday Addams in comparison. "I'm not too early. You're not late. Everything is just right. Now let's go!"

I huff and sigh, then follow Cam up the next few blocks toward Chinatown. We each reveal the book, flyer, and box in turn as we walk, but agree to keep them all sealed away in my backpack unless we find something really, really good. In the meantime, we work off the photos Gabriel sent us digitally. Cam zooms in on the bottom left section of the scroll.

"Look at her," he says, pointing at the drawing of a woman in a long, boxy floral dress with her arms outstretched. "I saw a statue up here that reminds me of her."

He leads us into St. Mary's Square. We walk through basketball courts and past rows of flagpoles until we're standing right across from a tall metal sculpture.

"Dr. Sun Yat-Sen," I read from a plaque in front.

Cam and I take a long step back to study the sculpture next to the drawing.

"Well . . ." I say. "The robe is similar. Ish. But this is of a man, not a woman."

"The point of the picture is to disguise the landmark, V. He can't just draw the same statue exactly."

"Right, but there has to be a clear connection somewhere," I argue. "The robe isn't as boxy as the dress. The hands in this sculpture are folded rather than pointing. It's just not the same."

Cam looks back and forth between his screen and the figure of Dr. Sun Yat-Sen in front of us.

"It's not the same," he says finally. "Dang. I was sort of hoping we could solve this part and skip the rest."

I look at him, surprised. "How could we have skipped the rest?"

He points at a small oval pendant hanging around the woman's neck in the picture, with the tiniest charm key dangling next to it.

"It's the necklace from the box," Cam says.

I blink at the detail. He's totally right—this is our necklace. Gilbert Baker wouldn't put it on this particular figure unless she was important to the ultimate solution. Crucial, even. I stare at the woman, trying to see something in the pattern of her dress, which is crawling with flowers, vines, and random fruit buried in the center. I look at the woman's arms, at her face . . . but there's no recognition there. I haven't seen a single statue around the city that looks like this.

We head up Kearny Street and stop for dumplings in the middle of Chinatown. I'm always so fascinated by the combination of shops here—the mix of bakeries and restaurants that look like they could have been around forever, alongside strange, shiny art galleries with human-sized Transformers and giant knock-off balloon dog sculptures. The new crowds in on the old, less a harmony of different stores mixing and more like a wrestling match of stores vying for the heart of the neighborhood. One type speaks to the past, the other to a cold, garish future.

We finish the dumplings and toss the empty bag into a trash can outside of Portsmouth Square.

"Oh, here's something," Cam says, pulling his phone back out of his pocket.

He brings us over to a narrow boulder with a small three-dimensional house chiseled inside. We look over the inscription below the house.

"The first public school in America. That's cool." He begins searching around the drawing on his phone, scrolling and zooming into different parts.

"I don't think it's in here," I say, looking at the image on my own phone screen.

Cam sighs. He checks over his shoulder, then does a double take. "Hey!"

He jogs across the square to another monument, this one a large, smooth rock like a tombstone. A brass ship sits on top of the stone, with gold lettering carved into the side. The first three words glint in the sunlight.

Robert Louis Stevenson.

"This is interesting," Cam says, searching through the image on his phone again.

I pull up next to him. "I think that's the problem," I say. "Everything's sort of interesting, isn't it?"

"What do you mean?" Cam asks. He motions to the top of the stone. "Robert Louis Stevenson! As in—"

"As in *Treasure Island*," I say. "I know. But imagine how many Robert Louis Stevenson monuments there are. Imagine how many Harvey Milk monuments there are! There are too many possible connections out there. We can't just turn everything into a clue."

"Okay . . ." Cam tucks his phone back into his pocket and faces me, his arms crossed tightly over his chest. "So what do you suggest we do?"

"I don't know," I say, stepping away from the stone. "Maybe we don't try to force things so much. Just look around and see if anything sticks out."

Cam gives me an almost imperceptible eye roll. "Fine."

We agree to head up to Coit Tower to get a bird's-eye look around the bay.

"Maybe we'll match up the angle of the Golden Gate Bridge from there," I say helpfully.

"Umph," Cam grunts as we settle onto the bus at Kearny and Jackson.

I stare out the window for a while, watching the storefronts and buildings blur outside, wondering what they looked like fifty years ago, when Gilbert Baker was deciding where to hide his treasures.

"That necklace thing is so weird," I say. "Good catch on seeing it in the picture."

Cam shifts next to me. He rests his chin on his arm, so we're both looking out the window.

"How is it weird?"

"Well, what's the deal with the necklace, you know? Is it a clue, or is it part of the treasure?"

Cam shrugs. "Maybe it's both. I'll bet the necklace itself is pretty valuable."

"Yeah, but it can't be the actual treasure," I argue.

"Why not?"

"Well, it's so . . ."

"What?" Cam asks. "Dull?"

I think back to when I first saw the necklace in the wooden box. How it looked like any necklace sitting in an antique store window. Just gold and nothing else.

"It's too straight-coded," I say, laughing a little.

Cam doesn't laugh with me.

"How does a necklace read as straight to you?"

I can feel the budding anger in his tone. I swallow. "I more meant . . . it doesn't have any rainbow stones, like the Judy Garland treasure did. Even the Marsha P. Johnson treasure was super colorful."

"So you meant to say 'colorful,' then."

"Yeah, I guess so."

Cam looks at me pointedly. "Then just say 'colorful,' Ivy. You don't have to code an object as gay or straight. Gay people all look different from one another. Some of us might be more colorful, and some of us are . . . I don't know. We're just trying to be ourselves, you know?"

I stare down at my lap and knit my fingers together. "You're right. I'm sorry."

"It's fine," Cam says. He sighs and stares out the window.

The bus stops. We get off near Coit Tower and begin strolling around the neighborhood. As we turn onto Sansome Street, Cam peers up ahead, using his palm as a visor.

"Hey. What's that?"

He's looking at a mosaic square at the intersection on Green-wich. We walk up to it until the tiny white stones come together, forming a single word, along with an arrow: "Steps."

"Mysterious." Cam looks at me. "Have you ever been up this way?"

I shake my head. "Nope."

We turn into a quiet cul-de-sac and weave between several large trees to find an open staircase that seems to ascend into the branches.

"This is cool," I say.

We walk up together, sardined side by side instead of sin-gle file. We both want to see what's in front of us too much to cede the front spot to the other. The stairs wind up and up. Yellow flowers dangle from the foliage overhead like strings of heavy lights. Flower beds with blooms in every color spring up around us. A life-sized tiger made with mosaic pieces watches from a high ledge.

"This is magical," Cam says.

The word instantly reminds me of Julia standing at the edge of the mirrored pond inside Golden Gate Park.

"Yeah," I say. "It is."

We walk through the garden, past more mosaic sculptures. The path leads us to a labyrinth-like wall, which only at the last moment reveals a hidden archway to the left. Cam turns for the arch, but I pause in front of a small copper fountain. It's mounted to the false wall and framed in the same style of mosaic tiles. The shape of the fountain is strange. Familiar. And those four blue stars and white moon hovering over the tile frame . . .

"What is it?" Cam asks.

I point at the fountain.

"Remind you of anything?" I ask.

Cam peers at the fountain for a moment, until his eyes go wide. He looks over at me and I nod. I pull my bag around to the front, unzipping the main pocket and taking out the wooden box. We pull out the scroll and open it between us.

We don't even have to confirm with each other—our focus goes immediately to the drawing of a grandfather clock in the top center, with four stars and a full moon arched over the clockface.

"It's the clock," Cam says. "You found another piece!"

He tilts his head into mine, as if we were clinking cheers to the thought.

The map is coming together.

CHAPTER TWENTY-SIX

We emerge through the brick archway and out of the secret garden.

"Come on," Cam says, turning for downtown.

"Wait." I motion to the next flight of stairs. "We're not going all the way to Coit Tower?"

"We don't need to. The fountain marks a point on the map—just like the Golden Gate Bridge. If we're going to figure out the rest of it, we have to move to a different part of town."

The bus back down to Market Street passes us by twice, but neither Cam nor I suggest hopping on. Walking downhill feels almost too easy, too floaty and weightless, to go ruining it by catching a ride.

Something delicious explodes inside me—the first sip of sparkling cider, when it's all crisp and fizz and hasn't yet turned into a stomachache. I sneak a look at Cam and am equal parts embarrassed and thrilled to see he's already looking at me.

"What?" he asks.

"What *what*?"

"What are you smiling about?"

I make a vague circle with my hands. "Um . . . everything? Just now? This is real."

"It was always real," Cam says.

The ground gives way a little. I feel a hole inside me open, a little window to Cam next to me on the bed, smiling at the corners of his eyes and looking so deeply into mine that my bones turn soft. This is the way Cam speaks. He pulls on sincerity like a cloak, using some stupid, vague term and acting like it means everything I want it to mean. Only, when I try it back, when I reach out to him, he runs away so fast that I blink and he's a dot in the distance.

Nothing was real, I want to say. *You wouldn't have left me if it were real.*

My eyes land on a building ahead to focus on. "I mean, the hunt was always real," I say. "But solving it didn't feel so real then. Not like it does now."

"That's true." Cam nods. "It does feel different now."

We walk the next block in silence.

"I think it's cool we found the fountain especially," I say after a while.

Cam laughs. "You're only saying that because *I* found the bridge and *you* found the fountain."

"That's not true! The bridge is cool too. I just think the fountain's neat because it's hidden. We had to walk right up to it to recognize it. Like"—I open Gabriel's photo of the scroll on my phone and zoom into a corner—"at some point, we might come across a statue of a bear, a snake, and an octopus in a wrestling match. But until then? It's a totally random part of the drawing."

Cam stops walking. "What did you just say?"

"I'm saying, the pictures look really random unless—"

"No! About the octopus!"

I take a step back. "Okay, why are you acting like I've committed some serious crime in mentioning the octopus?"

"I didn't know it was an octopus!" Cam cries out. He looks over my shoulder at the drawing on my phone screen. "I thought it was a bear fighting a pack of snakes!"

Two older businessmen on the opposite side of the street throw us apprehensive glares. I give them a very unconvincing smile in return and close the space between me and Cam.

"I think you're freaking people out," I murmur.

He looks from the phone to me, a crazed glint in his eyes. "I know this octopus!" he says.

Before I can react, he pulls one of my hands into his and begins running down the sidewalk.

We run for such a long time that I begin to think that, actually, probably only elite runners could run this far, and maybe I should have been on the cross-country team, maybe even some Olympic-level team. Then we get to a crosswalk intersection and I realize we've only run a single block, and I would never in this lifetime have made the cross-country team. But, really, screw the cross-country team anyway, because they're all just show-offs.

Then the walk sign turns green and we repeat the whole thing again.

Finally, Cam pulls me off the sidewalk.

"Here!" he yells.

He brings us over to a high stone column standing in the middle of a triangular plaza. At the top of the column is a small statue of an angel, arms outstretched as she holds a book overhead. At the bottom of the column is a large statue of a boy waving a pickaxe in one hand and an American flag in the other. I read the inscription below the boy.

"THE UNITY OF OUR EMPIRE HANGS ON THE

DECISION OF THIS DAY" —W. H. SEWARD

ON THE ADMISSION OF CALIFORNIA, U.S. SENATE, 1850

"Okay . . ." I say slowly. "What does it mean?"

"Who cares?" Cam answers. He's already circling to the other side of the column. I roll my eyes.

"Of course you wouldn't care—"

"Octopus!" Cam screams. "Octopus octopus octopus!"

Nearly the entire faction of people around us twist over their shoulders to give Cam worried stares.

"Shut up!" I hiss as I step around the column next to him. "You sound like a little kid at an aquarium touch pool."

Cam blinks at me. "They don't let people touch the octopi."

He steps to one side and motions with his entire body, arms fully out, toward our second fountain of the day. A bear head juts from the smooth stone face, water trickling from its open mouth. A snake entwines over the top of the bear's head like a victory crown. Just below the basin of the fountain, an octopus made of copper curls into a tangled little ball where the column meets the sidewalk.

"Well?" Cam asks.

"Well, I'd say the bear and the snake absolutely kicked the octopus's ass in that wrestling match."

Cam huffs. It's surprisingly delightful to see him so flustered. He turns again to the fountain, studying the little mangled octopus on the ground. Then he looks left, the way we came.

"Where's Golden Gate Bridge?"

I do a slow spin. "That way," I say, pointing over my shoulder.

Cam follows my finger. He frowns.

"It doesn't make any sense," he mutters. He holds up his palm. "Can I see the scroll again?"

I sit on one of the plaza benches and take the box out from my bag, then pass the scroll over. He unrolls it carefully, then shifts it back and forth, like he's turning a steering wheel.

"Shoot," Cam says after a while. "I guess it's not a map, after all."

I lean into him. "What do you mean?"

"Look where the bridge is. And then here's the mosaic fountain near Coit Tower. If I shift the drawing to make them line up . . ."

"It's impossible," I say, finishing the thought. I point to the bear, snake, and octopus on the page. "That would be sitting out in the middle of the water." I look up at Cam. "Hey! You think there might be another column or fountain like this out on Treasure Island?"

Cam shakes his head. "No chance." He sighs and taps the woman in the long dress again, the one wearing the necklace with the key. "We have to find her," he says.

I nod. "Yeah, we do."

We catch the Judah train on Market Street and begin to head home. But right before we reach Sunset Tunnel, Cam tugs the stop line and stands up.

"Let's hang out at Duboce Park," he says. "For old times' sake."

My stomach wrings itself like a washrag. "I'm not sure."

"Please?" Cam presses his palms flat together, then extends one arm out toward me. "What if there's a hidden statue of a lady we don't know about?"

"In a dog park?"

"Yeah! The patron saint of dogs or something."

The closing-doors bell rings out. Before I can overthink it, I've left my seat alongside Cam and leapt off the train. I watch it drift away into Sunset Tunnel.

Cam lets go of my hand. Our knuckles sweep across each other. The lightness of the touch nearly makes me jump. I take a deep breath and look over at the park. Dogs are running, free and happy, all over the place while their owners stand in clusters, chatting and holding dangling leashes in their arms.

"I don't see a statue," I say.

Cam shrugs and offers a meek smile. "Let's look around anyway."

We start down the winding path that cuts across the grass.

"You know," Cam says. "You're not the only one who did research that summer."

"Is that right?" I ask.

Cam nods. "The reason I kept bringing us back here to look is because of Harvey, actually."

I stop walking. "What?"

"Yeah. He took a famous photo right . . . about . . . here." Cam hops off the path and draws a circle in the grass with his shoe. "It was a publicity stunt to help get public parks cleaned up in 1978. Harvey invited a reporter to Duboce Park, and then, during the photo shoot, he stepped in dog poop 'by accident.' But, really, he wanted to make a point about how gross the parks were getting. It helped pass his bill."

I pin my hands over my hips. "Are you saying you thought the treasure would be buried under a pile of dog poop?"

"Historically significant dog poop!" Cam says.

He pauses and looks at me, and after a full second of silence, the two of us completely break down in laughter. We're each doubled over, tears streaming. Several of the dogs hear us and bound over, thinking we're playing some sort of game. One jumps onto my side, and I tumble forward into Cam. He catches me around the middle and we land on the grass, still laughing and breathing heavily. Another dog comes over and licks Cam's cheek.

The owners whistle and wave their dogs away, leaving Cam and me tangled in the grass. For a moment, I don't want to move. My limbs are sleepy and heavy against Cam's body. The warmth of his chest feels like gravity pulling me closer. We got into this configuration purely by accident, but now any move either of us makes feels like a decision.

I have no idea what Cam's thinking next to me. I can feel his heartbeat through his shirt, wild and thrumming, then slowly coming back down to a steady *thump, thump, thump.* We both gaze up at the sky.

"I didn't know you did your own research," I say.

"I like doing research," Cam answers.

The clouds slice through the sky like ships. The combination of wind from the ocean and the cross breeze from the bay moves them so quickly that it's like watching a time-lapse video. I keep my thoughts up in the clouds, far away from my body, trying to figure out this whole situation.

We could keep wandering through the city like this, checking behind trees and buildings again, the way we did that summer. Or, now that we have the images in front of us, we could speed things up. I know Cam and this hunt—he's like me. He doesn't want to wade through it. He wants to get right to the end.

"The San Francisco History Center opens on Tuesday at noon," I say aloud. I remember Gabriel telling us the hours, then explaining how we couldn't possibly cut school to go before Saturday. I remember how frustrated and lonely I felt right then, like no one cared about the hunt the way I did. "It's filled with old photos of landmarks and monuments around the city. If you like that kind of research."

Cam twists toward me without untangling us.

"I like that kind of research," he says steadily.

And to my credit—even though his voice is low and sounds like velvet, and he's giving me that same deep look and stretching those words into things I'm certain he doesn't really mean—I simply nod and sit up in the grass.

"Okay, then," I say. "Let's make our case to the group tomorrow. We could find the exact answer to this whole thing by Tuesday night. We could actually do this."

Cam smiles and sits up with me. "Let's actually do this."

CHAPTER TWENTY-SEVEN

Mom and I juggle the coffeepot in the kitchen the next morning, passing it nimbly back and forth without making eye contact.

"Have a day," she says as she leaves.

It would be a funny mistake if she meant to say "Have a *good* day," but with Mom, I never can tell what she really means, so I say nothing.

At school, Cam catches me after lunch, clasping me gently around the wrist as I walk past him in the hall. I stop at the touch and backtrack until I'm right in front of him.

"Yes?" I ask.

"What are we saying at the meeting?"

"We tell them about what we found," I say evenly. "The fountain. The octopus. They'll have to agree to come back to the history center tomorrow to figure out the rest."

"And if they don't?"

I bite my lip. I know what Cam's really asking: *If they don't want to skip school, do the two of us go anyway?*

I don't like the idea of leaving school on our own. I don't want the yearbook team to feel like Cam's barging in and ripping the treasure hunt away from them. Still . . . I don't know if I can wait a whole additional week before going back. Everything is at our fingertips right now.

"They *will*," I say firmly. "We'll all go tomorrow."

Cam gives me a little salute. "Whatever you say, Captain."

I make a face. He winks and walks off in the opposite direction.

—⚿—

I slink into the Bat Cave as soon as class gets out. Sunny rises from her chair the moment my foot touches the last step.

"You're late."

I check my phone. "It's 4:01."

"Exactly," Sunny says. Her voice sounds strained and flustered. "We thought maybe the British interloper kidnapped you for some X-ray glasses or something."

"Who, me?" Cam bounds down the stairs behind me. "Wow, Sunny—you're getting almost *too* good with your *National Treasure* references. Trying to impress someone?"

Sunny rolls her eyes. "Shut up. I guess we're all here, then."

I take my usual place between Gabriel and Julia. Cam starts to pull another chair toward the group, but Sunny holds up a hand and stops him.

"Over there," she says.

For the first time, I notice a chair sitting right in front of the projector screen.

I look at Sunny. "What's going on?" I shift and see the heading on Julia's notebook next to me.

Trial of Cam.

"What?" I say, standing. "Why are we holding a trial?"

"Relax," Gabriel says. "It's not like we're charging Cam with a crime or anything."

"Even though he *stole* our flyer," Julia grumbles.

I look down at her, surprised. I didn't realize that Julia of all people could sound so angry.

"We're just trying to decide if we want to let Cam into the group," Sunny says. Her mouth is pinched in a way that tells me what her personal feelings on the question already are. And with Julia pissed off too . . . we're barely two minutes into the meeting, and already the history center plan seems like an uphill battle.

Cam goes and sits in the front chair without any protest. He slaps his hands over his knees and waits expectantly.

"Cam," Gabriel says. He turns on the projector so the light shines directly into Cam's face. "Why do you want to join Treasure Island Hoes?"

Cam stifles a laugh. "Is that . . . is that the official name of this group now?"

Gabriel shrugs. "Either that or Dorothy and Friends. I haven't decided yet."

"I see." Cam interlocks his fingers. "Well—hoes or friends, either way—to the best of my knowledge, this is a group interested in treasure hunting. Which is a hobby I happen to enjoy. And, on the plus side, I look very, very sexy holding a shovel. Ivy can attest to this."

I bury my face in my palm.

"He's not taking this seriously." Julia shakes her head. She points the end of her pen at Cam. "You're not even taking this seriously."

Cam raises his arms. "I'm sitting in a chair with a freaking spotlight in my face! I would say I'm taking this plenty seriously. I do bring a lot to the table, and if we could just get over this damn trial, Ivy and I can present our actual updates on the treasure hunt!"

Sunny freezes. Slowly, she turns to me. "What updates?"

I look up. "Oh. Um—" My voice retreats to the bottom of my throat. I pull out my laptop and plug it into the projector. Gilbert Baker's mysterious drawing fills up the back wall, the woman's boxy floral dress covering Cam's face. He gets up from his trial chair and stands to one side of the screen.

"We found the clock, bear, snake, and octopus," Cam says for me. He points at the clock on the screen. "That's a fountain hidden near Coit Tower. And the bear, snake, and octopus are on a monument downtown near Union Square. Ivy found the fountain yesterday. I remembered seeing the monument."

I notice he doesn't tell the others we found and remembered both of those things while together.

Gabriel nods. "Okay. This is good. So it is a map, then."

"It's not," I say. "The three landmarks don't make any sense spatially. They're not connected."

"So let's figure out all the others," Sunny says. "Once we know what everything means, I'll bet the picture will get clearer.

I can research the woman with the dress. Julia, you can get the eagle and shield. Gabriel, can you do that gross floating head in the sink?"

"On it," Gabriel says. He powers up his desktop computer.

"Okay, then that leaves the sad little naked ladies for Ivy."

Cam raises his hand. "I can work with Ivy on the sad naked ladies."

Somehow this entire conversation has gotten miles away from me.

"No." Sunny points a finger at Cam. "You're not officially in this group. Not yet, at least."

He looks down, crestfallen.

"Come on, guys," I say softly. "Cam gave us the key to the poem. He figured out the Golden Gate Bridge and the octopus. Plus, he and I were talking earlier, and we were thinking that tomorrow maybe we all could—"

"I vote no," Julia says. She sets down her pen and looks at the rest of us. "I don't think Cam should get to stay."

"What?" Cam lifts his eyebrows.

Gabriel swivels away from his computer. "I also vote no." He looks directly at Cam. "The Friends of Dorothy Treasure Hunting Brigade—which I might have just renamed our group—is fabulous and gay, yes. But we're also friends first and foremost. Cam, no offense, but you don't really exude friend energy. You're a little too sneaky and self-obsessed. You don't fit our vibe."

I raise my hand and step forward. "Well, I vote yes. And

I'm technically editor in chief of the Friends of Dorothy Treasure Hunting Brigade, so if there's a tie, I'm breaking it."

We all turn and look at Sunny. She stares reproachfully at Cam, then makes eye contact with me.

"Sorry," she murmurs. She shakes her head slightly. "I just don't think he deserves to be here."

A ball of lead settles in the pit of my stomach. For some reason, it feels like I just got kicked out of the group too. Or at least a part of me.

Without a word, Cam picks up his messenger bag and heads back up the stairs. As I watch him take step after step, I start to feel like a circus act: the Elastic Woman, stretched from one group to another. I grab my own backpack and run after him.

"Cam, wait!"

By the time I reach the top of the stairs, he's already at the far end of the hallway, leaning against the side exit. I keep running until I've closed the distance between us. I can see how flustered and hurt he looks now that I'm right in front of him. His vulnerability makes my chest ache. I'm reminded of when we were kids, open to the world in a way you can never be again once you've been properly hurt. It never occurred to me until now that Cam's closed himself off too. That he's been badly hurt too.

"We can still do this," I say, breathless. "You and me. Tomorrow."

Cam looks at me, confused. "What does that mean? Are you leaving your own team?"

I shrug. "I don't know, Cam. I don't know what's going on. Maybe, if we figure this thing out, everyone will change their minds. And they'll want you back in."

His eyes flash with some expression I don't fully recognize. His pupils dilate slightly.

"Is that what you want?" he asks me.

I nod. Cam opens his mouth to say something else, but before he gets the words out, we hear steps echoing across the linoleum floor. Sunny appears at the top of the stairwell.

"See you tomorrow, then," Cam whispers. He ducks out of the side door.

I sigh and turn toward Sunny. We meet each other halfway down the hall.

"Don't be pissed," Sunny says once I reach her. "We work better as a team without him."

"Do we?" I ask, my voice tinged with sharpness. I nod toward the stairwell. "The three of you already had your minds made up about him before the meeting even started. Am I right?"

Sunny levels her gaze at mine. "Yes, you're right. But not just because of what Julia and Gabriel said downstairs."

"Why, then?"

"Because of *you*," Sunny says. "It's obvious Cam likes you, or that you like him. It's a power he has over you, Ivy. It's going to cloud your thinking."

Just as I am about to retort that Cam absolutely does *not* have any power over me and that he is definitely *not* clouding my thinking, my mind suddenly gets cloudy. I think this is a trick phrase, really. It's like telling a person that they're blushing. There's no way to refute it, because the accusation itself seems to spark the action into existence.

Does Cam like me? I don't want to let this question become real in my brain. I want to leash it, to hold it directly in the conversation between me and Sunny. I've followed that path before, picked up all the little what-if breadcrumbs. But no, it doesn't make sense. Two years ago, I basically threw my whole heart at Cam, and he—well—he taste-tested it and decided it wasn't for him.

"Do you like him that way?" Sunny asks, clearly impatient for an answer.

There is no right way to respond to this question.

"I . . . can't," I say finally. I clear my throat. "I mean, I don't."

"Mm." Sunny nods to herself. She hugs the tops of her arms rather than giving her usual formidable stance. Her thumb wags back and forth over her shirtsleeve, and I begin following the movement with my eyes like a clock's pendulum.

"Well, I think he's wrong for you," she murmurs. She stares at the floor between us, then cuts her eyes up at me through her lashes. "And he's not the only one who cares about you, you know."

"Wait." I step toward Sunny. "What does that mean?"

"What do *you* think it means?" Sunny says knowingly. She swallows, her cheeks going deeply red, then turns and flees back down the stairwell.

CHAPTER TWENTY-EIGHT

Sunny's right. My mind is officially cloudy.

It feels like the San Francisco sky, with every thought thick and crowded and constantly racing.

Sunny likes me, I think as I get on the train the next morning, heading not west toward school but east. I stare out the window at the crest of Strawberry Hill, then the final eastern swath of Golden Gate Park. I stare into the deep black of the Sunset Tunnel.

Sunny likes me.

On paper, this is very good news. Sunny is smart and funny, not to mention extremely hot. I have personally felt my knees get weak whenever I've seen her whip out her round reading glasses during yearbook meetings to take a close look at photo layouts. I should have followed her back down the stairs yesterday. I should be texting her something cute and flirtatious right now.

Instead, I get off the Judah train and walk the several blocks to the main library. I slink into the reference section.

And the whole time I'm paging through reference books, looking for entries about Harvey Milk and the gay rights movement in the 1970s, I'm not thinking about what to text Sunny or when I should see her. I'm thinking about Cam walking around the corner. I don't understand it. My mind is totally overcrowded. There are too many good ideas I should be following and even more bad ideas I want to follow instead.

Cam brushes through the front doors of the library just before noon. He strides across the foyer and looms over my notebook.

"Now who's the early bird?" Cam says, smiling.

The corners of his mouth make two tiny dimples—one in either cheek.

"Found some stuff," I say, not quite looking up.

Cam sits down next to me at one of the reading tables between the shelves. He leans over far enough that his Old Spice deodorant floods my senses. I want to hate it, I want to hate it, I want to hate it.

My lungs breathe in deep, traitors that they are.

"What did you find?" Cam asks.

"Well . . ." I flip back to my first page of notes. I'm not nearly as neat and organized as Julia, but as long as I'm translating my own chicken scratch, it's fine. "Remember what the octopus monument said? About the unity of the empire?"

"Uhhh, no," Cam admits. He grins and looks up at me from the notebook. "But I have a feeling you're about to remind me."

"It was a monument made to memorialize the state of California officially joining the Union."

"Union," Cam says. "Got it."

"Turns out, there are a lot of reference entries for Harvey Milk and unions. Did you know one of Harvey Milk's biggest movements as an activist was to lead a boycott over a beer company whose union workers were on strike?"

"Hmm. Union . . . union." Cam taps his chin in thought. He pulls a face. "That's a little bit of a stretch, V. It might be something, though."

I turn to the next page in my notes. "Okay, well, how about this? Do you know where the Stonewall riots took place?"

"New York City?"

"At the Stonewall Inn," I tell him. "In Greenwich Village."

I let Cam work out the next connection.

"And you found the clock fountain along the Greenwich Steps," he says slowly.

"*We* found it there, yeah."

Cam motions to the open books around me. "So . . . what does this mean? What do we do?"

I check my phone. "First we keep our twelve p.m. appointment upstairs. But maybe these facts, these little gay history footnotes, can be a sort of confirmation system for each drawing. I'm not sure yet."

Cam helps me pack up the books and place them on the return cart. When we arrive at the sixth floor, I'm almost relieved to see a different librarian working at the check-in desk. Like as long as no one here officially recognizes me from before, I'm in the clear. The man seats us at a different row of tables, this time packed not with two but ten boxes of city archives.

"What is all this?" Cam asks.

"Every city park archive from 1970 through 1985," I say. "At least, whatever they kept around at that time. Oh, and be careful—we found a used tissue the last time we were here."

I hand Cam a pair of white gloves and a pencil stub. He immediately tucks the pencil stub behind his ear, which looks simultaneously stupid and strangely hot. He then makes a show of putting on the gloves like a doctor heading into surgery, except the gloves at the library don't snap the way medical gloves do, and, thank God, this time he just looks stupid.

"Okay, which images are we looking for again?"

I pull up Gilbert Baker's drawing on my phone, zooming in and scrolling to the four remaining images we haven't yet figured out. There's the eagle with the shield. The head in the sink. The three women in the middle of what must be debilitating menstrual cramps. And, of course, the woman with the necklace, wearing that long floral dress.

"She's holding something," Cam points out. "Right there. In the hand closer to the screaming ladies. Is it . . . glasses?"

"I think it's one of those fancy masks, like the ones people wear at a masquerade party."

"Maybe," Cam says. He squints. "It looks more like binoculars to me."

"But it has that long handle!" I say. "See, it goes all the way from her hand to her hip almost."

"Hmm. Let's put a pin in that for now." Cam pulls off a lid from one of the boxes. "So. We set aside anything that could be a match?"

"Yes. Anything that could be a match."

The two of us get started.

As the minutes collect into the first hour, it becomes clear that working with Cam is undeniably different than working with the yearbook crew. Cam has always struck me as the type of group partner who would want to goof off and talk the whole time. But here he's quiet and methodical. He doesn't even mind going through the occasional disgusting unidentified object.

"*The Three Shades*," Cam says an hour and a half into our appointment. He taps the bottom right corner of the scroll between us.

"Oh." I put down my stack of photographs and look closer at the drawing of the women. All three figures are rendered in slightly different styles—one in basic line work, one with some shading, and one almost entirely in shadow.

"I guess they are in three shades," I say. "I hadn't noticed that part before."

"No." Cam turns and shows me a photograph of three men sculpted in bronze, slumping over. They're in the exact same pose as the female figures from the drawing.

I shake my head. "Those are all the same shade, though."

He sighs and points to the caption underneath. "They're called *The Three Shades*, Ivy. It's a sculpture in the Legion of Honor museum. It stands over a larger piece titled *The Gates of Hell*."

"Sounds cheerful," I say, scrunching my nose. "What's the connection to gay history?"

"I don't know yet," Cam answers. "Plus, the sculpture's inside a building. And I'm pretty sure Gilbert Baker buried the final treasure outside. But maybe nearby . . ."

"The installation series."

Both Cam and I nearly jump from the table. We swivel toward each other in unison, then turn and scan the room. The entire place is empty except for—

The librarian at the head of the room coughs and sets the newspaper down in front of him.

"There was a series of temporary art installations just outside the Legion of Honor museum," he says gruffly. "Those have been over for a long time now, though."

"How long?" Cam asks.

The old man shrugs and ponders, curling his fingers around his unruly beard.

"They lasted through the 1970s, maybe? Used to occur around the same time as the annual gay pride parades down Polk Street. June of each year—that was it. But they stopped around '82 or '83. So perhaps not what you're looking for."

I stand so quickly that the empty chair next to me tumbles sideways onto the floor. "That's actually kind of exactly what we're looking for," I say, throwing a quick glance to Cam. "Do you happen to have any photos of those installations by chance?"

The librarian shakes his head. "You won't find photos in the official archives. They were unauthorized installations— technically vandalism." He offers us a devious little smile, then picks up his newspaper and rattles it like a breeze is wafting through the room. "But I'll bet something comes up in the *San*

Francisco Chronicle archives. You'll find all the reels for the issues printed before 2003 in the basement."

It only takes five minutes for us to pack up all ten boxes and book it all the way down to the basement. We check out every reel of the *San Francisco Chronicle* printed between 1975 and 1983. Luckily, the library has two microfilm readers, and Cam and I sit side by side as we divide up years—he takes all the even ones, and I take the odds—and begin searching through.

"Are we sticking to June issues only?" Cam asks. He slides a reel into the reader.

"June and July," I say. "Sometimes newspapers pick stories up late."

We scroll through, trying not to get snagged in every article about the Pride marches or protests or Harvey's trajectory to office. There's so much that happened in such a short period of time. It really is like going back and seeing an entire revolution unfold.

"Listen to this," Cam says after a while. "'Gay people, we will not win our rights by staying quietly in our closets . . . We are coming out! We are coming out to fight the lies, the myths, the distortions. We are coming out to tell the truth about gays. For I am tired of the conspiracy of silence.'"

The last word manifests itself, stretching between us.

"It's from Harvey's speech at the 1978 parade," Cam says softly. He shifts away from the microfilm reader. "Is that how you felt? When you came out to me?"

My entire body goes numb. Neither of us has mentioned that specific day since it happened. Secretly, I guess I sort of hoped that in his weird, new surfer-guy phase, Cam had forgotten about it. That he might've looked back and figured we had simply grown apart as friends.

I go over Harvey's speech in my head, mining it for an answer that sidesteps my and Cam's personal history.

"I think it's important to come out on a community level," I say steadily. "I think Harvey's talking about the fact that a lot of people are scared to come out because they think coming out will get them stereotyped or"—I spin my hand around, trying to remember Harvey's exact wording—"distorted, in society. They stay in the closet because they're not a *specific* kind of gay person, you know? But being gay is a spectrum. It always has been."

I realize I haven't answered Cam's question at all.

"If you're asking if I came out for gay people's rights," I say finally, "then, I mean, yes! Obviously!"

"No, I'm not asking you that."

Cam pushes even farther from the microfilm reader, shifting closer to me. He clears his throat. "Harvey said, 'For I am tired of the conspiracy of silence.' But what does that mean, the conspiracy of silence? It's the idea that silence is telling a lie, right? Or, at the very least, that silence is covering up the truth."

I make a face. "I'm not sure I'm following."

"Forget the gay rights movement for one second," Cam says. "I'm talking about us right now. You and me. I want to know: When you came out that day . . . was that your way of trying to tell me the truth?"

CHAPTER TWENTY-NINE

I pull away from Cam on instinct. Self-preservation kicks in like a backup generator.

"The truth about what?" I bite into the last word so hard that he has to know I'm shutting down his question more than asking my own. I'm not doing this again. I'm not opening myself up to Cam just so he can smash my feelings to bits and then pretend like the whole exchange was a silly game.

I turn toward my own microfilm reader and press my face into the lens. I dive into the 1983 reel of the *San Francisco Chronicle*, speeding through a whole spring's worth of headlines. Serial thefts. Business closures. New election candidates. Time blurs into a buzzing haze of ink.

March 1983.

April 1983.

May 1983.

The dial clicks.

"Holy shit."

Cam sighs next to me. "Don't pretend like you found

something great just to avoid saying you don't want to talk to me."

I pull away from the microfilm. "Oh, I'm not avoiding it. I *don't* want to talk to you. But it turns out I also found something pretty great."

He stares at me, trying to decipher my expression. I shift the view over from the microscope to the front screen on the reader. "See for yourself."

The article takes a moment to come into focus.

TWELFTH YEAR OF LEGION OF HONOR INSTALLATION BY MYSTERY VANDAL

"Holy shit," Cam breathes.

I smile. "Told you."

Under the headline is a grainy photograph of what looks like a clock growing right out of the ground. Each slice looks like a different kind of green plant. The clock numbers stand at the edges, spelled out in flowers.

Twelve Faces, No Hands, the caption reads.

I look back at the photo and realize it's not just the title of the piece, but a description of the clock itself. There are no clock hands or arms, nothing to signify the time. It's just an empty clockface out in the middle of a field. Gilbert could have found it and buried the treasure right outside the raised circle. He might even have been the mystery artist behind the entire thing.

But where exactly would he have buried the treasure, then? There are no markings, nothing that points to one particular spot.

"A clockface in the grass?" Cam asks from beside me. "That's a little strange, isn't it? You would think this would have matched up with the grandfather clock in the scroll."

I think about the drawing of the grandfather clock. "But that clockface wasn't empty," I say. My brain does a double take, and I suddenly pop up out my chair. "It wasn't empty! There was a time on it!"

"Well, yeah," Cam says.

I reach into my bag and pull out the wooden box. "No, you're not getting it. There's not a time on the clock in the installation. It doesn't have any hands. But the clock in our picture *does*!"

I peel the scroll open. Cam looks over my shoulder. "What time is that? 9:20?" he asks.

"I think so," I say. "But that still doesn't give us a specific place to look for a treasure. The arms are pointing at nine and four. So which one is the right one?"

"V. Look." Cam brings his finger from the grandfather clock down to the woman in the long dress. "Look at her arms."

I gasp. I don't know how we didn't see it before. The woman's two arms, outstretched in either direction, are in exactly the nine and four positions. Same as the grandfather clock hands. The left arm points at the edge of the page, where the paper cuts off. But the right arm, the one holding the strange glasses, is pointing directly at *The Three Shades* sculpture. Right where the clock installation used to be.

"Four o'clock," I whisper.

I look at Cam. "Gilbert must have buried the treasure right outside the four o'clock section."

Cam's mouth breaks into the widest, most all-encompassing smile I've ever seen on him. He looks at the other pictures in the scroll.

"The bear, the snake, the octopus. *The Three Shades*. The two boys in the sailboat hats. The head in the sink. The eagle. The woman in the dress. And the clockface. Oh my God." He looks back at me. "You said the piece is called *Twelve Faces*?"

I nod. "*Twelve Faces, No Hands.*"

Cam points at the scroll. "There are twelve faces here, V."

All the pieces are connecting.

I don't know if I have ever felt so giddy in my entire life.

We each take a quick photo of the article on the microfilm reader with our phones. Then we gather up the collection of reels from the *Chronicle* archives and turn them back in. As we step outside, it's already nearing four. We arrive at the rail station just as a train is leaving.

"Want to walk home?" Cam asks me. "I'm too antsy to wait for the next train."

I'm antsy too. I feel like I'm floating in the strangest dreamlike way that's both insanely cool and maybe a little bit terrifying. Cam offers me his arm, and because it feels like it is the only possible thing to tether me to this Earth, I hook mine through his. We walk down Market Street. We walk through Duboce Park. Every single tree waves. Every building window glitters. It's like San Francisco knows we have a secret. Or maybe it's the other way around, and at long last we finally know what this city has kept hidden away for so long.

When we get to Divisadero Street, Cam pauses. He cranes his neck and looks north, in the exact direction of the Legion of Honor.

"You want to catch a bus over?" he asks me, grinning.

"Absolutely not," I say, feeling more like his tether now. "We have to bring this to the whole group, remember? We need them to like you."

"Ah." Cam nods, barely concealing his dejection.

We cross Divisadero and reach the Panhandle of Golden Gate Park.

"It's kind of funny, isn't it?" Cam says as we cut past the entrance and walk through the greenery.

"What's funny?"

"That Golden Gate's not part of the solve."

I look up at the sea of trees in front of us. "Maybe it was too big to be a part of the solve. You know, too obvious or something."

"What an oversight." Cam shakes his head. "See, I think it's too big *not* to be part of a treasure hunt about gay history in San Francisco. In the 1970 *Chronicle* issue on the first anniversary of the Stonewall riots, there was a full-page article about a 'gay-in' at Golden Gate Park."

"What's a gay-in?" I ask. "Like a sit-in? Except everyone is gay?"

Cam blushes a little. "The article made it look . . . slightly more titillating than that."

I let out a guffaw. "Did you, of all people, just use the word 'titillating'?"

"It was in the article!" Cam yells, but he's laughing too.

"So, what in particular was titillating?"

He waves a hand. "Nope. Absolutely no comment." The blush spreads farther across his cheeks. I feel the heat rise in my own face. The "titillation" seems to be contagious.

We smile shyly and duck around the various sections in the park until we close in on the music concourse. A live jazz band is playing in the outdoor band shell. Couples are pressed together on the surrounding benches bolted down between the trees, nodding and bobbing their feet to the tune. Cam and I stand at the very back. He looks at me and extends a hand.

"Shall we?"

I take hold of his hand, and suddenly we're swaying and spinning to the music. The clouds in my head are swirling into the most beautiful concoction. Cam dips me once, low, and holds me there. We look at each other for a long time before he pulls me back up to standing. The song ends, vibratos eventually fading to quiet.

There's too much silence between Cam and me right now. I don't want to go back to that moment in front of the microfilm readers. I don't want to talk about the day from two years ago.

"Sunny said she has feelings for me," I say instead. The words come out by accident, like a glove tumbling from a coat pocket.

"Oh." Cam's eyebrows jump. He takes a step back. "Oh, wow, that's—that's pretty huge, isn't it?"

"I don't know," I say. "She told me yesterday. I don't know what to do."

The band starts up their next set, but the urge to dance again is gone. Cam and I look around awkwardly. He motions toward the park entrance next to our neighborhood, and I nod.

"She's really attractive," Cam says as we walk.

I side-eye him. "Go sweep her off her feet, then, Casanova. You've stolen every other girl from me."

Cam stops the both of us. "That's not what I meant. I'm not trying to steal anyone from you. I'm saying you should go for it."

I cross my arms. "So you want me to go for it?"

"If it's what you want."

"Why wouldn't I want that?"

Cam throws his hands up. "Jesus, Ivy! Don't twist this into something complicated. I'm just trying to be a supportive friend."

"Oh, is that what we are again? Sorry, I didn't get the no-tice that we're officially resuming our"—I make air quotes—"'supportive friendship.'"

We glare at each other.

"Forget it," Cam says.

"Already forgotten," I say, turning out of the park.

I march ahead of him, crossing the street before the signal so I can go straight home. I'm fuming the whole time—mostly at Cam, but maybe a tiny bit at myself too. Why did I have to tell him about Sunny? What was the point of bringing it into that moment? What *was* that moment, even?

I already have my front door unlatched before I realize Cam's standing directly behind me.

"Ahhhh! Why are you following me?"

"I want my book back," Cam says.

"What?"

"We didn't end up needing it! And it's my book." He's fuming even more than I am, which really isn't fair. I feel like I should get all fuming rights between us from now until eternity.

"Well, it was my flyer," I say. "And you went right ahead and stole that anyway."

Cam makes a face. "And I gave. It. Back. When are you going to stop holding that against me?"

"Um, probably never."

I scowl at Cam until it's clear we're in some kind of standoff.

He is right, though, I remind myself. We don't need the book anymore. And at this point, I just want him to leave me alone. I sigh and hold the door open.

"Fine. Take the book. It's in my room."

Cam squeezes in between me and the doorframe. He storms across the living room and down the hall. Sometimes I forget that he used to be here all the time. I forget he knows everything so well. I follow him into my bedroom.

"Where is it?" he asks.

I point to the nightstand next to my bed. Cam reaches over and scoops up *Gay Treasures* under his arm. He turns and looks at me, his eyes flashing with anger.

"What?" I motion to the book. "You have what you want now. Aren't you happy?"

I can see Cam's nostrils flare as he takes his next breath. "No."

"No, you're not happy?"

"No—I don't have what I want," he says.

He tosses the book onto my bed and reaches for my waist.

CHAPTER THIRTY

He doesn't even have to pull me in.

My chest is drawn, magnetized, right to his. My hand snakes up Cam's shoulder and curves around his neck, touching the feathery ends of his hair. His fingers flex and curl as they knead into my shirt. The touch is surprisingly gentle. But there's so much tension in the restraint. I can feel how hard he's working not to crush his body immediately against mine.

The spaces left between us are going to make me explode.

His eyes go heavy as they slip down my cheeks, landing on the center of my mouth. I raise my other hand and cut his jawline with my thumb. He inhales sharply, lips parting.

I cannot believe I'm going to do this.

Again.

I swallow and tilt my head to one side.

"What do you want?" I whisper.

His breathing is thick and strained. I move the tiniest bit closer, until I feel his breath over my skin. I repeat the question.

"What do you—"

His mouth is on mine before I can finish.

I catch his bottom lip, savoring the exact flavor of him. Not even a specific brand of lip balm or a leftover fruity taste from some sports drink. There's just Cam—warm and spiced.

I'm aware that now would be a great time to close my eyes, but for some reason, I can't. I've spent too much time in this room, twisting under my covers late at night and imagining this scenario playing out in my head. Because the truth is, I *have* wanted Cam so badly. Wanted to have him want *me*, like this, so badly. I have to at least try to capture every detail of this moment in my memory.

I catch a glimpse of the ceiling through the curls in Cam's hair as our lips pull away and come back together, and I know I'll never see my ceiling the same way again. The late-afternoon light spills in through the curtains behind him. This is a mirage. It's a dream. It's blurring the line holding fantasy back from reality. Cam's hands move down my hips, and I feel high and giddy and half asleep. I realize this moment is so surreal that I might, in fact, be dreaming. But if I am, I'm in no hurry to wake up.

The light from the setting sun gets stronger. It pulls Cam in until he's a silhouette across from me. He tips his forehead against mine. It's so easy to lean into him, to have the two of us meld into one figure, one statue, as if we were always destined to come together this way. The light gets brighter, and I finally close my eyes, sinking fast into him. There's only one speed when it comes to kissing Cam, and that speed is quick, hungry, hurried.

My mouth presses hard into his, and it's like falling down a rabbit hole.

And down.

And down.

And down.

As I fall, the scent of his mouth, his neck, his arms, grows sharper. The more I kiss him, the more I start to smell something else too.

Fresh-cut grass. Damp earth. Rain somewhere in the distance.

I open my eyes.

Cam's lying in the meadow, across from me.

Pale shadows are scattered over us from the canopy of trees way up high.

A shovel at Cam's feet.

A book under my arm.

Our mouths were still tingly and buzzing. I reached for Cam and found a tiny strip of exposed midriff. My fingertips inched under the fabric of his shirt. His breath hitched, and my heartbeat dipped down below my stomach.

"Cameron," I whispered then.

"Cameron," I whisper now.

His rib cage goes from shuddering to completely still. Then, all at once, he jerks away from me. It takes me a minute to figure out what's going on. I look around.

We're back in my room.

The afternoon sunlight has dissolved into a pale pink tinge. We're no longer standing next to my bed but draped over it, propped up on our sides, facing each other.

The same way we were lying in the meadow that afternoon.

The day I came out as gay.

Cam sits up and swings his legs over the edge of the bed. I push myself into an awkward pose, my legs half curled under me. I try to find something to say. My lips are raw and puffy. I'm exactly at the point of beginning to process the fact that whatever has just happened between us—dream or otherwise—is now very, *very* over.

Cam drops his head into his hands. "I cannot believe I'm doing this shit again."

This shit.

The insinuation is a sudden gut punch. I turn my head away so he won't see my face.

"I'm . . . sorry if you made another mistake," I say through clenched teeth.

I'm pretty sure that's what he said last time.

This was a mistake.

My lips were still warm from the hum of his kiss—it was my very first kiss ever, with anyone—when Cam stood up in the meadow, spat out those words, and didn't talk to me again for more than twelve months.

Cam doesn't answer me now in my room. He takes a shaky breath. He's going to stand up again any second. He's going to leave knowing that, even after two years, all it took was one well-placed hand on my side, and I was ready to fall right back into him. This is beyond mortifying.

There is no way I can possibly wait another few months

before leaving the country for art school. I have to leave for Paris right now. I had to leave five minutes ago. I wonder if I can pack my bags in the next few seconds and beat Cam out the door.

This isn't fair, I think angrily. *This isn't even my fault.*

I didn't ask for this stupid game between us. I didn't ask for anything between us! I'm the one who's been trying to move on since he first rejected me.

"Why did you kiss me again?" I whisper. I'm still too embarrassed to face him.

Cam sniffs and stands from the bed. He takes a few steps toward the door, then swings around, reaching for the book next to me.

"I don't know, Ivy. I thought things would be different, I guess."

"Different how?" I wave toward my room, which has been in the same exact configuration since middle school. My billowy black clothes now are almost identical to the baby gothic outfits I wore in middle school. I have the same Doc Martens, sized up. Same sarcasm, if only slightly edgier. I'm the same person who's known Cam for years. The same person who fell in love with him the first time.

"You shouldn't kiss someone if you want them to be someone else," I say. I'm vaguely aware of the tears collecting at the inner creases of my eyes. It takes everything I have not to blink and fall completely apart in front of him. "I have always been the same."

"Right," Cam murmurs. "You've been pretty damn clear about that from the start, haven't you?"

He mops his face, then shuffles through my bedroom door.

I stand up from the bed.

"What do you want from me?" I yell out. "It's like you've made it your entire mission in life to torture me! You want every girl I go out with, except you don't. We're friends, except we're not. You want me, you don't want me. You like me, you don't like me. You're playing this stupid game and only telling me half the rules, then walking away when I don't do exactly what you want. Well, you've already done this, Cam. We've already played this round."

He whirls back through the doorframe, gaping.

"That's really what you think?" he asks.

I shrug, unable to answer. He hasn't said a word, hasn't done a single thing, that explains otherwise.

In two giant strides he's crossed the room again. He cups my chin in his hand and tips my face up to look at him. Is he seriously about to kiss me again? The absolute nerve of this guy.

But before I pull away or lean in—my frontal lobe and amygdala haven't finished hashing it out, gladiator style— Cam stops just short of kissing me.

"Take everything you just said, Ivy, and reverse it. You have it entirely backward," he says. "Entirely."

He drops my chin and heads out the door. And this time he doesn't come back.

CHAPTER THIRTY-ONE

The next day I am essentially a human-sized exposed nerve. It seems unfair, unethical even, to make me go to school in this state. Unfortunately, last night my mother learned that I in fact did not go to school yesterday. So I'm currently walking down the block not only with a ripped-out heart but also with a metaphorical stiletto heel jammed up my ass.

Cam's mom is pretty lax compared to mine, but she'll probably make Cam go to school too. I will have to do everything I can to avoid him at all costs.

It's confusing, because I'm *nearly* certain I'm avoiding Cam purely out of embarrassment. I practically fell over myself to kiss him. I listened to him tell me—*for the second time*—that kissing me was a mistake. He pulled me in and then pushed me away completely. There is not a hole deep enough for me to burrow into to recover from that.

And yet.

Tendrils of another feeling are mixing in with the one I already know. I'm filled not only with searing embarrassment but also . . . a strange, cold guilt for some unknown reason. Like icy fingers wrapped around a hot mug.

"Why should I feel guilty?" I mutter to myself as I round the last corner to school.

Cam's the one who stole my flyer and turned the treasure hunt into a race. Cam chased us down at the art museum. He forced us to add him to the group. He made me track clues across the city with him when all five of us were supposed to be taking a break.

He's the one who stormed into my house, into my room, and pulled me to him.

If anything, I'm only culpable of being *too* complicit in all of Cam's demands.

The mysterious guilt still lingers.

"Hey, Sunny," I say as I walk down the main hallway.

I veer toward her locker, but as the door slams and Sunny looks at me, I realize I have absolutely made the wrong move. Her face is flushed and blotchy. Her eyes are all sharp edges. She scowls at me like I am a rat-sized cockroach that just crawled out of the gutter in front of her. I immediately take a step back.

Monday! my brain pings. Sunny told me she had feelings for me on Monday. And today is Wednesday, and I haven't said one word to her since then. Until right now.

But Sunny doesn't particularly look like she's waiting on a response from me. She shifts to face the opposite direction, then begins shuffling through the books in her arms.

"God, Sunny. I'm so sorry about yesterday. I was . . ."

Don't lie and say you were sick.

"Sick," I say anyway, because it is literally the only reason my mom ever allows me to miss school. She even schedules all my medical appointments for Saturdays. Nobody should have to schlep to a freaking dental cleaning on a Saturday.

Sunny makes a weird, choked laugh. "Oh. Sick. Is that right?"

Should I cough or something? This entire conversation feels like getting trapped in a spider's web. If I struggle, I'll only make it worse. I decide to sidestep yesterday entirely.

"I thought a lot about what you said on Monday."

"No you didn't," Sunny says dully.

"Come on, Sunny. I'm trying to talk to you about this. I . . . I was caught off guard after the meeting. I didn't think you liked me that way. I thought you barely liked me at all."

She flicks her eyes at me over her books. She's still glaring.

"Maybe you feel the need to go through this whole song and dance," she says. "But I really, really don't. Just talk to yourself and pretend I'm still listening if that's what you need to do."

She starts walking down the hall. I follow her.

"Wait!"

She waves me off with the back of one hand. "It's fine, Ivy. Go have your little happily-ever-after moment with Cam."

I stop just short of her. "What are you talking about?"

"I saw you on a date," Sunny says. "At the music concourse yesterday? You two were dancing."

"That wasn't a— We were just— Hang on, why were you even *at* the music concourse?"

"Researching!" Sunny's voice cracks. She swallows and glances around furtively. "We all split up images on the map, right? I was looking for matches in Golden Gate Park after school. But, honestly, screw all of that. I'm over this stupid treasure hunt."

She jabs her index finger into my chest. "You used us as placeholders, Ivy. You really had us convinced Cam was the bad guy in your story. But that was a total front. You just made him out to be the bad guy because that was easier than admitting you liked him. All this time, I bet you were wishing he would come running back to you and replace us. God, I feel like such an idiot!"

The guilt engulfs the humiliation from earlier, extinguishing it completely. Feeling hurt and betrayed is awful. But seeing yourself hurt someone else, the way I can see I've hurt Sunny, is excruciating. I'm not used to playing this part in the story. I don't want to be someone else's bad guy.

"You're not placeholders," I croak. Sunny rolls her eyes and takes off down the hall. I'm scrambling to keep up. "Sunny, you are *not* a placeholder!"

My mind races over what I could possibly say to convince her. I definitely cannot mention the kiss—or the fight—between me and Cam. But before that, Sunny already saw us at the music concourse. Now is my chance to share everything we found with the others. Yearbook crew and I can finish this thing together, just like we started it.

I can still fix this.

"Let me prove it to you," I say.

Sunny slows down on her next stride. "How?"

"The meeting." I'm already out of breath, mostly from

desperation. "Please, come to the meeting today. I'll bring what I have to the Bat Cave after school. Just us. No Cam."

Sunny shakes her head. "I don't know."

"You do, though," I say. "I know you care about this. And not because of me. Screw me. I'm awful—I'm not worth anyone's time. But this hunt *is*, Sunny. All of you have put so much into this. You deserve to know."

Sunny startles a little. She betrays herself and looks right at me.

"You know where the treasure is?"

I nod. "Yeah. I'm pretty sure I do."

I'm early to the meeting but am still the last one down into the basement lab. Gabriel, Sunny, and Julia are already in their chairs, facing the projector screen, which is currently blank and dark.

Sunny nods slightly as I make the final step in. "She's here. Okay, let's see what you've got."

Gabriel and Julia look up from their phones. I have no idea what Sunny's told them. She might've spilled everything she saw regarding me and Cam. Or she might've kept it to herself.

I go in playing naïve.

"I'm first to share?" I ask semicasually.

Sunny narrows her eyes at me. "None of us found anything. And you know where the treasure is, so—"

"WHAT?!" Gabriel pops out of his chair. His phone

clatters onto the desk behind him. He turns and gives Sunny a look. "You didn't say she knew where it was."

"I said she had something to show us." Sunny leans back and crosses her arms.

"The treasure?" Gabriel asks eagerly.

I shake my head. "Not yet. But its location, hopefully."

Gabriel runs a hand through his hair. "Okay, this is crazy. None of us came here with a clue, even, and somehow you have the entire thing figured out?" He pulls up the drawing of the scroll on his phone. "Which part of the picture were you working on?"

I bite my lower lip. "The three women in the corner. They're *The Three Shades* sculpture at the Legion of Honor museum."

Julia cocks her head. "Another art museum? I thought we were supposed to be digging for this."

"We are," I say quickly. "There used to be these outdoor installations near the museum that popped up every June during the Pride celebrations. In 1983, the installation was a clockface, but without any arms to indicate a time. Look at the grandfather clock picture on the scroll. I think we're supposed to dig where the clockface installation was, right outside the four o'clock mark."

No one says anything. Gabriel, Julia, and Sunny poke around the picture on their phones, squinting. I notice that Julia hasn't written anything down in her notebook.

"That's . . . interesting," Gabriel says finally. Except he makes the word "interesting" sound exactly like the word "stupid."

"Why not the nine o'clock mark?" Julia asks after a minute. "The clock in the picture is pointing there too."

I pull out my laptop, then connect it to the projector. Once the machine warms up and the image flashes over the back wall, I walk directly to it.

"See this woman?" I ask. "She's wearing the same necklace as the one we found in the box. And her arms are doing the same thing as the clock arms. They're pointing to nine and four. But there's nothing near the nine."

"Well, nothing in the drawing," Sunny clarifies.

"Which is important," I say, exasperated. But no one looks convinced. I rack my brain to figure out what I'm missing from earlier—why the solution felt so obvious when Cam and I first found it. "The boundaries of Gilbert's picture have to be there for a reason, right? There's nothing outside nine o'clock. But look where her four o'clock arm is pointing. Right at *The Three Shades* in the Legion of Honor museum!"

Gabriel folds his hands in his lap. He looks like a sad combination of confused and disappointed. "What about everything else? How is Harvey Milk connected?"

I throw my palms up. "I don't know! The librarian from the history center said the installations could be related to the San Francisco Gay Pride marches. They popped up in late June from 1970 all the way to 1983. I think that's pretty fascinating!"

Sunny lunges forward, elbows pinned on her knees. "Wait. You went back to the history center yesterday?"

Ohhhhh no.

"Is that why you weren't at school?" Gabriel asks softly. "You . . . you couldn't wait for us?"

Sunny tuts and shakes her head. She would be pulling off

the distant, judgmental vibe perfectly if her eyes didn't look so hurt. "So I guess you two lovebirds weren't just playing hooky for a date, then."

The room goes completely silent.

Sunny eyes me menacingly after dropping the bombshell. I can only look back at her, beyond guilt-ridden, as Gabriel and Julia put two and two together.

"Cam," Julia says. "You were with Cam."

I swallow. "He's a good researcher."

"So why are you standing in front of us right now?" Sunny asks. She motions at me with one arm. "If you and Cam wanted to sneak off and find this thing yourselves, why aren't you out digging it up together?"

"I wanted to bring it to you—"

"Bullshit," Sunny says. "You didn't say a word about this on Monday or in the group chat yesterday. If I didn't know any better, I'd say you're only here right now because something happened with Cam, and you're out looking for place-holders again."

I wince and close my eyes. I feel like I've just failed a lie detector test.

"You're not placeholders," I whisper. But even my voice refuses to prop up such slippery, spineless words.

Sunny stands and grabs her bag. She breezes by me and trots up the stairs without a word. Gabriel shakes his head as if in disbelief. Then he stands, resigned, and picks up his own backpack.

Julia studies me as the sound of Gabriel's footsteps fades

into the distance. Instead of tucking her notebook away, she holds it out to me.

"What's going on?" I ask as I take it.

Julia tries to smile. "I . . . I don't think I want these notes anymore," she says. "It was always your magic, anyway. Not mine. Good luck, Ivy."

She makes the fourth person to leave me in less than a day.

CHAPTER THIRTY-TWO

Losing every friend you've ever made is not the "Complicated" by Avril Lavigne song it's made out to be in *Bottoms*, one of my favorite sapphic movies. There is nothing complicated or layered about being abjectly despised—it's just unequivocally awful. Zero out of ten, do not recommend.

This is exactly how I feel on the bus ride to the Legion of Honor museum on Friday after school.

I've never been to the Legion of Honor, not even for a school field trip. When the bus first dips into Lincoln Park, where the museum is housed, I'm actually surprised by how expansive all the trees and hills are. Golden Gate Park is a total giant, but all the parks in downtown San Francisco are like tiny dots in comparison. I sort of figured Golden Gate was the one exception. But as we zigzag down the winding road filled with green, I get the uncanny feeling of driving through actual woods. I mean, I can see a sheared golf course in the distance, but still. This is nice. The perfect place to bury a treasure, really.

The bus pulls up in front of the museum. The building looks like an actual palace, with two statues on horses guarding the entrance and an open courtyard behind the front gate. I get off the bus and take out my phone to look at the fuzzy picture from the *San Francisco Chronicle* article. Maybe if I hold it up at just the right angle over the surrounding park, I'll figure out exactly where the clock installation was. It can't be that hard, right? This was the kind of shit yearbook worked on for months.

Yearbook.

My heart flinches.

The moment I begin zooming in on the picture, I realize that, actually, this might be insanely hard. The digital image probably would have turned out a lot clearer if Gabriel had been there to capture it on one of our official cameras. But, I remind myself, the picture was pretty blurry to begin with. Even on the microfilm reader, the clock installation already looked like a giant sepia-toned pizza.

I sit down on a stone bench and pull Julia's notebook from my backpack. It feels wrong to be taking over the official role of notetaker. But it would feel even worse to leave all her work behind. I turn to a blank page and set my phone down to one side. If I can sketch out every blurry outline I see in the background of this photo, maybe that will help me figure out where the heck this clock once was.

The more I sketch, the more I realize that the clock in the photo isn't on flat ground. It's on a hillside, facing out. This is good. Promising, even.

There's also a shape that looks like a small boulder to

the left. I can see a tall pole at the top of the hill in the background. I'm not sure if the pole is something man-made or just a long, skinny tree in the distance. But either way, it's good to note. I jot it down in the picture. Only when I look up do I catch sight of the exact same object across the road.

A golf course flag.

The installation was on the golf course! That would make perfect sense, really. The hills would be smooth. The grass would be short.

A niggling thought worms its way into the back of my head. I can hear Gabriel's voice from Wednesday.

What about everything else from the puzzle?

Where *is* all the Pride history here? The Greenwich Steps and Union monument from the scroll at least made some sense. But why would Gilbert Baker have us learn all that, have us solve the clues about Harvey's birthday party and Naval Station Treasure Island, only to lead us to a golf course?

I check the time and stand up. I need to get inside the museum before it closes. I want to see *The Three Shades* sculpture for myself. Maybe I'll feel something when I see it in person. Or, better yet, maybe I'll find some clue in the context, in the placard next to the art or something, that will make everything else make sense.

I turn and walk along the pathway between the two statues on horses. They each raise their swords at me—either in salute or in warning, who can tell?

As I walk, the clear ocean breeze from over the cliffside washes over me. A medley of birds crowded in a nearby tree chirps and hops gleefully. I'm hit with that overpowering feeling of love I get when I'm in a new part of the city. Like, if San Francisco were a person, he would be the type to have a totally different outfit for every occasion. Cold, gusty beaches with views of the bridge. Warm, open fields in the middle of downtown. Hills and mountains to hike. Art pieces around every corner. Giant buildings that chip away at the clouds. He could change again and again and again, and I would still love him in every form. There's just something about his bones, I guess. Whether it's smack in the middle of the city or tucked away out here in the woods, he's the same person.

And . . . I'm leaving him.

At least, that's what I want to do, isn't it? The whole point of finding Gilbert Baker's treasure is to impress the art school in Paris. So I can leave San Francisco and never look back.

Why did I not realize how messed up that whole objective was until now?

I walk through the museum's courtyard, past a larger-than-life-sized bronze cast of Rodin's *The Thinker*, then make my way to the front doors. The foyer is set apart from the rest of museum, so you can hardly see any of the art past the front room. But the person behind the desk waves me right on through.

"Admission is free after four-thirty," she explains. She makes a point of turning and looking at the clock behind her. "But the museum closes at 5:15."

I look at the clock over her head. 4:50.

"Got it," I say. "Thank you."

I grab a museum guide, then realize I'm going to need some help if the museum is closing in less than thirty minutes.

"Could you please tell me where *The Three Shades* sculpture is?" I ask the front desk person.

"*The Three Shades*?" The woman pauses for a moment, blinking. She snaps. "Oh, you mean *The Gates of Hell*. Third room down that way. The piece is on your right, but trust me, dear, you can't miss it."

"Thank you," I say again, placing the guide back on the desk.

I try to keep myself from running across the open hall. I make myself take in all the details—the lofty, vaulted ceilings and spiraling columns at every corner.

I step into the third gallery and immediately see a large bronze door towering against the wall. There are easily over a hundred figures sculpted inside the door in bas-relief. Figures falling, screaming, clinging to the edges. The whole thing makes my insides shudder. I find *The Three Shades* part of the sculpture at the very top, looming over the door itself. The placard next to the door explains that the sculpture—another one of Rodin's—depicts a scene from Dante's *Inferno*. *The Three Shades* represent the souls of the damned. In the scene, they're all pointing to an inscription over the door:

ABANDON HOPE, ALL YE WHO ENTER HERE.

Immediately, my mind goes to Harvey and all the quotes and speeches I've ever read by him. If I had to associate his legacy with one word, that word would be "hope."

You've got to have hope!

You gotta give 'em hope!

Hope will never be silent!

"Abandon hope," I murmur out loud. Abandon hope. Abandon hope. There has to be something to work out from all this. I just don't know what it is yet.

When I head to school on Monday, I have a fairly decent plan of what to do next.

I went back to the main library on Saturday—one of the people at the front even waved as I came in. I guess visiting three times in the span of a week does make me a regular.

The librarian in the basement helped me figure out the best way to digitize an image from a microfilm reel. Turns out, it's a lot like taking a screenshot. You send the direct image on the reader as an attachment file to an email. When I get the email and open it, I'm disappointed by how similar it looks to the crappy picture Cam and I took with our phones on Tuesday. But I still have a few more steps to take.

If I can just get into the Bat Cave and log on to Gabriel's computer, maybe I can use his programs to clean up the image the way he cleaned up the chapters from *Gay Treasures* that we found during the hunt. Technically, any student should be able to log on to any computer—we literally just took over the old computer lab for our club meeting space. But Gabriel's downloaded a bunch of digital editing applications on this machine specifically, and I'm nervous they'll only show up under his student account. Fingers crossed I find Adobe Photoshop when I log in.

The plan, in short, is as follows:

1. Sneak into the Bat Cave.
2. Access Gabriel's Photoshop program.
3. Fix up the photo from the *Chronicle*.
4. Go back to the golf course at Lincoln Park.
5. Dig up the treasure.

Obviously, doing all this on my own isn't exactly ideal. But if I can just get to Gilbert Baker's treasure, if I can see this full hunt through, I feel like—somehow—everything's going to turn out okay. Like winning can push some sort of reset button on my life.

I leave for school with high hopes for the day. But not even a block later, I see something that ruins my mood entirely.

At the corner of the first intersection, right next to the bodega my mom and I go to all the time, is a makeshift bulletin board—a wall that everyone tapes flyers to for band events, craft fairs, and dog-walking jobs. All those flyers look older and weathered now from the week's past rain. All except the one crisp white page taped to the center of the wall.

WANTED:
TREASURE-FINDING ASSISTANT

CHAPTER THIRTY-THREE

**WANTED:
TREASURE-FINDING ASSISTANT**

Interested in taking on the seven seas next to Blackbeard?

In becoming the quirky Riley to an established Ben Gates?

There is a treasure buried within San Francisco.

Seize on the opportunity to dig it up—THIS SATURDAY.

Considering all applicants Monday–Thursday.
Text the number below:

415-555-2267

The quirky Riley to an established Ben Gates?
How fucking *dare* he.
"I am Ben Gates!" I scream loud enough to accidentally scare the young mother walking past me with a stroller.
I am *always* Ben Gates.

I yank Julia's notebook out of my backpack and rip out a page near the end. I glance up at the stupid notice several times as I write. Finally, my own note is ready. I borrow a few pieces of tape from the guitar teacher who practically bonded their ad to the wall, then stick my flyer right next to Cam's.

WANTED: TREASURE-FINDING PARTNER

Forget the stuff of fairy tales.

Come dig up a real piece of San Francisco history.

Payment negotiable upon unearthing the treasure.

Text THIS number ASAP:

415-555-4897

There. I will not have Cam try to yank this hunt away from me again. He only knows about the clock installation because of me. It's my group that found Harvey's flyer. We're the ones who found the necklace and the scroll. By all rights, that treasure is ours.

I see Cam puttering around the hallway before class starts.

"Really?" I ask, barging right up to him. "Ben Gates?"

Cam shrugs, not quite meeting my eyes.

"One would think a tough guy like you could easily dig up the treasure without a 'quirky Riley' at your side, no? What do you need the extra help for, anyway?"

"None of your business," Cam says. His phone dings. He takes it out and opens the message against his locker.

"An applicant?" I ask, nostrils flaring.

Cam stares at his phone. "Like I said, none of your business." He makes a tiny sigh and tucks his phone away. Not an applicant after all, I guess.

I puff up my chest. "Well, just so you know, I put up an ad too."

He raises an eyebrow. "Why?"

Why? *Why?*

I nearly flap my arms up and down. "Because *you* did!"

"I thought you had your whole yearbook team behind you," Cam says cooly.

I pinch my mouth and stare at him.

Not anymore, my eyes say.

All because of you, the silence adds.

The sneaky, spy-on-a-mission energy I had been gathering all weekend dissipates in a moment. I stomp away from Cam and directly down into the empty Bat Cave. I sit at Gabriel's usual computer and log in. Thank God, Adobe Photoshop is sitting right there on the desktop screen.

I input the image file and start cranking the brightness, the contrast, the definition. For whatever reason, when Gabriel does these things, it's like a magic trick: The image goes from blurry to clear. But now that I'm the one doing it, the image goes from blurry and dark to blurry and brighter. It shifts from blurry sepia to blurry black and white. Even the definition feature just seems to define the blurred lines rather than defining the original things in the photo. What the hell even is this? I thought Photoshop was for the common man.

I send all the stupid, still-blurry images back to myself over email anyway and log out.

Throughout the day, as I sit in each class, I wonder if people are contacting Cam to be his treasure-finding assistant. I vaguely wonder if people are looking at my flyer, but I don't really care about hearing from anyone. Mostly, I'm hoping my flyer is canceling Cam's out. That anyone interested enough in his idea will see my idea next to it and second-guess reaching out to either of us.

I pass by Cam again on my way out of school.

"Any luck?" I ask nonchalantly.

Cam is already on his phone. He looks up, grinning. "As a matter of fact, I just now received an application. Thanks for the good luck!"

My mouth gapes open. I scramble for my own phone so I can check my messages.

"Well—ha!" I say loudly. "Because I just got a new applicant too."

"Good for you," Cam says. I can tell he doesn't mean it.

I quickly read the text.

Good afternoon. We have been made aware of your "treasure finding" notice. Please see the information at the link below and fill out an application form to be considered for authorization by the City of San Francisco. Your notice has been removed until completion of authorization.

An application form?

I click the link, and it takes me to the San Francisco Recreation and Park Department's website. The page I've landed on is for permit applications, specifically a section titled "Landscaping and Maintenance Permit." The section lists several requirements:

- Fill out an online application.
- Include the exact location for landscape maintenance proposal with latitudinal and longitudinal coordinates.
- Receive official authorization from the department.
- Contact the designated Park team member on the authorized date.
- Attend a mandatory Nature Safety course before proposed landscaping alterations.

The real meaning behind the text message and website link slowly becomes clear. This is a cease-and-desist notice from the city. Or at least a cease-and-desist-unless-you-do-things-our-way-and-we-say-it's-okay notice. But either way, there's zero chance of me being able to run into the park and dig up the treasure now. The Park Department will be on the lookout for anyone with a shovel. Heck, they wouldn't even have to go on a manhunt for me if I tried to be sneaky about it. They already have my freaking phone number thanks to my flyer!

From Cam's silence across the walkway, I'm guessing the exact same message has landed in his inbox. I wait for him to finish reading and look up from his phone.

"Are you happy now?" I ask him.

He shakes his head. "What are you talking about?"

"It was your brilliant idea to go around advertising your plans to dig up the city in the first place."

"Yeah, and it was your brilliant idea to copy it!" he says. "The city probably thinks there's an epidemic of treasure hunters now because of you."

"Because of me? You're the one who put up a PUBLIC NOTICE, Cam!"

He rolls his eyes and turns away.

I stand there, the link still open, considering.

"You're not going to be able to dig now," I say to Cam's back. "Not without getting permission first."

He looks over his shoulder at me. "Same applies to you."

"Right," I say.

I crane my neck and see the westbound Judah train approaching. I can catch the next bus to the Legion of Honor. From there, all I have to do is walk the golf course until I see the same hill from the photo. Golf flag at the top. Boulder to the left. I could have the coordinates within an hour. I could have my application to the Park Department in before dark.

I watch the train until it's right about to pull up to the stop across the street. I'm closer to it than Cam is. I'm not faster than him, but I am closer. And at this point, the one thing I've learned from Cam's tactics is that the only surefire way to get ahead is to take whatever shortcuts you can get.

I sigh and make the most disappointed *tsk* sound I can manage.

"Thanks for ruining this entire thing," I say.

I shuffle down the rest of the walkway until I'm out of his sight, then immediately sprint down the block and catch the train just before it leaves. I hop inside and sit down, then take my phone out to click open the permit application from the Park website.

I may not have Cam on my side anymore. Or Sunny. Or Gabriel. Or Julia. But I still have this hunt. And I am not letting it go for anything.

I am going to find that treasure first.

CHAPTER THIRTY-FOUR

In the summer before ninth grade, Cam's mom scooped me for a family trip to the Santa Cruz boardwalk. Somehow Cam convinced me to ride the Whirlpool of Death, a roller coaster that makes three full-circle loops.

"We're going to get stuck," I had told him as we strapped ourselves in. "The power's going to shut off at the worst possible moment, and we're going to be trapped on this thing while we're upside down."

But Cam said that wasn't possible because of something called kinetic energy. Apparently, roller coasters are designed to move through those loops with or without power. They only need power to get up the steepest hills. The rest is just physics.

When I ran away from Cam and hopped the Judah train, I figured the treasure hunt had the same kind of thing. *Kinetic energy*. That betraying the yearbook crew and racing ahead of Cam would be totally fine, because as soon as I found the treasure, everything would be okay. I could deal with all the consequences of my admittedly questionable actions while holding on to an actual piece of hidden San Francisco history.

I didn't think I would get stuck in the middle of a loop on the way.

It turns out, applying for a dig permit from the San Francisco Recreation and Park Department does *not* have kinetic energy. It has the opposite of kinetic energy. While I've waited for my dig to get approved over the last two weeks, I've had to watch Gabriel, Julia, and Sunny avoid me at every turn in the hallways. I've had to trade silent death glares with Cam while we've both been abnormally tight-lipped with each other. I thought I knew what it was like to be a loner before. I thought I had been mostly on my own since Cam left me. But that wasn't true. I didn't realize I had made new real friends until those new friends also disappeared. This really is what it's like to be stuck while completely upside down.

I check my watch again for the Recreation and Park ranger to finally lead me on the Nature Safety course and let me dig my hole. I'm waiting directly outside the Legion of Honor museum. I've visited the museum—or more so the golf course surrounding it—almost every day since submitting my application. Luckily, the place I want to dig is totally open, totally undisturbed. Aside from a random pile of sticks I found during one of the visits, there hasn't been a single sign of anyone else dropping in. I guess the permit requirement must have scared Cam off entirely.

Finally, a small vehicle comes rumbling over the hill. It looks like the byproduct of a pickup truck and a golf cart mating in the wild. A woman with long braided hair steps out of the minitruck/golf cart. She's holding a clipboard with two thick manuals stacked on top. She hands one of the manuals to me.

She looks around. "Waiting on one more."

"No we're not," I say. "I don't have a partner. It's just me."

Only then does it occur to me that she didn't say it as a question.

"Sorry!" someone yells.

I turn just in time to see Cam running up the last of the path. He's carrying a full-sized shovel over his head. "Bus was late."

I stare at him. "No. Absolutely not."

He stops and looks back at me. "What are you doing here?"

"My permit application was accepted."

He shakes his head. "Uh, no. *My* permit application was accepted."

The Park official eyes us back and forth. She lifts the other hefty manual and hands it to Cam.

"Actually, you two are lucky you both submitted an application. We don't usually accept any alterations to our parks. But with multiple requests, the department was concerned about managing unauthorized digs. So they've agreed on the condition of a single alteration."

Cam and I stand there stupidly.

"Excuse me," I say. *"A single alteration?"*

"One hole," the official clarifies.

Cam looks at me. "You didn't even bring a shovel," he says.

I point to the roller bag by my side. "I brought a whole set of gardening tools. Which includes trowels."

"But no shovels." He looks back to the official. "I feel like only people with actual shovels should get to dig."

She sighs and writes something down on her clipboard. Great—we're already annoying her.

"You get one hole," she says again. "I'm sure your combined shovel and gardening kit will suffice."

I don't love the way she said "gardening kit."

She asks us to leave all tools in her vehicle and open our manuals to page four. From there, we take off on foot in between the trees.

It's funny that this is called a Nature Safety course, which would seem to suggest staying safe while out in nature. But really, it's a course about keeping their nature safe from us. The "safety" isn't our safety but the park's. Any plant life will need to be cleared by an official before disturbance. If we encounter a PVC pipe, we are to stop digging immediately, as it protects the irrigation lines. If we encounter any signs of animal life, we are to stop digging immediately. If we encounter any signs of archeological significance, we are to stop digging immediately.

Cam raises his hand. "But what if we're specifically out here to dig up something of archeological significance?"

The Park official squints at a line on our forms. "The applications specified a burial date of 1983."

"Correct," I say.

She waves her hand dismissively. "That's not something we would deem significant."

Cam and I both turn to each other and share a combined look of exasperation.

"The treasure was buried by Gilbert Baker," I say. "He invented and created the first LGBTQ+ rainbow flag. He's a pretty significant figure."

"Is that right?" the official asks. She looks the slightest bit intrigued. "Is that what's supposed to be buried? The first flag?"

Cam and I both laugh.

"No," Cam says. "The first flag was humongous. Yards and yards of fabric. But Gilbert hid seven treasures to celebrate gay icons around the country. Two of the treasures have already been found."

The official does a small double take. "Really?"

"Really," I say. "One in Grand Rapids, Minnesota, and one in New York City. And San Francisco's is supposed to be the big one."

"Huh." She scratches the back of her head and flips through the last two pages on her clipboard. "Well . . . I think that about covers it for the Nature Safety course. Are you both ready to dig?"

Cam looks over at me. "Don't we have to agree on the same place first?"

"You already did," the woman says. She holds up a photo of my hill, but this photo was taken more recently. As I lean in closer to the photo, I see the pile of sticks I came across the other day. Except here they've specifically been arranged to form an X.

I look over at Cam. "You did this?"

He shrugs and nods. I want to be annoyed, but I can't help cracking a smile. "Now look who's the ex marking the spot," I say.

Cam smiles, frozen for a moment. I wonder if he remembers saying the same thing to me, back when we were kneeling in front of the pipe in the Chong-Moon Lee Center.

But then Cam blinks, and suddenly the smile's gone. He heads to the minitruck and grabs his shovel while I hoist my roller bag up and out of the truck bed. It clanks loudly as I drag it over the dirt path toward the hill. Cam carries his shovel up ahead.

He looks back at me. "You sure that thing is supposed to go off-roading?"

"Obviously not," I groan.

Cam sighs and swings the shovel down next to him. He offers it to me. I take hold of it tentatively.

"What is this? Am I in charge of digging now?"

"Obviously not," Cam says, mimicking my voice. He picks up my roller bag by the handle and hoists it the rest of the way across the golfing green. I can hear the things inside shift and clatter, but Cam doesn't complain about the weight even once.

We reach the base of the hill. Cam drops my bag and climbs up to the pile of sticks he placed along the hillside. He pulls out a printed photo from his pocket and holds it against the backdrop. I set down his shovel and scramble up next to him.

"What's that?" I ask.

"Printout," he says. "From the microfilm reader."

"You went back to the library?"

Cam lowers the photo and looks at me. "Oh, come on, like you didn't?"

I swallow. "I did. I just figured you would be too busy to go there again."

His jaw tenses. "I *told* you, I like research too. You just don't listen to me."

"Yes I do! You're the one—"

The Park official claps her hands from the base. We both jump and turn to her.

"You have one hour!" she calls to us.

Cam and I nod briefly and head back for our tools. I unzip my suitcase and pull on my gardening gloves. Cam moves the sticks aside and tips his shovel into the ground.

"You're sure about this?" I ask.

"Oh, shut up, Ivy."

He chops up and down through the grass, creating a two-foot-by-two-foot square. We set the sod carefully to one side, then bring a plastic tarp next to the gaping hole we've just made in the ground. From there, Cam's in charge of moving each shovel-load of dirt. He grabs as much as he can, then shifts so I can come in and break up the packed earth with one of my trowels. We actually make a ton of progress using this method in the first twenty minutes, to the point where even the Park official has abandoned her camp chair to sit near us and point out anything that looks remotely interesting.

Then, forty minutes in, we hit a wall.

Not a *wall* wall. But a level of dirt so horribly, densely packed that it may as well be a wall.

Cam shifts the loose soil and I keep chipping away, but we go from moving full shovel-loads to handfuls, and then to the equivalent of dirt crumbs. I only manage a single scrape on my last turn. When Cam approaches, he doesn't even try to move the loose soil away.

Instead, he tosses his shovel aside and climbs directly into the hole. He tucks his arms and legs in. Only the top of his head pokes out.

"What are you doing?" I ask.

My hands ache and we've found absolutely nothing, but there's still a firm countdown on the clock. According to the official's watch, we have less than fifteen minutes to dig.

Cam rubs his hands over his thighs.

"It's not here."

"Yes it is," I say. "We can't give up now. We are literally ten minutes away—"

"Away from making a slightly deeper hole," Cam finishes. He shakes his head, resigned. "But it's just not here."

I let my trowel fall onto the grass. "Well, who made you boss, Cam? When did we decide that because you're the one who found the book, you get to call all the shots?"

He gazes up at me, pondering.

"You know what?" he says slowly. "I am so done with this argument."

"Well, so am I!"

"You're not, though." Cam climbs out of the hole and stands in front of me. "Because you bring it up every other second. Which one of us gets to be in charge. Which one of us deserves the treasure more. I brought it to you to *share* it with you, you idiot. I brought it to you because I liked you and I wanted to share something special with you. But from day one, all you have cared about is taking over. *You're* the one who wanted to have some big talk about the title before we could even crack the book open!"

He makes a little squeaky voice. "'Oh, *Gay Treasures*, what does that mean? Are you gay, are you gay? You have to be gay to read *Gay Treasures* because I said so.'"

"I never said that," I say angrily.

"You said it all the damn time!" Cam yells. "You thought only *you* deserved to do the hunt because you were the one who came out first. I didn't want to talk about being queer because I was still figuring out what being queer even meant for me!"

I stare at him.

"And you," he says, motioning to me. "You kept making it worse, kept making it harder for me to figure out! Every time I tried to bring up something about *us*, you kept turning it into *you*. You made being gay your entire identity."

"Holy shit," I say. "I cannot believe you're shaming me for being gay right now."

"I'm not shaming you! I'm trying to explain this concept to you, because even now, years later, you're so freaking thick that you're still not getting it. I liked you, Ivy. I like you."

My teeth are practically chattering. My legs are shaking.

"Why the hell do you think I first came out as a lesbian?" I whisper. "I was trying to tell you I liked you too."

Cam stares at me. "But I'm not a girl."

"Obviously!" I throw my arms out. "But how was I supposed to know that two years ago? You said *nothing* to me. You kissed me and then ghosted me for an entire year! What the hell was I supposed to take away from that moment, Cam?"

He nods, head bobbing as he thinks. Then he turns and

looks directly into my eyes. "That you didn't know me," he says. "Not really. That's the heartbreaker for both of us, isn't it?"

"Time!" the Park official calls out.

Cam picks up his shovel and puts back the first load of dirt.

"Let's just be done with this, once and for all," he says. He sounds so worn and exhausted. "We tried our best, but it didn't work out. End of story."

CHAPTER THIRTY-FIVE

There is something about Cam that has always made me put my guard up.

Maybe it's his confidence. The way he seems to stride through life so smoothly. He gives out smiles like they cost him nothing, even though receiving one feels like winning the lottery. There's such an imbalance with him. You get the feeling that you could come and go and his life would stay more or less the same. But for you, his choices mean everything. His absence would be, has been, is still—even now—devastating. There's so much to lose, liking a person like that.

And I have always been terrified of losing.

The second the sod is replaced on top of our dig spot, Cam picks up his shovel and walks back out the way we came, around the hill and through the trees. The Park official and I watch him go. She turns to me once he's out of sight.

"Tough break," she says consolingly. "For what it's worth, I was really hoping you would find something."

She hands me a business card. "My email address is on the bottom, right here. I'd be interested to know more about this treasure hunt. Sometimes we do little exhibits inside McLaren Lodge at Golden Gate Park. Maybe see if you want to put something together."

"Okay," I say, taking the card. Even though, at the moment, I have no real intention of going home and making some stupid poster board exhibit. I can't treat the hunt like a kid treats a science fair project about honeybees. It's way too personal for that.

I wish I could leave my suitcase behind, dump it in a ditch somewhere, throw it off the edge of the cliffside and into the ocean. But technically, these are Mom's gardening tools, not mine, so instead I have to do the stupidest walk of shame ever and drag it back onto the city bus.

I get home and kick the bag into the side yard, then go upstairs to shower. I want to curl up in my bed and hide away there forever, forget that the treasure hunt, that me and Cam, ever happened. But I can't even look up at the ceiling without picturing the same view of it through Cam's hair. His hands on my waist. His heart beating so fast against mine.

What do you want?

"No," I whisper, sitting up. I can't replay that memory. It took forever to get the first kiss from the park out of my head.

I pull on my oversized gray denim jacket and slump out of the apartment. It would be nice to go nowhere—a black hole in the space-time continuum that can just suck me up. I pause, thinking. I don't know of any black holes, but I do have a spot that might work.

The sidewalk slopes down through the entrance to Golden Gate Park. I take the familiar path winding between the highway and the fields, across the width of the park, to Lloyd Lake. I can see the Portals of the Past in the distance, looming over its own reflection in the water. The bushes around the portico are filling in with the sweet-smelling flowers of late spring. I brush past them, thinking of when I used to pluck the petals off fallen flowers as a little girl. I pick a flower off the stone steps now, pulling on its petals absently. He loves me, he loves me not. He loves me, he loves me not.

Not, the last petal says definitively. Ouch.

I poke my head through the entryway of the portal and look over at our tree. The large branch extends out to me like an open hand. I briefly consider climbing up onto the branch, but that was always Cam's spot, not mine. Instead, I sit right where I am, pressing my back against one end of the doorway and pushing my feet against the other side. I look down into the lake and see a version of myself reflected in the water. The image is murky and unclear.

"Gabriel could fix that," I say to myself. And despite the stupidity of that statement, it makes me smile. I imagine Gabriel smoothing the lake like paper, dialing in contrast, brightness, definition. Like every view of the world could be a picture for him to translate and make better.

As I look into the lake, it hits me: I wish Gabriel were here now. I wish any of my new friends—well, my old friends—my new-old friends were here to distract me from myself. I feel antsy in my own body. Like I've accidentally left the stove on somewhere in my head, and I don't know how to go in and turn it off.

I lean into the cool stone and close my eyes. If Julia were here, would she see magic in this? Sitting inside a doorway to the past? I want magic to exist so, so badly in this moment. I want to slip right through the Portals of the Past and be able to travel back in time.

I think about when I stood next to Sunny in front of the kintsugi display at the Asian Art Museum. Actually, if I could have any sort of magic, I'd want to spin gold out of nothing, Rumpelstiltskin-style, then use it to bond every relationship I've shattered back together.

A magical kintsugi to fix my own life.

I picture all the broken fragments in my head. When I think about my friendship with Gabriel, or Julia, or even Sunny, the pieces are bigger. It's like a bowl cracked in two. If I can just figure out the right thing to do, the right words to say, I can fix those cracks. The pieces already line up.

With Cam, it's a lot more complicated.

Putting the pieces of our friendship together feels more like doing a tricky jigsaw puzzle. There's the book, the hunt, the first kiss, and then the second. There's the day I came out to Cam. And the day he came out to everyone. The memories all feel barbed and untouchable.

I try to sort through them anyway.

I want to decode them, to understand why Cam keeps

pulling me in and pushing me away. He made that wanted poster for me to see; I just know it. But he's also the one who said getting close to me was a mistake. Why? What do I keep doing that drives him away, over and over? Why do we keep circling each other and repeating the past?

I think about Cam lying in my bed next to me. I can feel his skin, hot and clammy, under my palm as it skates across his stomach. His heart thrums against my ear. I whisper into his neck.

Cameron.

I open my eyes.

"Oh my God." I clap a hand over my mouth.

I don't think Cam has gone by "Cameron" since he came out. But that's what I said, with my hand under his shirt, inching dangerously close to his chest.

He thinks I was misgendering him.

That's why he stood up and said I didn't know him. He meant that I didn't know *him*.

The rest of the pieces start finding one another, start fitting into place finally. All this time I thought Cam was teasing me with his whole cool-guy routine, acting like a totally different person from the friend I first fell in love with. When really, he's just been trying to make sure I see him as a guy, full stop.

And the thing is . . . I do like Cam as a guy. I'm *attracted* to him as a guy. Which, I guess, technically means I'm pansexual.

"I'm pansexual," I say out loud to the lake. My reflection

smiles back up at me, as though she's saying, *Duh. Of course you are.*

I like that word for me. I like how it feels when I try it on. Maybe not as much as I loved identifying as a lesbian, but I'll get there with time. But Cam doesn't know all that yet. As far as he knows, I still think of myself as a lesbian. Which must be confusing as hell to him, considering that we've now made out twice, and he is very much *not* a girl.

My mind suddenly starts playing memories of us together like a highlight reel. Cam holding out his hand for a dance at the park. Cam waiting for me to find him in the library. Cam somersaulting into my room, holding *Gay Treasures* close against his chest.

It was an invitation. The whole treasure hunt was an invitation. This was always his adventure to share, not mine to steal.

Son of a bitch, I think.

He really is the Ben Gates of this whole scenario. And *I'm* his Ian.

A silhouette steps into the reflection on the water. I look away, tucking my head over my shoulder. People drop by this area from time to time—the Portals monument isn't a huge, touristy thing, but it's one of those hidden gems of the city that locals know about. Architecturally, it's sort of a marvel, having survived an earthquake that took out the rest of an entire neighborhood. Mom was the first person to bring me here, when I was really little.

"Ivy?"

I twist my head toward the lake. "Mom?"

She's standing there in a gray pantsuit, stunned, holding a to-go cup of coffee.

"I thought you were working today," I say.

"I was." She blinks at me a moment, then sits on the top step, right next to me. "I come here a lot, right after work."

She points at a bench just past the monument, curving around the west end of the lake.

I laugh. "I come here a lot too. After school." I point through the doorway, to the tree and the hillside behind the Portals.

Mom stares at the tree, contemplative. "Hmm."

"What is it?"

She shakes her head. "Oh, that's . . . I don't know. I think I might've met your father there."

I sit up straight, shoulder blades no longer touching the doorway.

"WHAT?"

Mom gives me a brief side-glance. "What, you thought you were the immaculate conception?"

"No, but— You never talk about that. Him or whatever."

"I don't," Mom says wistfully. She looks over at her bench. As I look at it too, I realize it's set at the perfect angle to see the branches of my tree through the Portals doorway.

"You don't talk about it with me," I say, understanding. "You just think about it on your own."

Mom says nothing.

"Does it help?" I ask. "To keep it all to yourself?"

"What do you think?" Mom says shrewdly.

What *do* I think? Every time I've sat with my mom at a Chez Moi lunch, it felt like we were both stepping into the future. That she and I got to live vicariously through fantasies unburdened by the past. But now I know that, outside of those lunches, we've each come back here on our own. We've both stared at the same tree tied to a personal history we can't really escape from, no matter how hard we try. It makes me think of a dog trying to get away from something that's tied to its own leg. There's no outrunning what anchors us down. The only way to actually escape it is to look right at it, to understand it.

And maybe, hopefully, untangle it.

I turn to my mom. "I'm not going to Paris," I say.

She takes a sip of her coffee. "They said no?"

"I'm not applying." I squint at her. "But not because the yearbook project doesn't count as art. It is real art, Mom. Maybe you were right, and maybe it wasn't really my story to tell. But it *is* an important story. Whether you're open-minded enough to see that or not."

Mom stares at me. Her shock only fuels me further.

"You know, I've made my whole life into a stupid competition, because I always felt like you and I were in one," I say, pointing between the two of us. "I wanted to be as good as you. I wanted to do something that would make you proud of me. But you know what? I am practical, like you. And that's great! It's a strength, not a weakness! And if you weren't so insecure about yourself, you would see how great I am, just the way I am.

"Maybe I'll be an artist someday, and maybe I won't," I say finally, "but it doesn't matter what I choose to do. You should have been proud of me the whole time. And it sucks that you haven't been, but that's not my problem. It's yours."

I stand and shake my head at my mom. She continues to gape at me over her coffee. I wait to see if she'll find the right words to say, but she doesn't. She doesn't have them.

As I look at my mom I realize that this right here—her sitting on that bench, thinking of what her life could have been, instead of being happy with what her life is now—*this* is what it looks like to be stuck in the past. And I don't want to be stuck in mine for one minute longer.

I walk back down the steps.

CHAPTER THIRTY-SIX

YEARBOOK CREW

HARVEY'S PARTY

TREASURE ISLAND HOES

DOROTHY AND FRIENDS

Gabriel has renamed the group chat so many times that it takes me a while to find it on my phone. When I scroll down in my messages, I see the current title is listed as LIAR AND BRIMSTONE. Which is both quite damning and, if I'm being honest, not really as on brand as the other group names.

Me: Guessing I'm the liar here?

Me: Is the designated liar at least permitted to say sorry to everyone? In person?

Gabriel: . . .

Gabriel: Sry, just came here from the BRIMSTONE ONLY chat. We will accept apologies on the condition that they are accompanied by copious gifts.

Sunny: (In caffeinated liquid form.)

Gabriel: Right, sorry! Copious gifts in caffeinated liquid form. And/or Chappell Roan concert tickets. Or quality jewelry. Or notebooks! Julia said notebooks.

I check the time. I have a few more hours until all the shops close down for the evening.

Me: Understood. Tomorrow morning okay? Or no because it's the Lord's day?

Gabriel: . . .

Gabriel: Tomorrow works. God will understand. (BIG Chappell Roan fan.)

Me: You know I'm not going to have Chappell Roan tickets, right?

Sunny: FOR THE LOVE OF CHAPPELL ROAN, JUST BRING US SOME FUCKING COFFEE, IVY.

I'm waiting for everyone by the school's side door the next morning. Sunny turns the corner first. She slows down the moment she sees it's just me standing there. I watch her go from a brisk stride to slumped over, shuffling the rest of the way across the street.

"Sorry no one else is here yet," I say. I rotate the coffee tray so her drink is facing out. "You don't have to talk to me while we wait."

"I won't," Sunny says curtly. She takes a sip, looking away. She turns back and points at my backpack. "What did you bring?"

"Copious gifts, of course."

Sunny rolls her eyes. I catch the slightest hint of a smile, but I don't linger on it. Gabriel and Julia show up at the same time around the corner.

"Thank you," Gabriel says as they each pluck their usual orders from the tray.

"Where's yours?" Julia asks.

I shrug. "Gifts are for the Brimstone Only group chat today. But there's more. Let's go inside."

Hands now free, I unlock the door and hold it open as Sunny, Julia, then Gabriel tromp down the stairs to the Bat Cave.

Sunny sinks into her seat, then takes an enormous gulp of coffee. She wipes her mouth with the back of her hand. "I assume you're here to show us the treasure?"

Julia leans forward in her chair.

"No," I say. "We didn't— Cam and I didn't find it. Our theory was wrong."

"So, that's it, then?" Gabriel asks. "You're done?"

I picture Cam's face at our dig spot. The way he looked as he walked away from the hill. Like all the light was taken right out of him. All the magic of the hunt was used up.

"Yeah. We're . . . done."

I snap out of the memory and reach into my backpack, mentally queuing up the speech I wrote last night. "I totally wrecked this adventure for everyone and I'm so, so sorry. Each of you deserves an adventure that's all your own."

Sunny pulls a face. "Okay, Chuck E. Cheeseball. Cheers to that. Thanks for the coffee." She starts to get up.

"No, wait!"

I fumble inside my backpack until I find the small pink envelope. I pull it out and hand it to Sunny.

She holds the edge of the envelope hesitantly. "What's this?"

"AGB," I say.

"What's AGB?"

"Open it and find out."

Sunny flips the top open and pulls out a small note.

"Remember that girl at the front desk of the Chong-Moon Lee Center? Her name's Beiye, and she's part of this really cool group: Asian and Gay in the Bay. Mr. Wong was one of the original founders, but it's really huge now, apparently. Lots of clubs and social events and stuff."

I tap the phone number at the bottom of the note. "Not that you have to be interested," I add, "but I think Beiye was sort of hoping you would text her too."

Gabriel lets out a low wolf whistle.

Sunny reads the note to herself. She swallows and folds the flap back down, then looks up at me. Her expression is unreadable. "Why did you do this?"

"Because you deserve to be at the center of things," I say. "And not always feel like an outsider. Plus . . . Beiye is very hot. I basically *had* to let her add her number when she asked."

Gabriel claps his hands. "My turn, my turn! I want a hot date!"

I turn to him and smile. "Okay, so here's the thing about your date. I don't have a specific person *yet*. But picture an absolutely gorgeous European guy or girl or nonbinary hottie sitting across a café table from you in Paris."

"Paris?!" Gabriel leaps out of his chair. "You got me a ticket to Paris?"

"What? You can't get just one person a ticket to Paris!" Sunny cries. "What the hell is this?"

I hold up a hand. "Wait! Wait. Calm down. This *might* be a ticket to Paris; I'm not sure. I had wanted it to be my ticket earlier, when we started this whole thing." I pull out a guide to the Paris College of Art. "I was going to submit our yearbook as a portfolio for an art program in Paris. But I've thought a lot about it, and the thing is, *you're* the one who made this yearbook truly special, Gabriel. I realized that I want to tell stories about the past and the present. I don't necessarily want to create visual art out of it. You're the visual artist. You deserve to be in this program. And our yearbook, your yearbook, would make an amazing application."

I hand the guide to Gabriel. He takes hold of the pamphlet,

cradling it gently, like I've given him an actual, real-life treasure. It reminds me a lot of the way Cam held *Gay Treasures* when he first showed it to me.

"Thank you," he says. His voice is unusually soft.

I turn to Julia and smile. "New notebook, right?"

I pull out a hardback journal covered with archival linen and embossed in gold foil. Julia's eyes widen as she sees the intricate design. She opens her hand.

"Thank—"

"Ah, no." I stop her. "Not yet. You also need something to write about."

I remove the last item from my bag, a manila file bulging with loose papers.

"I'm sorry I couldn't get another copy of *Gay Treasures*," I say. "But I went back to that message board online and found and printed every scan of the book that I came across. There were seven treasures hidden. That means there are still at least four other hunts out there to complete. You were right— these *are* magical. And you're the perfect person to make a fairy-tale treasure come to life. You know how to make magic real, Julia."

I hand her the notebook and file stacked together.

"Well, there you go. Coffee and gifts. So, now, here's my official apology."

Gabriel, Julia, and Sunny stare up at me.

"I messed up—big-time. But the truth is, I messed up way before I went back to the history center with Cam. I shouldn't have been working on the hunt in the first place without Cam's permission. I shouldn't have pulled you in and pushed him out, then pulled him back in and pushed you guys out. This was always his thing, and I was petty, and I wanted to beat him at it. I thought if I found the treasure and used it for my application to Paris . . . I could finally get away from thinking about the time when he and I used to be friends. But that's not how the past works, is it?"

Julia smiles.

"We're supposed to learn from the past," I say. "Like, we have to first know it, so we can understand it. I think that's why Gilbert Baker made this hunt. And it's funny, because I did learn a lot about Harvey and San Francisco . . . but I was also using the whole thing as a distraction. I didn't want to look into my own past. But I'm doing that now."

I hear a small snort from one of the chairs. Gabriel and Sunny both turn toward Julia, who is nearly shaking as she presses a balled-up fist against her mouth.

"Are you laughing or crying?" I ask.

"I'm sorry." Julia takes her hand away and dabs at her eyes. "I'm sorry. I was laughing, because—well—you're totally doing the Wizard of Oz thing right now."

"I'm . . . what?"

Julia sniffs, beaming. She holds up the file and notebook I've just given her. "This is going to give me the courage to find my own magic, right?"

I nod, hesitant. "Yes . . ."

"And you didn't exactly hand Gabriel a diploma, but you did just hand him a college guide. And Sunny—"

Gabriel gasps and brings his hands to either cheek. "You gave her that girl's number! Like a heart for the Tin Man!"

Sunny cackles. She waves the note in the air. "Can you hear that? It's ticking!"

"Hang on," I say, folding my arms. "So, I'm the Wizard, then? Isn't he the bad guy?"

"Kind of," Gabriel says. "Depending on your perspective."

I groan and plop down into my own chair. "Oh my God. I *am* the Wizard. How am I both Ian and the Wizard?"

"Just lucky, I guess," Julia says, still clearly amused. She gives me a hug, wrapping her arms around both me and the chair. "For the record, if I do one of these new hunts, I definitely want your help. All of your help."

Gabriel joins the group hug. "Shovels and Hoes forever," he says into our shoulders.

I pull back and look at him. "Excuse me?"

He holds up his phone screen. "Oh, that's the new name of our group chat. I'm going to change it now."

"Maybe don't put our group name in your application to Paris," I say.

"I won't!" he says, mock offended.

I grin. Something about his voice makes me know, right then, that he's really going to apply. My heart hurts as it swells, like a sore muscle flexing.

It's different from the kind of pain I've felt with Cam over the last two years. There's the kind of pain you get from pressing on a bruise or accidentally rubbing hand sanitizer over a paper cut. It's sharp and acidic, something to breathe through, to get over, to move beyond and never look back. As I look at Gabriel and Julia and Sunny in front of me now, I feel the kind of pain I want to get better at. I want to keep caring about people like this. I want to be cared for by people. Even if we'll hurt each other sometimes. I want to keep trying again and again.

Julia tucks the files into her backpack. Gabriel hugs the brochure to his chest.

"You know," he says. "There's a saying about treasure hunts. 'Even if you don't find gold, the real treasure—' "

Sunny turns to him. "Don't you dare," she growls. "I cannot handle that level of corniness right now."

But Gabriel just winks at Sunny. " 'The *real* treasure is—' "

Sunny claps a hand over Gabriel's mouth and muffles his voice. Julia and I grin at each other. We have to finish the corny quote for him.

" 'The friends you make along the way!' "

CHAPTER THIRTY-SEVEN

After a few more group hugs, Julia and Gabriel tromp up the stairs together, arm in arm. They're acting like the Lion and the Scarecrow from *The Wizard of Oz*, singing their own version of the main song from the movie.

"We're off, thanks to the Wizard! The Wonderful Wizard of Ozzzzzz!"

I shake my head and smile faintly as I listen to their voices fade away into the stairwell. Finally, it's quiet in the Bat Cave again. I turn to Sunny, who's been unusually restrained during the impromptu show tune exit.

"Do you want to go for a walk?" I ask her.

Sunny sighs. She looks at me and bites her bottom lip. It's funny to recognize that she looks extremely attractive right now and also realize in this moment that I'm not personally attracted to her. I've never really thought about the difference before. But there is a difference.

"Sure," she says. "Why not?"

I lock up the school behind us, and we lean into the tilted

streets, letting gravity lead us gently down to Golden Gate Park. The wind can't quite decide whether it wants to be refreshing and breezy or tip into blustering. But the sun peeks out from the clouds at little moments, and Sutro Tower waves hello between the sporadic sheets of fog, and it feels like the most perfect day I can imagine.

"Strawberry Hill?" I ask after we cross Irving and step under the tree-lined canopy.

Sunny laughs. "No freaking way. I'm not in hiking gear."

"Okay, then." I point up ahead. "Shakespeare Garden?"

"That I can do."

We walk under the delicate arched wrought-iron sign and past the sundial. Sunny finds a bench in the shade. She slides onto one side of the bench, leaving the other side open. I sit down next to her. Sunny shifts and faces me as soon as I've sat down.

"I've kind of wanted to tell you something," she says carefully. "Over the last few weeks, I mean."

"Oh," I say, a bit surprised. I had thought I was going to have to be the one to dive into this subject. But I'm glad Sunny's bringing it up. It's good that she's leading this conversation. "Okay. Yeah, tell me."

"Don't get mad."

"I won't be mad," I say.

"You might get mad."

"*Sunny*. Just tell me!"

She nods. "You're right. So, here's the thing: The day I saw you dancing with Cam, I was pissed."

"Rightly so," I say quickly. "I shouldn't have lied to you and the group. I should have been talking to you that day after school about what you had told me—"

Sunny holds up a finger to get me to stop talking. "But here's the thing, Ivy: When I saw you two together, I also felt this weird sort of relief."

Relief? I swallow and wait for Sunny to keep going.

"After we voted Cam out of the group, and I chased you upstairs and said I had feelings for you . . . Well, I regretted it almost immediately. I knew I had messed things up somehow."

"With our friendship," I offer.

Sunny shakes her head. "No. It was more like I had the wrong translation. I've never been a part of GSA, Ivy. I've never felt strong enough—or safe enough, really—to champion my sexuality. Like, I've never even let myself think about it the way that you have. But I still remember your poster on the LGBTQ+ acronym. And how you wrote about why the acronym starts with the letter *L*."

"You remember that?" I ask.

Sunny gives me a smirk. "I mean, they hung it up in the main part of the hallway. I couldn't avoid it. But it stuck with me, you know? Like it was a clue to figuring myself out. And this last month . . . it made me realize, I don't have a crush on you, specifically. But I do look up to you. I like how proud you are about your identity. And . . . yeah, when I ran upstairs after you, what I really should have said was 'I think I'm a lesbian.' Because, well, I am."

She looks down into her lap shyly.

I leap up from the bench. I can barely contain myself.

"Sunny," I say. "Sunny! That. Is. AMAZING!"

She looks up and smiles. "Yeah?"

"Hell yeah! The lesbians are lucky to have you!" I cup one hand to my ear. "I think I hear Hayley Kiyoko rejoicing at this very moment."

Sunny laughs and swats my leg. I sit back down next to her. We're grinning at each other at first. Then each of our smiles softens.

"I don't think you're a lesbian, though," Sunny says.

"No," I say in agreement. "I'm not. I'll have to bring you all my gorgeous lesbian flag décor while I redecorate my room with colors from the pansexual flag. Although . . . I did come across a *Reductress* article last week titled 'Five Doc Marten Looks That Say, "I'm Attracted to All Women and Two Men,"' and that feels even more accurate at the moment."

Sunny nods approvingly. "You do rock some very sexy Doc Marten looks."

"Thank you," I say. I give a silly bow.

The wind blows through the garden like a deep breath, and just like that, we're back to the way things were before. Except we're not, actually. Because now things between us are even better. Sunny and I are friends. We're really, really good friends.

A small tourist group filters under the archway, taking photos of the sign, the sundial, the bust of Shakespeare set inside the stone and brick wall at the far end. I look over at Sunny.

"Maybe we should give up our bench."

"Yeah," Sunny says, "give someone else a turn to have their own sexual-orientation awakening."

We leave the garden and walk back along Seventh Avenue. Sunny tugs me off the sidewalk as we pass by a coffee shop called The Beanery. I wait next to the front sandwich sign, certain that Sunny's off to grab her second (or possibly fifth) cup of coffee for the day. But then she surprises me by pulling my wrist and leading me inside the shop behind her.

"Come on. This round's on me."

We find a small table in the corner, and I wait while Sunny brings our drinks over. She sits across from me, and for a moment it's like I'm back in Lady Business with Rachel. Sunny's so beautiful. She would be a perfect date. But she's my friend. And my mind isn't really here at all with this gorgeous girl— it's fixated on a boy I'm hopelessly crazy about.

Sunny smiles wryly at me, like she knows exactly what I'm thinking.

"So, why didn't you find it?" she asks.

I blink at her.

"The treasure," Sunny goes on. "Why didn't you and Cam find it?"

"Oh." I sit up and take a sip of my coffee. "Well, the clock installation thing was a total bust. Just like you three said it would be."

I think of the inscription over *The Gates of Hell* sculpture, the one *The Three Shades* were all pointing to:

Abandon hope, all ye who enter here.

I should have known right then that the treasure wouldn't

be anywhere near the Legion of Honor museum. How could it? If *The Three Shades* were meant to be a symbol in Gilbert Baker's drawing, they might as well have symbolized the dead opposite of Harvey Milk's legacy.

"We were probably wrong about all of that stuff," I say.

"Naturally," Sunny says. She drinks her coffee and smiles. "But why did you give up?"

I give her a look. "Why do you think?"

Sunny purses her lips like she really is thinking about it. She places her index finger to her mouth in a pause, then points it at me. "Because Cam still thinks you're a lesbian?"

"Oh, right," I say, laughing. "I forgot. This treasure completely hinges on Cam and me figuring out our past and burying the hatchet or whatever."

"Or digging it up," Sunny says. She wiggles her eyebrows knowingly.

I squint at her. "No . . . I'm pretty sure the saying goes that you're supposed to *bury* the hatchet."

"Okay, fine, bury it," she says. "Dig up something better. I meant what I said earlier, about your mind being too cloudy to see the real truth. But maybe that's not Cam's fault. You know what I've noticed about you two whenever you're together?"

Sunny leans across the table. I can't help scooting my drink to one side so I can meet her in this halfway huddle.

"What?" I ask.

"You don't look at yourselves when you're around each other," she says. "Like, of course you're always giving each other these yearning sidelong glances. But whenever you two pass by a mirror or a window reflection, you clam up. You both look down at your feet. It's like you're afraid of what you look like together. As a couple."

I just stare at her.

"And maybe that's what's holding you back," Sunny continues. "That, right there, that's the cloud. You guys started this hunt at one point and now you're here at this new point, but you won't connect the two together. And I think you sort of need to. If you want to finish it."

She stands from the table. I watch as she pulls a small slip of paper from her pocket. It's Beiye's number, I realize.

"Now, if you'll excuse me," Sunny says. "I have a very cool club to look into and a very hot girl to ask out on a date."

I give Sunny a salute. "Bye, Tin Man."

"Oh, you're still the real Tin Man," Sunny calls over her shoulder. "I call Dorothy now and forever."

"Fine," I say, relenting. "Bye, Dorothy."

"Bye, Tin Man!" Sunny shoots me a coy smile. "Hope you get that weird-ass heart of yours fixed soon."

CHAPTER THIRTY-EIGHT

I'm squished into the corner of my room with another flower in my hand. This one's from our side yard, not the park. But I hope it will do the same job, will be my little oracle and tell me what I should do now.

Tell him how I feel.

Let him go for good.

Tell him.

Let him go.

Tell him.

"Let him go." I sigh and drop the now-bare flower stem next to me. "Fine."

I let my head fall back so it's resting on the mattress. There's the ceiling, and there's Cam's curling hair, and he smells so good, and he's kissing me hard, drawing my mouth open and closed like he's coaxing something out of me. And then I have to go and ruin it like a complete dumbass.

I groan and snap my head up. I keep ruining things. Maybe it's best to leave Cam alone for good, like the flower said. Then

I can't hurt him anymore. Then he can find another girl to start over with. And maybe I can start over too.

I study the flower stem a moment, then pick myself up off the floor.

"Screw oracles," I say. "I'm telling him."

I find myself in the mirror across the room and lock onto my reflection. It's not my job to decide what's best for Cam. He can be the one to decide that for himself. I think about what Sunny said at The Beanery. This is about me clearing my own head. This is about my real truth.

The truth is . . . maybe I'm not the exact kind of gay I thought I was two years ago. Maybe I was too chickenshit to tell Cam I liked him directly, so I sidestepped and made the smartest move I could think of at the time: come out as a lesbian with the hope that Cam would put two and two together. *But it's never actually been about being a lesbian*, I realize. It's about liking Cam. It's always been about my feelings for Cam.

Cam has always been himself—goofy and charismatic, eager and sincere. I'm guilty of so many things when it comes to him . . . but calling him Cameron that day in my room doesn't mean I don't know who he really is. It was a miscommunication, not a misgendering. And I would hate for him to walk away from all this thinking we didn't work out because I secretly wanted him to be someone else.

I want *him*, exactly the way he is.

And this time I have to tell him that. To his face.

I start riffling through my things, searching for Harvey's flyer, for Julia's notebook, for the box with the necklace and scroll. They all belong to Cam. I want him to have them, to decide what he wants to do with them. It's time for him to get to hold all the pieces of the puzzle.

I find the flyer and put it on my desk. Julia's notebook goes on top. I open the box to make sure everything's inside: the encrypted poem, the drawing on the scroll, the necklace with the key—

Wait a second.

I bring the oval pendant closer and inspect it. On the left side there's a tiny lump of metal sticking out. It looks almost like . . . a hinge.

"Holy hell."

This isn't just a pendant. It's a locket.

I flip open Julia's notebook and find the last two transcribed lines of the poem:

If you seek the lock and key
You will have to dig down deep

Lock and key. The necklace has both a key and a *locket*.

I shake my head. "Gilbert Baker, you tricksy minx."

I slide a fingernail between the thin layers of metal on the right side of the oval and pop it open, expecting to find another note or maybe even a photo of where to dig. But instead, inside the locket itself is . . . a mirror.

"If you seek the lock and key," I say, studying the locket. "So you need to *see* the lock and key before you know where to dig. But the locket is a mirror. Which means . . . to know where to dig . . . you have to look in . . ."

I lay the necklace down on my desk and pull out the scroll.

But this time I don't look directly at it. I unroll the page in front of my mirror and study its reflection.

Nothing jumps out from the picture at first. It's still the same

woman in the boxy floral dress pointing. The same bear and snake battling the octopus. The clock, the sink, the Shades . . .

The two boys with sailboat hats.

"Golden Gate Bridge," I say.

The craziest idea comes over me. Slowly, I rotate the scroll clockwise, still looking into the mirror. If the sailboat hats are the Golden Gate Bridge, then that clock-shaped fountain on the Greenwich Steps should be . . .

"Here," I say, pointing exactly where the grandfather clock falls in the picture.

The Union monument is just south of the steps, matching up with the drawing of the bear, snake, and octopus perfectly. And there's the Legion of Honor in the northwest corner, where *The Three Shades* are depicted in the corner of the scroll.

I can feel the little hairs rising on the back of my neck. Goose bumps travel down my arms, from my shoulders to where my fingers are now digging into the paper.

"Holy shit." I shake my head.

Gabriel and the others were right. The scroll really *is* a map of San Francisco.

Cam and I just had it backward.

We needed to look in a mirror to see it properly.

I look over at the woman in the floral dress, and suddenly, as if it only appeared in the last ten seconds, I notice it. Within all the flowers roping across her dress is a single strawberry over her rib cage. Exactly where Strawberry Hill is.

The woman *is* the aerial view of Golden Gate Park.

I read through the whole poem again.

Congratulations! You have found
The San Francisco Bonus Round
For of my treasures, far and wide
My home imbues the deepest pride
No added ciphers, codes to break
Ground yourself for what's at stake
Read the map, find the point
Grab the shovel to anoint
If you seek the lock and key
You will have to dig down deep

"Read the map, find the point." I start pacing back and forth across my room. "Find the point. Find the point . . ."

The woman's arms are outstretched, pointing in two different directions. There are two points on the map. So we have to figure out which one is the correct "point." Her right arm points directly at *The Three Shades*. I think of the actual *The Three Shades* sculpture within *The Gates of Hell* at the Legion of Honor museum, and the inscription just below them:

ABANDON HOPE

"It's the wrong way," I tell myself. "*That's* the clue."

I lean closer into the mirror, squinting at the object in the woman's right hand. It's not a mask. Not binoculars, exactly. But maybe some kind of fancy binoculars. I remember seeing them in a movie once.

Opera glasses!

But why would she be holding opera glasses? I mean, she would need them, I guess, to see all the way from Golden Gate Park to the Legion of Honor. But everything on the map is spread out. It has to mean something else. She needs to get a good look at something. She needs a good view, a *great* view, of—

I freeze, completely mid-thought. The next word explodes in my head like a camera flashing. I can barely breathe as I rush over to my desk and flip my laptop open.

San Francisco, I type into the search bar. I click on the maps tab.

I study the north end of the bay, checking over all the landmarks featured in Baker's clues. But the place I really need to be checking isn't marked on Gilbert's map. It falls just outside the boundary. I tilt my head and imagine Golden Gate Park as the long floral dress, superimposing the woman from the drawing onto the map over my screen.

I follow the direction of her left arm as I scroll farther down, moving just south of Golden Gate Park and deeper into my own neighborhood until I see . . .

The exact same stick figure from the locket.

I *knew* I had seen that shape before. I had just never recognized it as a person.

Grandview Park. *A GIANT BTWN STREETS.*

"There it is," I whisper.

The place where Gilbert Baker buried his treasure.

CHAPTER THIRTY-NINE

The stairs in Cam's house creak under my weight as I climb up to his room. His door is slightly ajar, and I can see his figure twisting up and down through the gap. Chin-ups, I'm guessing.

I tilt the stack of things in my arms against my chest for balance and rap my knuckles against the doorframe.

I hear a thump as Cam hops down from the chin-up bar he jammed into his closet frame sometime during freshman year.

"One second!" he calls.

"It's me," I murmur before he can open the door. I don't want him to be completely surprised when he sees me. And, okay, maybe I'm also hoping to avoid whatever facial expression he's making at this exact moment.

If he pauses after the forewarning, it's too short for me to register. He swings his door the rest of the way open.

"Yes?"

"Your mom still loves me."

He raises an eyebrow. "What?"

"She offered me a slice of cinnamon pear pie." I motion with my chin. "Downstairs. Just now. Moms don't do that to people they hate."

"Is that right?" He looks me over warily, then steps to one side.

I walk into his room and am met with a tidal wave of the smell of him. The Old Spice deodorant that smells horrible on every other guy at school, but for some reason, on Cam, crackles like a beach bonfire. Then there's his sandalwood shampoo. His citrus detergent. It all swirls together, mingling but not completely mixed, so I keep catching different notes of him. I take a deep breath, but it does nothing to help me focus.

"Are you okay?" Cam asks.

Of course not, I think. *I'm obsessed with you, and you hate me.*

"Chin-ups," I say instead, which is somehow an even worse response.

Cam looks at the bar over his shoulder. "Oh yeah, sorry. I was working out for a while, so it's probably pretty warm in here."

Steam might actually come out of my ears.

I thrust the pile of treasure hunt stuff—everything I've gathered this spring—toward Cam's chest. He looks down at the bundle in my hands.

"What's this?"

"It's yours," I say. "Take it. Please."

He shakes his head. "I already took my book back. You found these things fair and square."

"Well, that pipe sticking out of the wall was definitely more of a circle," I say, then grimace. "Bad joke. The point is"—I swallow and look up at him—"this was always your hunt. You brought it over as something special to share with me, and I basically ripped it away from you. I'm sorry I have the sharing skills of an only child during their first week at preschool."

He cocks his head. "That's . . . an oddly specific metaphor."

"It was a hard week for me." I push the things slightly closer to him, to the point where he finally brings his hands up to take them.

"Can we talk about something? Unrelated to all this?" I ask.

Cam sighs and sets the things down on his bed. "I don't know, Ivy. I don't think that's such a good idea."

"Or it's a brilliant idea, because all we've ever done until now is shout back and forth over the elephant in the room."

He rubs his neck and looks away. "Look, maybe we're just better off—"

"You're hot," I say. I step to one side to catch his gaze, even though my face feels like it's going to melt completely off my skull.

"You were hot when we were younger too," I explain. "I've always loved your eyes. And I feel like that one time I accidentally got my fingers caught in your hair was my first ever sexual awakening."

He lets out a gruff laugh but won't quite meet my eyes.

"But you're much, much hotter now. Your voice makes my skin vibrate. Every time you wear a sleeveless shirt, like now, for instance, I get really itchy."

A muscle on his bicep flexes involuntarily. My heart leaps into my throat.

"Why are you saying this?" he rasps.

I raise my hands and drop them to my sides. "I don't know, Cam. Because I'm confused. I like you, but I am also queer. I'm pretty sure I'm pansexual, actually. And both those things are important to me. I should've done a better job of explaining what my queerness means for me and, maybe, what it could mean for us."

Cam turns directly to me. "Why didn't you do that before? Explain any of this?"

"Because it was sort of terrifying," I say. "I was scared you would break my heart."

I see a trace of his lopsided smile. "And what exactly do you think you've been doing to me for the last two years?"

"I know." I dip my head. "Well, I didn't know before, technically. But now I know. And I'm sorry."

His hand moves forward, like a robot trying to decide if it has enough juice to jolt to life. He raises it halfway between us, barely grazing my arm with his fingertips. I hold my breath, willing every muscle in me to go completely still so I don't break the spell.

But he freezes up anyway.

"The thing is," he says, stepping back, "you say you like

me now. But I've tried leaning into you, twice. And both times . . ."

"I fucked it up," I say before he can get to it. "I used the wrong name. I touched you without asking you first. That's on me."

"It's not even that," he says quietly. "There's just too much history between us. Too many memories between you and a part of me I don't like to think about right now. It would have been easier if we didn't know each other before. If we could have met after, you know?"

He takes one of my hands in both of his. I sink into the comfort of his skin. It feels so good to have him hold my hand. It feels so good that I can almost make myself forget he's in the process of rejecting me.

I wrinkle my nose so I don't cry.

"I know."

The words are choked and strained, but there they are. He keeps holding on to my hand, and I think for the first time, I finally get the flavor of misery he's been going through. To have someone keep holding on to you even when they really should be letting go. But if both of us don't want to let go, where does that leave us? Does someone really have to walk away just because of things we couldn't help in our own pasts?

I extricate my hand from his.

"Can I just say one more thing?"

Cam gives me a look. "Um, all you ever do is say things, V. But, yeah, fine, go ahead."

I steel myself, knowing this may well be the last opportunity

I have to say the uncomfortable things, the things I don't know how to talk about, before we shut the door on this forever.

" 'Cam' and 'Cameron' are really similar," I say. "Name-wise. And I get it; that was probably the point. But me saying Cameron wasn't actually me thinking, 'Oh yeah, I'm with this girl named Cameron.' I didn't have your gender messed up in my head. I just hadn't realized what the name meant to you. And when I touched under your shirt—"

"Ivy . . ."

"Just wait, please. I'm not trying to convince you about anything when it comes to me. But maybe this can help for your next partner. When I put my hand under your shirt, both times, I had wanted to touch right here."

I lay my own hand, flat, over the center of my chest. My fingers tease the edge of my collarbone. I feel the steady *thump, thump, thump* of my heart in my palm.

Cam stares at my hand for a long time. At first he looks quizzical, like he's not sure if he can believe me. Then his jaw tenses, and his mouth goes taut.

"Shit." He closes his eyes and shakes his head. "So it's me, then. I'm too stuck in the past."

"That's not true. It's not me or you. It's both of us, Cam." I take one of his hands in mine, uncurl his fingers from the clenched fist, and lay his hand where mine was: just under my collarbone. My heart beats faster under him. I want him to feel it as I say what comes next.

"I don't think the past is meant to be left behind. The things that happened back then . . . their impact evolves, right? It changes. That's the point of *Gay Treasures*. It wasn't meant to be about certain names or objects gathering dust in a book. It's about looping people from the present into that legacy. *We're* the gay treasures too. We're growing and changing too. And liking someone . . . Well, it's less about liking who they are in one exact moment, and more about liking the ways they change. And I like the ways you change."

I feel sweat gather under Cam's palm. Something in my stomach curls into a thick knot. We have a dangerous habit of melting into each other like this. We get too close to see properly. And I desperately need to give Cam some distance here. So he has a chance to see things from another perspective. Maybe, hopefully, the clearer perspective.

I reach for the thin wooden box on his bed, then pull his hand away from my chest and set the box down in his palm.

"A few days ago," I say, "I couldn't have told you any of this. I wasn't here yet. Sunny was the one who said I needed to take a long look in the mirror. I think that might help you too."

I lean in and give Cam a tiny peck on the cheek, then pull away and tap the top of the box twice.

"In more ways than one," I add.

I slip out the door and leave him to it.

CHAPTER FORTY

I am completely rethinking my plan.

Plan A was Plan Obvious. I was going to write a poem, just like Gilbert's poem in the box.

Congratulations! You have found Cam and Ivy's Bonus Round

That's about as far as I got before realizing I was diving headfirst into a pool of cringe and would be in grave danger of never seeming cool again. But despite the cringe factor, the poem would have information! It would contain clarity! By the end of it, even if I did look like a total dweeb, at least Cam would know exactly where to find me now, one week later.

Instead, I went with yet another plan B. Plan Say Little and Look Smooth Doing It.

I left exactly one line in the box for Cam to find. Written in plain English—though it does have to be held up in front of a mirror to be read—is a day and a time. This day. This time.

And that was it. The hope, when I first wrote it, was that Cam would figure out the place on his own. Then he could decide, without me right next to him, without our hands touching or hearts racing, if he wanted to come out and finish what we started two years ago.

The minitruck comes bumbling up the road.

As it gets closer, it somehow looks even smaller. The truck pulls into a spot along the side street, trembling and chugging in place until the driver kills the engine.

The same Recreation and Park official with the long thick braid—Ranger Merilyn, I've since learned—steps out.

"Morning, Ivy."

"Good morning, Merilyn," I say.

"He here yet?"

I grip the handle of my roller bag tight, then let it go. "No. Not yet."

She slams the door and walks over, hands jammed into her pockets against the cool ocean air coming in from the west.

"Loved your application," she says as she walks. "That's exactly the kind of thing I was hoping we could put on display in the lodge. Tells a story, you know? About what the parks meant to the queer community of San Francisco in the seventies and eighties."

"Right," I say.

A sharp wind whips through the street, rustling my hair and making me clutch at my jacket. Ranger Merilyn tamps down her bangs and looks up toward the top of the dune. That's the main part of Grandview Park. Right now we're standing to one side of it, where the neighborhood clusters together in strange, wavy lines, mimicking the dune's topography. But even from here, through a slice between the houses, I can see the fine red lines of the Golden Gate Bridge just over Strawberry Hill.

I did a little research on this place last week. Apparently, it not only offers the best views in all of San Francisco but is also probably the oldest remaining sand dune in the entire Bay Area. One historian called it "the last window into San Francisco's earliest past," which is, well . . . pretty fitting.

I check the time again and sigh. "I definitely appreciate you meeting me here. But like I said in the email—"

Ranger Merilyn stops me. "I know, I know. No dig unless the boy shows up."

"What boy?"

We look up to see Cam striding around the last block of houses. He's wearing a white T-shirt, no jacket, and has his shovel swung over one shoulder. I can't stop smiling as he marches the rest of the way to us.

"You made it," I say, oozing unbridled joy like the disgusting little creature I am.

Cam stops just short of me. "Yeah, I did. Holy hell, what a ride. Those opera glasses?"

"Right?"

"Grand. View. Grandview! Totally genius."

"Totally," I say, grinning.

Ranger Merilyn looks at the two of us, slightly amused. "As I told Ivy before, this is a highly specialized permit request. We can't normally grant access to historical parks like Grandview. But, given the information Ivy shared with us, we are allowing a one-time, one-hole dig. This is it, folks. You have an hour once the first shovel goes in." She claps her hands. "So, where are we going? Up to the top?"

I look at Cam, waiting.

"No," he says. He looks back at me. "We're digging here."

He points to the northern tip of the dune beside us.

"So you got that too," I say.

Cam nods. "If the aerial of Grandview Park is a person, then right here is the chest, yes? Exactly where the locket fell on the woman in the scroll. But more importantly . . ."

He takes out a sheet of paper from his pocket and shows it to me. It's his own version of the poem from the box, this time transcribed in his writing.

"If you seek the lock and key," Cam reads aloud. "So we need *both* the locket and the key. But the key on the necklace is useless, right? It's not the real key."

"It isn't," I say in agreement. "You're right."

Cam holds up the poem again. "And look, here it says, 'No added ciphers.' Which means preexisting cipher keys are fair game. You and I had it from the very beginning."

He walks to the tip of the dune, right next to a street sign. One side for Fourteenth Avenue, the other for Fifteenth Avenue. They converge at this exact point.

"A giant between streets," I say, walking next to him.

"Grandview's the giant. And right here is the only point where a person can be between Fourteenth and Fifteenth." Cam spins his shovel around and drives the tip into the ground. "So, let's dig."

Ranger Merilyn settles into her camp chair to watch us dig. I unzip my bag and pull out my gardening trowel from last time. We lay a tarp next to us and begin to move the dirt.

The soil is soft at first and moves easily. Then, once we reach twelve inches down, the ground becomes thick and densely packed. Cam's turns get shorter and mine get longer, with me putting every bit of strength I have into chipping away at the earth before he hauls the freed dirt away.

"Twenty more minutes!" Ranger Merilyn calls.

My chest deflates. This is starting to feel like last time. But everything is supposed to be different now. Cam and I, we're supposed to be getting things right, finally. We *need* to get this right.

"Let's switch," Cam says. "I'll poke around, then you clean up."

He offers a hand to help me out of the hole, then jumps in with his shovel.

"You want this?" I ask, holding out my trowel.

"Nah," he says. He takes his shovel in both hands and plunges it into the ground with all his strength. Then, as if he were removing Excalibur from its rock, he pulls the shovel back out again.

On the third plunge, we each hear it.

A distinctive, delicate crack.

Cam freezes and looks up at me. He tosses his shovel out of the hole and pulls me into it alongside him. We drop into the dirt, arms and legs overlapping as we dig with our bare hands.

"I've got something!" I scream.

"Me too!" Cam yells.

Slowly, shakily, we both rise, each holding a piece of an ornately sculpted casque. It's painted in beautiful, glimmering colors, shimmering with every shade of the rainbow. There are figures carved in bas-relief on the outside. I recognize some of them. Harvey Milk. Marsha P. Johnson. Judy Garland dressed as Dorothy from *The Wizard of Oz*.

Each figure is so delicate, so beautiful, that instantly I know I could see a piece like this in a museum. It reminds me of the ancient bowls and vases found from hundreds of years ago. I think Gilbert Baker did that on purpose. He wanted people to know that gay history is nothing new—it's as ancient as human-kind itself.

Ranger Merilyn leaps out of her chair and bounds over.

"You found it!" She runs until she's standing just outside the hole. "Oh shoot. It's broken."

Cam twists his piece to see the damage. "Yeah . . . that was my fault."

"It's okay," I say quickly. "I already know how we can fix it."

I assess the clean break between each of our pieces. I can already imagine the resin filling in the cracks. The gold-leaf kintsugi being painted over the fracture. It's a celebration of brokenness, of resilience, of things coming together again.

Ranger Merilyn brings an empty bin and two clean towels from the truck. We wrap each piece and set them gently inside the bin. As she loads the bin back into the cab, I step next to Cam and touch his hand.

He looks down at my palm, then lifts it and places it flat

on his chest. I take his other hand and place it flat on mine. We study each other for what feels like ages—seeing all our past versions, all the ways we've changed in knowing each other. Cam nods slightly, as if I've asked him a question and he's only now said yes. He leans into me and parts his lips. I lean up to meet him in the middle.

If our first kiss marked a fracture in the friendship, and our second a total split between us . . . then this third kiss is the one that puts us back together.

This one is pure gold.

San Francisco Chronicle

ECCENTRIC GROUP OF TEENS FIND LOCAL BURIED TREASURE

JUNE 28

It was a whirlwind afternoon for the Sunset High Yearbook Club—who fondly call themselves "Shovels and REDACTED"—as they approached city hall on a warm Sunday, carrying a giant treasure chest between the five of them.

The day held a weighty significance across the country as the nation celebrated nearly 60 years of gay pride and rebellion first ignited by the Stonewall riots that took place in Greenwich Village on June 28, 1969. The streets of downtown San Francisco were crowded with color, rainbow flags waving and drums rap-tap-tapping as the annual Pride parade made its way to city hall. This year the Shovels and REDACTED group were the main and final event.

Inside their giant wooden treasure chest was, curiously, another treasure chest, an intricate and fine piece of art rumored to have been crafted by famed San Franciscan Gilbert Baker, inventor and creator of the rainbow flag. Baker passed away in New York City in 2017. Thirty-four years earlier, he anonymously published and distributed a treasure hunt book based on gay American history, titled "Gay Treasures." The book details the lives and work of seven key figures throughout the United States who were instrumental in the early gay rights movement of the 1960s and 1970s.

The elaborately carved casque found in San Francisco features portraits of all seven of the chosen gay icons: Harvey Milk of San Francisco, Lorraine Hansberry of Chicago, Stormé DeLarverie of New Orleans, Marsha P. Johnson of New York City, Barbara Gittings of Philadelphia, Jackie Shane of Nashville, and Judy Garland of Grand Rapids, Minnesota. Only the treasures representing Milk, Johnson, and Garland have been recovered thus far.

The Shovels and REDACTED crew is composed of five plucky teens: Cam Leonardo, Ivy Wethington, Sunny Noguchi, Gabriel Velasquez, and Julia Karlsson. When questioned, the group insists that credit for the find is split evenly among them. Baker's treasure hunt book is filled with a vast array of tricky riddles and confounding codes, presenting a multistep challenge that required the critical eye and vital role of each player. In particular, the group claims that Leonardo is credited with cracking the first pigpen cipher, Velasquez is credited with digitally editing a set of nearly illegible book cipher code, Noguchi is credited with translating the book cipher, Karlsson is credited with linking the solution to the proper address, and Wethington is credited with locating the stowed "lock and key" that led directly to the buried treasure.

The treasure chest itself has already been restored and appraised, with its estimated value at $2.6 million. The teens have decided to forgo a private auction and are willingly relinquishing the chance to split a lottery sum among them in favor of sending the treasure chest on exhibition across the country. The chest will begin its tour here in San Francisco, in the Chong-Moon Lee Center for Asian Art and Culture, where, thanks to the chest's restoration via gold bonding, it will reside as the centerpiece of the kintsugi gallery.

The teens may not be walking away with a fortune, but they are certainly not ending the hunt empty-handed. Thanks to his diligent work in handling the archived materials, Gabriel Velasquez currently has a scholarship to the Paris College of Art, where he will be attending their highly sought-after digital arts program starting later this summer. Sunny Noguchi has been named as the student ambassador for the Chong-Moon Lee Center, where she will help curate a rotating exhibition of local queer artists. Julia Karlsson is the new head of GAY 4 TREASURE, a previously archived website that has since been resurrected with a surge of new treasure hunters keen on locating the remaining four treasures.

This leaves Cam Leonardo and Ivy Wethington, the two members of the group deemed the "queer king and queen" of their local school, Sunset High. As the original owners of the "Gay Treasures" book and the book cipher's key text, respectively, Leonardo and Wethington will earn a small stipend from loaning their materials to the traveling exhibition with the treasure chest. When pressed for further individual developments, the so-called queer royalty remained tight-lipped. But although they are not personally jet-setting to Paris, chairing local art exhibitions, or taking over one of the fastest-growing sites on the internet, the pair seem almost suspiciously content with their own fortunes. Perhaps the mystery of "Gay Treasures" continues on, and these two know something we do not.

"Redacted?!"

Gabriel slams down the paper. "This is absolute bullshit," he cries. "I was told they would be including our full group name! What's wrong with the word 'hoes'? Hoes are a type of tool!"

"You're a type of tool," Sunny says cheerily.

Beiye laughs and kisses Sunny's cheek.

Despite there not being one window into the outside world, the Bat Cave is uncharacteristically bright as we lounge across the tables, sipping on sparkling lemonade. Julia and I dragged about seventeen more twinkle light strands into the room yesterday. We draped streamers down from the ceiling, taped balloons into every corner, and hung a giant banner over the projector screen.

CONGRATULATIONS, GABRIEL!

"Look at it this way," I tell him. "When you get to Paris next month, everyone will want to know what exact word 'REDACTED' was in the articles. This is drumming up interest!"

He rubs his chin, pondering. "Okay, fine. I see it." He looks up suddenly. "Oh! Is this going to give me a sexy and mysterious edge?"

"Absolutely," Julia says, beaming. "I bet that on your very first day, a Nico Hiraga look-alike will find you after class and ask you all about it."

"You're teasing me now," Gabriel says, but he's smiling too.

"What about you, Julia?" Cam asks from beside me. "Will you be traveling before school starts up again?"

"Probably not," Julia says. "I've barely had any time to dive into the other treasure hunts. But it's crazy." She holds up her phone and shows us her email inbox. "I keep getting all these donations for when I do eventually travel. Everyone wants me to come to their city to help them look."

"Where do you think you'll want to go first?" I ask. "Like, once you have an idea of where to look, I mean."

"Hmm." She scrunches her mouth. "New Orleans, probably. There's just something about those old houses and trees.

Ooh, and the Mardi Gras parade routes! Old necklaces dripping off magnolia branches, sparkling in the sunlight. It almost seems—"

"Magical?" I offer.

We grin at each other.

Julia nods. "Exactly."

Cam squeezes my hand.

"So, what about you two?" Sunny asks from the opposite table. She kicks her foot out so it nudges my shoe. "The paper made it sound like you guys have something exciting going on."

I look at Cam. "Not really," I say. "No Paris trips. No solving mysteries in New Orleans. No curating exhibitions at the Chong-Moon Lee."

"Just worldwide fame as treasure finders." Sunny shakes her head in mock sadness. She clicks her tongue at us. "Poor you."

"Hey! You asked!"

We raise our cups all together for Gabriel and toast to an amazing trip filled with hotties and lattes. And hopefully some good grades in his digital art classes or whatever.

Sunny and Beiye are the first to leave. Off to a club meeting at the art museum. Gabriel says he needs to start thinking about what he'll pack. Especially since, in his words, he'll need a whole new wardrobe if he wants to be the new "Emilio in Paris."

"Want me to close up?" I ask Julia when it's just the three of us.

"Nah," Julia says. She sets down her cup and parks herself

at her desktop computer. "I kind of want to work on the New Orleans chapter a bit."

I toss her my custodian key to the side door and start up the stairs. Cam nods and joins me.

"Wait." Julia spins around in her swivel chair.

Cam and I pause. "Yeah?" we say in unison.

"If I find any leads . . . you two will still help me, right? I seriously don't think I could do one of these alone."

"You could," Cam says encouragingly. He smiles. "But, yeah, we're definitely down to help. You know where to find us."

Julia sighs in relief. "Okay, good."

She starts typing away at her computer.

Cam and I climb up the stairs and onto Sixth Avenue. We turn west and snake through the neighborhood as it shifts from straight grid lines into gentle curves. It leads us up and up, above the rest of the city, until we've scaled the final rickety wooden staircase of Grandview Park. Cam sits on our bench first, making barely enough room, so I have to press my hips into his to sit down next to him. I tilt my head and rest it on his shoulder as we look out at the skyline.

"What should we do next?" I ask after a while.

Cam leans back to look at me. "What should we do?"

I think about the version of myself I used to picture at Chez Moi. The future me bustling into the restaurant, filled with stories and news about my exciting life in Paris. The part that stands out the most, weirdly, isn't even the art school thing. I used to think I had to go to school in France to be interesting enough for my mom to want to hang out with me. But the unease between us was never about me. It was about her and her own past. For me . . . I just want to have a future where I'm happy.

I turn to Cam.

"Point," I say. "Point to a spot somewhere out there. And we'll go find it."

"For what?" he asks, smiling.

"For an adventure."

He laughs and tips his head into mine, kissing me gently. He looks around at the empty park, then leans in and kisses me harder, one hand cradling the back of my head, bringing it closer to his. I get completely lost in him, in the newness and oldness of us mixed together.

As we kiss, Cam picks up one of my hands and stretches it out toward the city. He pulls back, his eyes deep and dilated, then looks at my hand in his.

"There," he says, as I turn and look to see where we're pointing.

Together, we mark the spot.

AUTHOR'S NOTE

Although the treasure hunt in this book is fictional, *Gay Treasures* was inspired by several real armchair treasure hunt books. I earned my master's degree in the critical study of children's literature and wrote my thesis about Kit Williams and his debut picture book *Masquerade*, which was published in 1979. Previously known solely as a fine artist in Britain, Williams wanted a way to get his readers to look closely at the illustrations in his book instead of quickly flipping through them. In tandem with his debut's publication, Williams buried a handmade jeweled necklace valued at over $10,000, with clues leading to the treasure's whereabouts in the book's illustrations. For two and a half years the entire world was obsessed with Williams's treasure hunt.

One of the obsessed fans of Williams's hunt was American publisher Byron Preiss. As Preiss watched *Masquerade*'s sales soar into the millions, he decided to try his hand at his own armchair treasure hunt book. Preiss published *The Secret* in 1982. In *The Secret*, Preiss presents readers with twelve paintings and twelve verses. In press interviews leading up to the book's release, Preiss revealed that he had buried a separate treasure in twelve different cities throughout the United States and Canada. In order to locate these treasures, readers had to first decide which verse paired with which painting, and then use clues found in both the verse and the painting to home in on the city, the area, and the exact location to dig for the treasure.

Three teenage boys unearthed the first *Secret* treasure in Grant Park, Chicago, one year after the book was released. Two lawyers from New Jersey unearthed the second *Secret* treasure in the Greek Cultural Gardens, Cleveland, over twenty years later in 2004. Finally, with the help of a local construction crew and the show *Expedition Unknown*, a family unearthed the third *Secret* treasure in Langone Park, Boston, in 2019. The nine remaining treasures have, at the time of this book's publication, not been located. Preiss passed away unexpectedly in 2005, leaving the whereabouts of the official solution to *The Secret* riddles unknown.

I first learned of *The Secret* in June 2023, during a solo writing retreat in the New Mexico mountains. During the retreat, I had planned on turning my master's thesis on *Masquerade* into a nonfiction book on treasure hunts—their origins, their lore, and their perpetual appeal, especially in American culture. I was reading up on Forrest Fenn's treasure hunt in Daniel Barbarisi's *Chasing the Thrill*, and I found myself fascinated by Barbarisi's assertion that in order to fully understand the appeal of treasure hunting, he had to join in on the hunt itself. Barbarisi introduced several unsolved or partially unsolved armchair treasure hunts, including *The Secret*. Right away, I was drawn to Preiss's treasure hunt. I loved the seeming simplicity of the verse and painting formula. I loved that Preiss was a history nerd. I especially loved that many of his clues seemed grounded in the parts of American history he wanted to honor and remember.

I had been a fan of armchair treasure hunt books long before I came across *The Secret*. But *The Secret* seemed to unlock (excuse the pun) something new within me. A huge problem with treasure hunting as a narrative trope is that so often, the treasure hunting involves stealing. Pirates stole valuables from ships and then buried them in the ground. Indiana Jones and Lara Croft were literal tomb raiders. Even Forrest Fenn came by his treasure after essentially looting it from the peoples and cultures those treasures rightfully belonged to. I love that Preiss commissioned new treasures in order to honor the past. As soon as I finished reading *The Secret*, I was already thinking about a fictional treasure hunt that could pay that same kind of homage, but specifically to the history of the American LGBTQ+ community.

Anyone who reads this book and then picks up *The Secret* (or vice versa!) will find many Easter Eggs hidden in these pages. The drawing that Cam and Ivy find bears a strong resemblance to the painting in *The Secret* most associated with the (still hidden) San Francisco treasure. Even the final location of the treasure in *Buried Feelings* is my own little Easter Egg to the place I first thought Preiss might have buried his treasure in SF. But a word of warning to anyone who finds their own interest piqued by the world of treasure hunting: Digging in public parks without permission is a crime. San Francisco has the coolest Recreation and Park Department in the world, and they will work with you on an authorized dig to look for Preiss's treasure. But you have to contact them and go through the proper channels. Their "Secret Treasure Hunt Dig Request" form is available online.

ACKNOWLEDGMENTS

Here's a riddle: What kind of ship has two mates but no captain?

Skip ahead to the end for the answer (cheater!), but this riddle reminds me a lot of what it's like to produce a book. No one captain calling the shots, just a whole host of mates running around, trying to keep this strange little ship of a story from capsizing. Making *this* book in particular feels like that process times ten, so naturally there are a lot of mates to thank here.

Lauren Spieller, we finally got to write the treasure hunt book!!! You don't have to hear me pitch another treasure hunt book ~~ever again~~ for at least a few years! Hannah Teachout, you are the person who got this story off on the right foot. You informed me in the kindest way possible that my first version of Ivy was *not it*, and your invaluable feedback ultimately led to the story that I most wanted to tell. Ali Romig, as usual, you found the heart of this book before I did. More hijinks! More swooning!! More nuanced explorations of sexual identity!!! Thank goodness I'm lucky enough to work with you, because your voice often feels like the good angel on my shoulder, steering me toward the best version of myself.

When a writer puts their work on submission, they are

often crossing all their fingers and toes that *anyone* will want to buy it. The fact that I am working with **Delacorte Romance** of all imprints continuously blows my mind. I cannot believe how fortunate I am to tell stories with this talented and hardworking team of individuals. Thank you, Kristin Guy, Jasmine Ferrufino, Tamar Schwartz, Shameiza Ally, Megan Shortt, Carol Ly, Sarah Maxwell, Jamie Johnson, Kaitlyn San Miguel, Starr Baer, Lillian Boyd, and everyone else who has had a hand in this book's journey. *Buried Feelings* is all the better thanks to your direct involvement.

I have a rich personal history with treasure hunts, both real and fictional. Every step in this history was aided by someone helping me leap from one stone to the next. Chip Sullivan, thank you for agreeing to act as my advisor for my bonkers treasure-hunt-book thesis. Kit Williams, thank you for being my friend after I sent you two hundred bound pages I wrote all about you. Phoebe Judge and Lauren Spohrer, thank you for accepting my pitch for what would become the episode "Masquerade" on your podcast *Criminal*, and for reigniting my love of treasure hunt stories. Thank you to the entire *Secret* community, but most notably Brian Zinn and Andy Abrams, the New Jersey lawyers/triumphant *Secret* treasure finders, for graciously granting me interviews, and to John Jude Palencar and Byron Preiss for creating the enigmatic paintings and verses. Thank you to the San Francisco Recreation and Park Department for designating some of your valuable staff as "treasure rangers." Also thank you very much to the Lyft driver who didn't reject me as a passenger on sight after one of my treasure digging expeditions. (A stranger later asked if I fell into a swamp.) You, sir, are a gentleman and a saint.

Thank you, Gilbert Baker, for playing such a crucial role in

LGBTQ+ history, and for creating the ultimate gay treasure in the form of the beautiful rainbow flag. There was never a doubt in my mind who the fictional treasure hunt creator would be. Thank you, Harvey Milk, for leaving such a tremendous legacy in your wake, one that I could create a hundred clues around that all emphasize your deep connection to and compassion for the queer community. Thank you to everyone who has ever stood up, sat down, marched, spoken, or listened in order to advocate for queer rights. You are ALL gay treasures in my book! And thank you sincerely to the trans individuals who read early versions of this story and who wish to not be outed as trans in these acknowledgments. Your input and perspective have been invaluable. I identify as a genderfluid person, but not trans, and having these readers was a crucial step to getting this story right. All remaining blunders in the pages are solely my responsibility.

While I continue to flail at social media, the one BRILLIANT thing it has given me is so many beautiful connections with writer and reader friends, whom I now count among my most cherished book community. Brian Kennedy, Matthew Hubbard, Cale Plett, Erin Cotter, Julian Winters, Becky Albertalli, Kelly Quindlen, Dahlia Adler, Jason June, Erin Baldwin, Jenna Levine, Amanda Sellet, Jennifer Dugan, Rachael Lippincott, Erica Waters, Wendy Heard, Susan Metallo, Khadijah VanBrakle, Zahra Marwan, Laurel Goodluck, Alder Van Otterloo, Lauren Blackwood, and everyone else who I've ever giggled with and vented to about writing, I love you. Thank you for being here.

Mom and Dad, thank you for watching *Expedition Unknown* with me and letting me pause every two seconds to talk your ears off about *The Secret*. Loriel Ryon, thank you for listening to and then validating all of my ridiculously awful treasure hunt theories. Brooklyn Watters, my forever partner in (alleged!) crime, thank you for going to the ends of the earth to search for actual, real-life treasure with me. Remember that moment when we hit the edge of a stone in Golden Gate Park?? Holy cow, what a thrill.

David Rosewater, how do you manage to make every aspect of my life so perfectly romantic and wonderful? I am currently looking at the striped lighthouse figurine on our bookcase that reminds me of the FOUR HOURS you drove from your work trip destination in the summer of 2023 to do some on-site treasure investigating for me. It's such a magical thing that you take me seriously, down to my bones. When my heart is set on something, then yours is too. If that isn't true love, then I don't know what is.

Last, but certainly not least, thank you to my beautiful children: August and Rowan. If you didn't get the dedication reference in chapter thirty-six (which is fair . . . you can't even read yet), **the two of you** are the real treasure in this whole ordeal—the wild adventure that my life has been. You have always been, and will always be, the real treasure.

PS: The answer to the riddle is a *relation*ship! Get it? Hahaha.

ABOUT THE AUTHOR

KIT ROSEWATER lives in Albuquerque, New Mexico, with her partner and two small children who are bent on destroying the universe. She is the author of the romances *Buried Feelings* and *All's Fair in Love and Field Hockey*, as well as the Derby Daredevils, an illustrated middle grade series. Kit has been a theater and English teacher, a bookseller, a children's literature academic, and a Flamin' Hot Cheetos addict. That's all behind her now. Well, most of it.

KITROSEWATER.COM
@SAVETHEKITROSEWATER

IT'S A LOVE STORY.